Irresistible in Love

~ The Maverick Billionaires ~

Book 4

Bella Andre & Jennifer Skully

IRRESISTIBLE IN LOVE

~ The Maverick Billionaires, Book 4 ~

Meet the Maverick Billionaires—sexy, self-made men from the wrong side of town who survived hell together and now have everything they ever wanted. But when each Maverick falls head over heels for an incredible woman he never saw coming, he will soon find that true love is the only thing he ever really needed...

Evan Collins is the man with the Midas touch. Having left his hard childhood behind him, the financial genius vowed to one day have everything. But when he discovers that his marriage is built on lies, the only people he can trust now are the Mavericks—and the woman who has always been there for him: Paige, the sister of his soon-to-be ex-wife.

Paige Ryan has always loved Evan Collins, a secret she's hugged close to her heart for nine long years. But when her sister's devastating betrayal is revealed, Paige can't keep her feelings hidden any longer.

Paige is a beacon of light for Evan. Despite believing he needs to keep the walls around his heart stronger than ever, he's irresistibly drawn to her sweet, pure heart—and the undeniable sparks flaring between them. She's the only one he trusts to help him face the darkness of his past head on before it destroys him. But will their forbidden romance end up destroying them both?

A note from Bella & Jennifer

Right from the start, each of the Maverick Billionaires touched our hearts. But we've always had a special soft spot for Evan. More than anything, we wanted him to find love. Real love that would make him stronger, rather than tearing him apart. True love that would bring him joy, instead of pain.

Fortunately, Paige Ryan wanted exactly the same thing.

We hope you love reading Evan and Paige's romance as much as we loved writing it!

Happy reading,
Bella Andre & Jennifer Skully

p.s. Daniel's story, *Wild In Love*, will be out next! Please sign up for our New Release newsletters for more information about upcoming Maverick Billionaire romances. BellaAndre.com/Newsletter & bit.ly/SkullyNews

Chapter One

It had all been lies.

From the moment Evan Collins met Whitney Ryan to the day their marriage ended a month ago, right after Thanksgiving. But that was all over now. He was setting his world to rights, reclaiming his life, moving on.

And he was home again.

Evan stood in the arched living room doorway of Susan and Bob Spencer's Chicago home. Their house was fragrant with Christmas pine, mulled wine, and joy. The decorations still hung, stockings along the fireplace and brilliant poinsettias brightening the corners of the room, which was big enough to handle all of Harper Newman and Will Franconi's wedding guests tomorrow.

When the money had started to flow for the Mavericks, the first thing the five friends had done was move the Spencers into a good neighborhood. At the time, this home was a palace compared to the apartment in the dreary, backwater neighborhood they'd grown up in. Now that millions had turned to billions, the Mavericks wanted to buy them a better and bigger house. But Susan and Bob insisted this was their dream home.

Now it would be the dream setting for Harper and Will's wedding.

No one had noticed Evan's arrival yet as he hung back, watching his foster family. For the past twenty-five years, they'd been a tight unit, going back to when they were kids out in the schoolyard. None of their childhoods had been innocent, and they'd each had their fair share of scars—both physical and emotional— by the time they left Susan and Bob's home and headed out to conquer the world.

But only Evan had made the mistake of marrying the wrong woman.

Damn it, he'd already lost enough time over her— including the month he'd just spent in isolation in Europe beating himself up over his mistakes. It was long past time to move forward.

God, he'd missed his family and friends. All the people who were closer to him than blood. Closer than the wife he'd thought loved him.

Harper and Will would be married tomorrow, on New Year's Eve, and tonight was the cusp of a new life for them. No matter how badly his life had imploded, he would never miss their wedding.

Harper was radiant in a burgundy dress that made everything about her shine—Will's eyes certainly followed her everywhere she moved. He lit up with each of her smiles, every time she laughed. Harper's brother, Jeremy, circled like a satellite, his usual enthusiastic, joyful self.

Sebastian Montgomery and his fiancée, Charlie Ballard, flanked her mother, Francine, who was perched in a wing chair. Francine's lined face beamed with happiness—she and Charlie were a perfect addition to the Mavericks. Sebastian's hand stroked over Charlie's red hair, and she leaned into his touch.

Matt Tremont sat beside them, one hand on his son's back, the other around the waist of his girlfriend, Ari Jones. Evan's chest tightened at the sight of little Noah, who was almost six now, in Ari's arms. Evan had planned to have his own kids by now, his hope growing with every passing year for the miracle of a healthy baby. Only to finally discover the horrible truth, a month ago, about why that had never come to be…

He put the brakes on the runaway locomotive of his thoughts. He'd deliberately left his raw, battered emotions behind after his European travels. From here on out, he was moving full steam ahead into a new world unmarked by his past.

Evan Collins had started over more than once in his life.

This time he vowed to get it right.

Thankfully, his friends had already gotten it completely right. Will had found his perfect match in Harper. Evan felt Sebastian's joy in being with Charlie and was ecstatic that Noah now had a brand-new mother in Ari. Not for one minute would Evan let his own loss tarnish this celebration.

There had been so many moments during the last month when he'd wanted to punch in Will's number, or Susan's, or Matt's, or God help him, call all his friends at once. To bare his soul. To tell them everything. And yet, in answer to all their queries after telling them a month ago that he was divorcing Whitney, the most he'd managed was a single curt text saying he was doing fine.

At least he'd sent them a response. Whitney's sister, Paige, had reached out to him too.

Whitney just told me everything. I know you must be in shock right now. Call me as soon as you're up to it.

But he hadn't gotten to that point, not knowing what to say or how to say it. So he hadn't replied at all, ignoring not only her texts, but her emails and phone calls as well.

Evan's gut clenched as he realized Paige was nowhere to be seen tonight, as though she no longer felt welcome now that Evan and her sister had split up. As if she actually believed she was the "hanger-on" Whitney had always called her. He'd never felt that way about Paige. No one had.

At the very least, thank God Whitney hadn't shown up. She'd been on the invitation they'd received before their marriage imploded, and he knew all too well how much she would relish causing her own special brand of trouble at the wedding.

At last, Daniel turned and spotted him. Evan could easily read the emotions on his friend's face—shock, concern, maybe even a little anger. In a split second, however, it all disappeared beneath Daniel's smile of welcome.

The Mavericks always accepted each other unconditionally. They didn't take crap, but at the same time, they understood when a guy had to work things out on his own. And Evan swore that he had worked out all his emotions about Whitney. Even if it had taken a brutally lonely month spent halfway around the globe.

Separating from the group laughing at one of Bob's hilarious stories, Daniel headed his way. "Glad you made it for the wedding." He gave Evan a quick, hard hug.

Despite owning a home improvement retail conglomerate and hosting a DIY TV show, Daniel Spencer was the most muscular of the bunch. Making boatloads of money had never gotten in the way of his outdoor activities, which included personally building a cabin in Lake Tahoe.

"Glad to be here." Evan glanced at Harper and Will. "I wouldn't miss the wedding."

"Some of us had our doubts. But we all know it's been a rough month."

Rough was an understatement. Evan's mission in

Europe had been about more than visiting his subsidiaries in London, Berlin, Paris, Rome, and Stockholm. The arms of The Collins Group, his investment corporation, reached out globally, and he believed in hiring local expertise. After all, they knew the markets, the economies, the politics, all of which affected investment decisions, and those people were the best at keeping him fully informed. He'd been determined to work himself out of the dark pit he'd fallen into when he'd learned the truth about the full extent of Whitney's betrayal. At first, he'd fermented in that dark place, hating Whitney, hating himself for not seeing the truth. But now he refused to keep handing her that power over him, not when he'd just come home to his family again.

"It's over now," Evan said. "I'm moving on."

Daniel smiled wide. "Sure you are." But his next words belied the easy smile. "Need to talk? One on one?"

Evan drank in the laughter in the room before answering. "No." He didn't want to destroy the homecoming. Didn't want to plunge back into darkness either. "I'm fine."

Daniel nodded, and for a moment, Evan thought his friend might let it go at that. Until he added, "We're here if you change your mind."

Thank God for friends. They had always been there, since he was a skinny ten-year-old. They stood up for each other then and now. He knew they all thought he was better off without Whitney, that none of his friends ever really liked her. Evan was the one who'd made excuses for her behavior, who'd told himself that the Mavericks didn't really know her.

Only to find out that *he* was the one who hadn't known his wife.

Not at all.

Across the room, Susan laughed delightedly as Bob gave the punch line to his joke. They always laughed together—not *at* each other, but *with* each other. Over Bob's shoulder, Susan finally saw Evan, her features freezing for a moment with deep motherly concern.

She whispered something to Bob, and he immediately pivoted. As if their moves were a signal to the rest of the group, the conversation fell silent.

Susan was soon enveloping Evan in a hug. He was transported back to childhood, to the heat of Susan and Bob's kitchen, to the warmth generated by the unconditional love she and Bob showered on all the Mavericks. The Spencers had taken them in, fostered them, treated them like their own sons, giving them the same love they'd given to Daniel and his sister, Lyssa. In Susan and Bob's house, there was always more than enough love to go around.

"I missed you, honey."

"Missed you too," he answered as he hugged her back, not wanting to let her go.

Bob knuckled his head, and Sebastian punched his arm lightly. "Dude, I knew you wouldn't miss the food."

Evan clapped his friend on the back. "It's Matt who's all about the food."

Matt snorted. "Give me a break. Daniel's the free-food king."

As they all laughed, Evan's heart clenched tight again. Only, this time it wasn't out of pain—it was because he no longer had a doubt in his head or his heart or his gut that he'd been right to come home.

Noah squirmed out of Ari's grip and launched himself at Evan. He scooped up Matt's son, burying his face in Noah's blond curls as the boy chattered excitedly. "I swam the pool end to end five times without stopping. It must be a whole mile."

"You're a superstar," he said, giving Noah a high five before putting him back down on the floor so he could run off to play with Jeremy.

Turning to Ari, Evan asked, "Where's your brother?" Evan had met Gideon only once, at Thanksgiving. The guy was enigmatic, having recently come back into Ari's life after spending seven years in the military, and another nine years working construction all over the country. Evan wasn't sure he trusted him, and he worried about Ari because of it.

"Gideon was so grateful for Harper and Will's invitation to the wedding," Ari replied, "but he wasn't able to get out of work to come." Evan knew that Daniel would have given him the time off, but he didn't refute her.

The front door opened, and seconds later, a snow-dusted woman threw herself at him. Lyssa, Daniel's sister, had always been a handful. She was the kid sister he'd never had, a toddler when he'd moved in with Susan and Bob a couple of years after his mother ran off. All the Mavericks felt like they'd raised her—and they would go to any length to protect her.

"You big lug. Where have you been this past month?" She smacked a hand on his chest. "I desperately needed to talk to you because—" She lowered her voice to a conspiratorial murmur. "—I hate to admit it, but I detest my job. You're my financial wizard, so I know you'll give me good advice."

"I'll help you out any way I can," he promised.

"Thank you," she said, giving him one of her sunny smiles as she let him go. "I definitely need a sage old man's advice."

Lyssa loved to needle him about their ten-year age difference. And the truth was that he *did* feel incredibly old. The last month had aged him. Hell, the last couple of years had.

Working to keep the bleak thoughts from his face—and wipe them from his mind—he turned to Will next and pumped his friend's hand, then pulled Harper into a hug. "You're radiant, Harper. The perfect bride-to-be."

She smiled, her cheeks pinkening. "Thank you, Evan." Concern flashed in her eyes, just as it had in Susan's, but thankfully, before she could press him on how he was doing, Susan guided him into the living room.

"Have you eaten? Do you need something to drink?"

"I'm fine," he said, his constant refrain. "And I need to say hello to this lovely lady." He hunkered down by Francine Ballard's chair to give her a hug and let her know how happy he was to see her again.

Charlie's mother's fingers were gnarled with arthritis, her legs shackled in braces, and getting up and down quickly was hard work. But she still walked a mile a day.

If she could keep going, keep moving forward, so could he.

Evan's family was full of smiles. Hugs. Unconditional love. But he could see that they were also walking on glass, with no one pushing. No one prodding. No one demanding to know how he could have left for a month with nothing more than a text to Susan, Bob, and the other Mavericks.

Getting divorced. I'm heading out to visit my European offices. I'll be back for the wedding.

He'd answered their shocked and concerned texts with his new stock phrase, *I'm fine.* And then he'd gone dark.

"Honey, you must be starved after your long trip here." Susan signaled him with a wave into the dining room. The sideboard was set with a spread of appetizers, casseroles, and salads. "Let me get you something to eat." She loaded up a plate with his favorite dishes, then sat beside him at the dining room table. "Will insisted I use a caterer for the rehearsal dinner. And the wedding too. He said he didn't want me exhausting myself with all the cooking. I wasn't sure how well it would work out, but the food is good, don't you think?"

"This curry rice is mouthwatering." He wasn't hungry, but he ate for Susan.

"You've lost weight." She frowned in concern again. "How are you really doing, honey? We've all been so worried." The Maverick chatter carried through the living room archway, with everyone careful not to intrude on their private moment.

"I've moved on. I'm not dwelling on the past. It's over. I just needed a few weeks to figure things out, that's all."

She locked eyes with him for a long moment. One in which he tried not to squirm like a little kid under his mother's all-seeing gaze. "We understand why you needed time to process what happened." She put her hand over his, sorrow and fury mixing together on her face as she said, "Paige told us what happened. About the things Whitney did."

He should have known Paige would spill the whole sordid tale to Susan and Bob, to the Mavericks. After all these years, she was family too—and family turned to one another when they needed help dealing with difficult issues. He should have done that too, but the deep shame of having been blind for so long to Whitney's true nature had held him back...

He squeezed her hand. "You didn't need to worry. You and Bob taught me to deal with the tough knocks and keep on going."

"I have to admit you look better than I thought you would." She shook a finger at him. "Except that you're too skinny."

He laughed for her, because she needed it and he wanted to make up for the worry he'd caused her. Then he made himself pick up his fork and eat a few more bites as Susan told him all about the wedding preparations. But he wasn't really there with her.

Because no matter how hard he tried, he couldn't stop himself from rewinding back four weeks, far away from this warm and loving family home...

Chapter Two

One month ago...

Whitney had decided to spend Thanksgiving in the south of France. Evan should have missed being with his wife during the holiday, but he was actually relieved. It meant the Mavericks and their families could all have a nice day together, without any of her inevitable drama.

The dinner conversation was as lively and entertaining as ever. But when they went around the table to each say one thing they were thankful for this past year, emotions went deep. One by one, each person at the large table in Matt's dining room bared a piece of their soul. By the time they got to Evan, he found himself blurting out, "I'm thankful you've all been there for me through three miscarriages."

The table fell silent. Until Paige said, "I'm sure that if Whitney were here, she would say that she's thankful for how you were always there for her. Especially since she wasn't comfortable reaching out to any of us."

Paige's statement was clearly intended to be kind, but her words hit Evan like a punch to the gut, nearly doubling him over with guilt. Because every time Whitney had miscarried, he'd been out of town on business. Yet, Whitney hadn't called her sister or any of the Mavericks for help or comfort. Each time she'd lost their baby, she'd gone through the pain and loss all alone, until he could get home to her from whatever locale his business dealings had taken him to. Even though he always rushed home as soon as possible, that sometimes meant it had taken more than a day for him to make it back to her.

But why hadn't Whitney gone to her sister for consolation? Or called Susan, who'd always been so good to her? Was it because he'd failed her so badly as a husband that she'd felt ashamed for miscarrying? Had she blamed herself?

During the past few years, Whitney had been increasingly difficult to live with—and he didn't want to make excuses for the nasty things she'd said and done far too often. But that didn't change the fact that they'd gotten so out of touch with each other that she obviously hadn't been able to call for help when she needed it most. It was long past time to step up to fix things between them, not just let his marriage keep falling apart because they couldn't talk anymore.

He strategized exactly how to do that during the remainder of the weekend, coming up with alternatives, vowing to make things right. By Monday, when Whitney walked in the front door, he was armed with fresh, new plans to build the family they'd always dreamed of.

"Whitney, welcome back."

She looked surprised to see him at home in the middle of a workday. "Oh, hi. Since you're here, you can help me with my bags. The shopping was *fabulous* in France." She was a stunning woman. But the smile she gave him didn't reach her eyes.

Or maybe that was just his guilt talking.

Ignoring her bags, and the open front door, he moved to take her hands. "I'm sorry I wasn't there for you."

She frowned, clearly confused. "In France?" She shook her head. "You would have been bored senseless at the spa and boutiques."

"No, not France. I'm sorry for not being there for your miscarriages. And for not making sure that you felt comfortable going to Susan or the Mavericks for help in my absence." No matter how badly she might have behaved in the past, Evan knew his friends and family would unconditionally support her.

She slipped her hands from his to wave away his concern. "It happened very early on each time. You know I recovered easily." Then she added quickly, "At least physically."

"I know you did, but I should have gone with you to your doctor to discuss the situation. Especially after you miscarried more than once."

"No!" She looked horrified by his suggestion. "You didn't need to talk with my doctor. She'd simply have told you the statistics on miscarriages in the first six weeks just like she told me."

"I know how hard it is for you to talk about this, Whitney." She'd never wanted to talk about the medical specifics of why she'd had three back-to-back miscarriages, and he hadn't wanted to deepen her distress. But now there was too much bottled up grief between them. And he was determined to fix what was broken. "But there's still a chance. We can figure out what happened and try again."

She whirled away, her high heels clicking loudly on the marble floor, one hand to her forehead. "It's too late for all that."

He put a conciliatory hand on her back and she turned back to face him right before he said, "We'll talk to the doctor together, and if nothing can be done, there are alternatives."

Flinching, she jerked a step back, nearly stumbling over one of her bags on the floor. "I don't want to have children right now." She huffed a breath, her nostrils flaring. "I simply can't go through all that again." She stared at him with misting eyes. "Can't we just be together, the two of us?"

Losing the babies had torn his insides out. But he knew that it must have been so much worse for Whitney, especially going through it all alone. "You're right. I completely understand how hard it would be to try again." Would either of them survive if she lost another baby?

Which was why he turned to the entryway table where he'd left the papers he'd worked on over the weekend. "Let's try this instead, then." He handed her the adoption forms, which he'd already filled out. "I've made some calls, and the good news is that we're prime candidates for adoption." Surely everything would change for them when they had the family they wanted. It was what he'd told himself every time they'd been on the verge of having a child.

"Are you crazy? I *don't* want to adopt." She tossed the papers back onto the table without even looking at them.

His guts twisted. He was doing everything he could to try to fix things, but Whitney was as distant as ever. "I know we planned to have our own kids, but we can still have that big family we've always dreamed of."

"You know you don't really want to raise someone else's child." She pursed her lips, tiny lines flaring out from her mouth. "And I can't take the blame when you finally come to that realization."

"I would love a child with all my heart, whether or not he or she is mine biologically."

The silence was long, echoing in the huge marble foyer. "Well, I'm not sure *I* can."

"Whitney." He held out his hand, but she didn't take it. "Once you have a beautiful boy or girl, I know you'll see the baby as your own. As ours." Again, the silence beat at his eardrums. "We can do this. We can be parents like we've always talked about being."

Something hard, something cold, flashed in her eyes. "You mean like *you've* always talked about." She made a face. "I don't even want children."

Everything went still. As if they were posing for one of those mannequin challenges he'd seen on the Internet. "Of course you do." She couldn't mean what she'd just said. It had to be frustration, grief talking. "We've *always* talked about having children together. Right from the beginning. Even before we were married."

"You brought it up," she snapped. "But you never *asked* me. And I *had* to agree to keep you happy. My whole life is about making you happy." She dropped her voice, a little sob creeping in. "But I just wasn't ready, Evan. And I didn't know how to tell you because you wanted a child so badly. You can't even imagine how I felt, always having to walk that tightrope with you. I didn't want to disappoint you. But I'm *still* not ready for a child, and I don't want to adopt."

His brain, which his colleagues always told him was so quick, couldn't process her words. "But if you hadn't miscarried," he said slowly, trying to get the pieces of his life to add up to something that actually made sense, "we would already have a child. Three children."

He could hear a clock ticking somewhere. Maybe it was inside his head, a time bomb seconds away from going off.

Then it exploded as Whitney said, "No, we

wouldn't." She sighed, as though she wished he would simply connect the dots she'd laid out for him. "I made up the pregnancies and the miscarriages so you'd stop harping on me. What else was I supposed to do? You didn't give me a choice. You wanted what you wanted without any consideration for me."

She didn't hang her head in guilt or shame. She didn't even seem to recognize the horrific nature of the lies she'd told. The worst possible lies about the worst possible thing. The utter anguish she'd caused. And she'd been doing it for *years*. He'd never questioned her. Hell, he'd actually blamed himself.

Until, in one fell swoop, at two p.m. on this late fall Monday afternoon, the blindfold was ripped from his eyes.

Suddenly, he could see that every facial expression, every gesture, every smile, every tear she'd shed were all designed to manipulate him.

Struggling not to lose it, his voice was almost too measured as he asked, "Has anything you've ever told me been true?"

"Of course it has." She rolled her eyes as if he were being ridiculous and overly dramatic. "You know I love you."

Did he?

Five minutes ago, he would have accepted those three little words at face value, despite how difficult she'd been to live with for the past few years. But the last five minutes had changed everything.

"What else have you lied about?"

"Do you really want the truth, the whole truth, and nothing but the truth?" She threw down her words like a gauntlet.

"I do." He'd said those same words to her at their wedding, but they held a vastly different meaning now.

"Fine." She arched her brow as if she were doing him a huge favor by finally admitting the truth. "I don't ever want children. And since you never asked me what I really wanted and kept forcing the whole baby thing on me, I had no choice but to take matters into my own hands and have my tubes tied."

He should have been shocked. He should have been furious. But in that moment, he was simply numb.

He couldn't wrap his mind around the immensity of her lies. From the moment they'd met, she'd told him everything she thought he wanted to hear, even down to planning the family she now denied ever having wanted.

"Does Paige know?"

Why those were the words that came out of his mouth next, he couldn't say. Maybe his brain was still trying to catch up with the last few minutes.

"Do you really think I would tell that little Goody-Two-Shoes anything? Especially since she's always had her eye on you. I see the way she moons over you when she thinks I'm not looking. As if she'd ever have a *prayer* of stealing a man away from me. Her crush is so pathetic."

"Get out."

Of all the things to make him finally snap, it was the callous way she spoke of her sister that did it. Hearing Whitney disparage Paige—who had never hurt a soul—was the final straw.

Whitney stared at him, her lips parting in disbelief. "I know this must be coming as a bit of a shock to you right now—" She moved against him the way she'd done so many times before when she wanted something from him. "—but once you have a little time to think things through, you'll see I did the right thing for us. We'll be so much better without kids. Freer. Happier. In fact, since I've already got my bags packed, why don't we go away together? Just the two of us. You'll see how good it can be for us to be all alone, all day and all night."

He pushed away from her, walked to the open front door, then signaled to the car and driver who were still there. He turned back to Whitney, the woman who was no longer his wife in anything but name. "Take your bags. I'll have the rest of your things shipped to you. You can give your new address to my PA, because I won't be taking your calls."

She gaped at him, as if he were being horribly unfair. As if she didn't understand the ruthlessness of what she'd done. Or maybe because she couldn't believe, after all these years, that he'd finally seen right through to her rotted soul.

"You can't throw me out of my own home without even talking about this."

"We have talked. And now there's nothing left to say." He put her bags on the front step, and she had no choice but to follow. "Good-bye, Whitney."

Less than two hours later, he'd gotten out as well, flying halfway around the world to get away from the memories.

And most especially from her.

★ ★ ★

Present day in Susan and Bob's house...

"I did make the wedding cake, though," Susan was saying, and Evan realized he'd totally zoned out. "It's a princess cake, with that fondant icing you roll on. But don't tell Will and Harper anything. It's a surprise." Her eyes were shining. She was so happy with all her family around her.

Doing his damnedest to shove away his dark thoughts and return fully to the present, he zipped his lips. "Mum's the word. It's going to be great."

The doorbell rang, and all heads in the living room turned. As Bob crossed to the front hall to answer, Susan rose from the table. "Oh good, Paige must be here."

Evan's heart started to pound hard and fast as Paige stepped inside. The other Mavericks closed around her with hugs and kisses on the cheek. He watched like he was wrapped in a fog, like his limbs couldn't move.

Thanksgiving had been momentous for more than just the unveiling of Whitney's lies. Other things had been revealed that weekend. Things that had made his guilt skyrocket.

He hadn't had a clue about Whitney's lies the day he'd looked at Paige in her gorgeous peacock-blue dress and thought, *I married the wrong sister.*

It was crazy. He'd told himself repeatedly that it was just his frustrations with his marriage that had been talking. Paige was not only his sister-in-law, she was also the girl next door. She was sweet. Gentle. A nice girl. He had no business thinking that way about her.

Yet even now, as he tried to reason with himself, the sight of her stole his breath. For the flight, she'd worn jeans and a soft sweater that fit all her curves. Curves that made his heart beat faster.

When she'd texted him while he was away, he hadn't answered her. It was only now that he finally admitted to himself the real reasons why he'd been avoiding her.

Because of the way he'd reacted when he'd seen her in the formfitting Cleopatra costume at the Halloween party.

Because of the desire he'd felt for her over the past month, no matter how hard he tried to push it away and pretend it wasn't there.

Because of the dreams he'd had about her in the

dark of the night when he couldn't control his thoughts.

Evan was still sitting in the dining room, reeling, when Paige headed in his direction. Standing with an awkwardness he hadn't felt since he was in his early teens, he counted every one of her steps as she approached, then held his breath as she rose on her toes to hug him.

Her body was full and lush against his, her scent surrounding him. Her hair brushed his cheek, her breath teased his ear, her heat singed him. And he was damned for noticing, for feeling. Damned for his thoughts.

Damned for his desire for the one woman he could never have.

Chapter Three

Evan's hands remained on her waist as Paige stepped back to look up into his eyes. She'd missed him so much this past month—especially his smile, which had never failed to shine a bright light into even her darkest corner.

He was thinner now, his face a little pale, the circles beneath his hazel eyes darker. She wondered when she'd see his smile again—there wasn't even a hint of it in the flat line of his beautiful mouth.

She wanted to put her hand to his face and smooth away the lines across his forehead. But she wouldn't. Because while she felt terrible for what he'd endured in his marriage to her sister, Paige was also furious with him for running out on his family.

"Paige, I'm so glad the whole family is here now that you've arrived. You must be starving after your flight," Susan said. She was always looking out for everyone. "We have plenty of food laid out."

"Thank you, it all looks delicious." Paige smiled her appreciation. She wished she hadn't missed the wedding rehearsal, but the holidays were a difficult time for many of her therapy clients, full of bad memories, loneliness, feeling apart rather than together—so she'd driven straight from her last appointment to the airport.

Truthfully, she'd also been unable to fully push away the worry that, with Whitney out of the picture now, Paige didn't really have a place in the group anymore. But Susan had quickly dispelled that worry with her comment about everyone in the family being here now that Paige had arrived. And of course the other Mavericks had welcomed her with open arms. It was only Evan whose thoughts, whose emotions, whose response to his soon-to-be ex-wife's sister, remained a mystery.

"Evan, since you haven't finished eating yet," Susan continued as she took Paige's coat, "why don't you help Paige fill up her plate at the buffet, and then the two of you can catch up?"

Susan spoke in a light voice with a smile, but they both knew it was an order rather than a suggestion. Clearly, she could see they had plenty to hash out tonight—friends who were also linked by a sister and a wife who had hurt them both—and she wasn't going to let either of them escape doing just that.

As Evan moved into the dining room with Paige, a wary shadow filled his eyes. He damn well should be wary of her, considering that he hadn't responded to any of her texts, emails, or phone calls during the past month. What's more, she'd bet money that no one here had confronted Evan about his behavior.

Susan, Bob, and the Mavericks had continually told her they thought it best to give him room, to let things settle. But as far as Paige was concerned, all that had accomplished was enabling Evan to go deeper into hiding with every passing week. If not for tomorrow's wedding, he'd probably still be thousands of miles away.

Well, Paige was happy to play the bad guy if it meant getting Evan to wake up and realize how much everyone cared for him—and how badly they all wanted to help him rebuild his life without Whitney. Hopefully, their friendship could survive some hard truths. Because Paige couldn't imagine her life without Evan in it.

Deciding there was no time like the present, even if they were currently standing in front of the vast array of food set out at the buffet, she said, "Everyone has been frantic about you." She made sure to modulate her voice so that only Evan could hear what she was saying. "You ran out on them all—Susan, Bob, the other Mavericks." And *me.* "It didn't help that your text left way more questions than it answered. Daniel told me all about it when he called to see if I might know anything that could allay Susan's worries."

"The bean casserole is good." Evan added a lump of it to her plate before saying, "I needed some time. They all understand that."

"Of course they understand. But you still *deserted*

them. The wedding was coming up. The holidays. It was supposed to be a happy time, but they were all too worried about you to really enjoy it."

Emotion moved through his eyes even as his mouth settled into an increasingly stubborn line. He took her plate and plunked it down next to his at the end of the dining table, far away from everyone else in the house. But though his family tried to pretend nothing was happening in Susan's prettily decorated dining room, Paige still felt as if they were on display.

"I know how bad it was for you," she continued in a low voice. "But you still blew it. You've been there for them when they needed help. You should have let them be there for you." She'd gotten herself so wound up, she couldn't hold back anymore. "And you should have let *me* be there for you too." She swallowed hard before adding, "I'm sure that my being Whitney's sister made it hard for you to talk to me, but I thought we were friends."

"We are friends," he said in a low voice. But he followed up with, "What exactly did she tell you?" The tenor of the question told her he suspected the worst.

"She admitted that she faked the pregnancies and miscarriages…and took steps to make sure she wouldn't get pregnant by accident either." The horrible way Whitney had abused Evan's love and devotion sickened Paige. She shook her head, unable to adequately express the monstrosity of those lies and the utter ruthlessness of her sister's actions. "I don't know how she could have done that—and I can't even begin to imagine what learning the truth must have been like for you."

The shock of discovering Whitney's horrible lies must have been devastating. Beyond devastating. Paige had been so sure Evan would need his family, his friends. She'd waited for his call. A text. An email. Some word from him.

Instead, there'd been total silence.

Even now, his face was a steely mask as he worked to hide every last ounce of emotion. But that was no good. Not with her. Not when she knew him well enough to see the grief—and fury—that flickered in his hazel eyes, darker now with the emotions he couldn't fully conceal.

"She claimed it was all because of me," he said in a grim voice. "That I pushed her to have kids when she didn't want to. That she had no other choice."

"She's always been good at putting the best possible spin on things for herself," Paige said. "Gathering her supporters around her, revealing exactly what she wants them to hear, eliciting the necessary sympathy."

He held her gaze for a penetrating moment. "Did it work?"

She stared at him in shock, an actual physical pain tightening around her heart. "How can you even ask me that?"

Whitney was two years younger, the baby of the family, and though Paige hadn't wanted to admit it, she'd long known that her sister had a dark side. How could she pretend it didn't exist when she'd been the recipient of that darkness herself so many times?

But this was beyond anything she could have imagined Whitney was capable of.

As a psychologist, every single day Paige helped people manage their emotions—which often included dealing with difficult family members. Somehow, though, none of her schooling or experience helped her when it came to her own sister. Whitney always managed to make her feel like she wasn't good enough.

According to her sister, the men Paige dated were losers. She didn't wear the right clothes. Didn't live in the right neighborhood or have the right kind of friends. And every time Paige looked into the harsh mirror her sister held up, she would question her decisions, asking herself if Whitney might be right.

Evan's question pricked that nerve all over again, making her angry enough to snap, "You should trust me more than that. Yes, there are as many sides to every story as there are people involved. But there's no way I could be on her side in this. It doesn't matter that I'm her sister. I abhor what she did."

Paige's breath was shaky as she dragged it in. Despite her irritation—and how painfully aloof Evan seemed right now—her whole body ached with the need to throw her arms around him, to absorb his pain, to make it all better. Whitney had ripped his heart out and shredded it into pieces. Even if he wasn't admitting it.

During the past year or so, Paige had felt him withdrawing more and more from everyone, and she hadn't known what to do for him. It was so much easier to analyze from the outside than it was to examine your own emotions. And the truth was that hers were too involved to offer the solace he needed.

Which was why she should get up from the dining table, and away from Evan, before she said anything she'd regret. It was okay to make sure he understood how much he'd hurt his family with his desertion.

But if he ever found out why it had hurt *her* so much…

She didn't have to be a psychologist to know that little piece of forbidden truth wouldn't help any of them.

"All right, I've gotten things off my chest." She stood. "Now I'm going to enjoy some girl talk with Harper and the rest of the gang."

She marched from the dining room and back into the herd of Mavericks. But she left a piece of herself behind with Evan.

Just the way she always did, whether she wanted to or not.

★ ★ ★

Paige was right. Evan hadn't simply gone dark—he'd deserted everyone. Especially Susan, the foster mother who'd taken him in when his own mother had abandoned him.

In the living room, Will laughed at something Jeremy said. Sebastian high-fived Jeremy, and Matt ruffled his hair, while Daniel pulled out his phone to take a picture of the group.

Evan had come home, determined to enjoy himself. Yet he was still standing on the other side of a chasm from everyone who mattered to him. All because he was too full of pride—and too ashamed—to admit that he'd been completely duped. His career was based on seeing deep inside a situation, making accurate judgments, having good instincts, assessing things correctly. But he hadn't been able to see inside his own marriage.

Finding Susan alone in the kitchen, he slipped his arm around her waist. "I'm sorry."

"You don't need to apologize, honey. It's okay."

He remembered an old movie line, something about love meaning you never had to say you were sorry. He'd always thought that was total crap. Love meant you *absolutely* had to say you were sorry when you'd been an ass.

"It's definitely not okay, Mom. I was wrong about a lot of things. Paige woke me up to some hard truths just now."

Susan glanced at Paige, whom they could see through the open kitchen door. She wasn't looking at them as she chatted with Harper, but Evan had a feeling Paige knew exactly what was being said in the kitchen right now. She was always able to see through to the heart of people. Unlike him.

Susan's face softened, a hint of a smile creasing her lips. "I'm glad she woke you up. But I do understand, even if I was worried. I remember when you were a boy how hard it was for you to talk about your feelings. Your way has always been to keep things inside."

When he'd first come to live with the Spencers at age eleven, after his mother abandoned him and his father gave him away, he hadn't allowed himself to be part of the family. If he'd felt like Susan was bossing him around, he'd given her the silent treatment. Of course, "bossing him around" had consisted of things like making him take a bath so he didn't stink, or asking him to remove his muddy boots before he tracked dirt inside. And if he hadn't been shutting her out, he'd done stupid passive-aggressive stuff, like when she'd asked him to take out the trash, he'd leave the bag just outside the door so that the rotting smell would seep inside. He'd done specifically what she'd asked and no more.

He'd been so afraid to let himself believe he actually belonged with them, no matter how good Susan and Bob were to him. Until their love taught him how to finally trust.

The trust that Whitney had done her damn level best to destroy all over again.

"I still should have called you, should have told you

what happened instead of leaving it up to Paige to give you all the whole story. And I should have realized there was something wrong with my marriage long before I did." He'd been nothing more than a pawn in Whitney's games. He'd spent the past month trying to figure out how he could have been so gullible…but he still hadn't found any answers.

Susan shook her head sadly. "I can't believe she made up the pregnancies, the miscarriages. The pain she caused you. But to have an operation without even telling you?" Her jaw flexed as she gritted her teeth. Susan was always the calm one, totally unruffled by just about anything life had ever thrown at her—and life had thrown a lot. Clenched teeth weren't her style, but Whitney's actions had pushed even Susan's limits. "I made so many excuses for her. So you can't beat yourself up for not seeing the truth, honey. Because I certainly didn't see it. She was so convincing." She sighed, her brow furrowed. "I just hope she won't keep hurting you now that you're no longer together."

"While I was gone, I had my lawyer draw up the divorce papers. I'm letting her have the flat in San Francisco and the apartment in New York." She'd picked out both, and the spaces had frankly always left him more than a little cold. "But the business stuff is all separate, so she can't touch it." Thank God.

"I'm glad you protected your business ventures. I never thought I'd have to say that. But then, I didn't realize she was so devious." Susan actually shivered, before curling her arm through his. "I want you to remember that we're here for you while you go through this. You don't have to do it alone. We all love you."

He pulled Susan in close, hugging her off her feet. "I won't shut you out again, I promise. And I'm done giving Whitney even one more grain of our lives."

But instead of nodding, Susan frowned. "Some things are easier said than done. Especially after we've spent so much of our lives with someone, good or bad." She glanced toward the living room. "Paige was wonderful while you were gone. She knew all the right things to say. I'm sure she wants to help you through this difficult time too."

His chest squeezed at Susan's words, even as he reminded her, "She's Whitney's sister."

Susan clucked her tongue at him. "Which means that she knows her best. When you add in the fact that she's a psychologist, I'm confident she can help you navigate the obstacles in getting over Whitney."

Susan was only trying to help, but Whitney's sister was the last woman in the world he should ask for help. Not when he couldn't stop noticing how the deep red of Paige's sweater made her auburn hair shine and that the gentle curve of her hips in jeans was mouthwatering.

And definitely not when every second that she'd been reading him the Riot Act in the dining room, his urge to kiss her had grown to near irresistible proportions.

Chapter Four

Paige grabbed her coat and stepped outside to enjoy the snow. She was a California girl, so the only snow she ever saw was up in Lake Tahoe. Unfortunately, she didn't get up to the mountains often enough.

Standing on the deck beneath the overhang, she gazed out over the backyard, the porch lamps bathing the snow with a soft blue light. The snow-covered lawn was pristine, with only the tiny footprints of a squirrel running from one side to the other. Flakes fell gently, floating in the air like wisps of magic.

The beauty of the scene reached deep inside her, easing the tension of the past weeks. She loved the career she'd chosen—helping families come together again, teaching people to see the good in their lives instead of only the bad, watching the growth of their spirits. But none of that happened overnight, and the process could sometimes be draining. When Paige added in her own personal issues—including not only the devastation Whitney's lies had caused, but also Paige's unrequited feelings for Evan—she had ended up feeling more than a little plowed under herself.

Thankfully, the serenity of the snowy night restored her. It also helped that Evan had spent the past couple of hours making his rounds inside, giving apologies and explanations about all that had happened. He was doing the right thing. Surely he would have gotten around to it even without her putting his feet to the fire, but she was glad he'd done it tonight so that nothing left a blemish on the wedding tomorrow.

Behind her, the sliding glass door opened, but she didn't turn at the sound of footsteps. She already knew it was Evan. He had a subtle scent all his own, something that always made her heart beat faster. As he stopped beside her at the railing, all it took was his nearness to heat her up.

For a long moment, they stared out at the yard that was as pretty as a calendar picture. She'd been angry before, but now she was simply glad to stand in the silence with him.

Finally, he said, "Thank you for your advice."

"It wasn't advice. It was righteous indignation."

He laughed softly. She hadn't realized how good his laugh could sound when it had been absent for so long. Or that it would fill her up in the places where she'd felt so empty this past month.

He put his hand on hers for a brief moment. "I'm sorry, Paige. It wasn't fair of me to put you in the position of having to explain to everyone what happened. And I shouldn't have left you to handle Whitney alone either."

Over the last month—at least until her sister had left for the south of France just before Christmas—Whitney had called several times, always trying to convince Paige that she was in the right—and Evan was at fault. For her part, Paige took her sister's calls out of hope that she could get Whitney to see the terrible betrayal in what she'd done, to convince her that she had to change, that she needed to atone. But that hadn't happened…and, if Paige was totally honest with herself, it likely never would.

Instead of going through the play-by-play of the last weeks, however, Paige simply told Evan, "Her calls came less often when she realized I wasn't sympathetic."

"She tried to punish you for my kicking her out, for wanting a divorce, didn't she?"

After a moment, Paige admitted, "She said my mother wouldn't have been surprised that I'd failed her yet again."

"Your mother wouldn't have approved of what Whitney did."

"She certainly wouldn't have," Paige agreed. But her mother would have made excuses for her sister anyway.

Because Whitney was the baby of the family, her parents had indulged her. Buying her toys when she cried, rationalizing when she behaved poorly, giving her money instead of insisting she earn it herself.

Their mother had passed from cancer three years

after Whitney married Evan. As she lay dying, she'd made Paige promise to take care of her father and sister. *"You're all they have now,"* her mother had said.

Paige had only just started her family therapy practice, and while she was still in the weeds of her new business, somehow her father had floundered before she even realized it. He hadn't taken care of himself, and when the flu turned into pneumonia, he wasn't strong enough to fight.

After horribly failing her vow to look after him, Paige had sworn she would do whatever it took to support Whitney. She'd stuck with her sister no matter what, listened to Whitney's complaints, given advice she knew her sister wouldn't take, even made excuses for Whitney when she was cruel, selfish, or hurtful.

But once her sister betrayed her husband in such a monumental fashion, Paige had to finally draw the line.

"Apart from being angry with me," he said softly, "how are you doing?"

Paige was always the one who asked that question. She wasn't used to being on the receiving end. "I'm fine."

He raised an eyebrow. "I know a thing or two about those words." He held her gaze. "I also know they're not always the whole truth, even if we wish they were."

She turned slightly, brushing his arm with hers. "You're home, and your family is ecstatic to have you back. There's going to be a beautiful wedding tomorrow." Yes, she was burying her head in the sand, but she didn't want to talk about Whitney anymore. She turned back to the snow. "And we've got this gorgeous sight laid out before us. Like a Norman Rockwell painting."

When Evan's mouth curved slightly as he took in the scene, her heart lifted. He *would* be fine. There'd be days or even weeks when it would all drag him down again, but in the long run, he'd be better off without her sister. Paige would make sure he was.

"Look, the snow is coming faster," she said, leaning over the railing to catch the big, fat flakes. They melted quickly against her skin, and she wiped her wet hand on her coat, the cold suddenly shivering through her.

She was surprised when Evan pulled the lapels of her jacket together. "It's freezing out here. Let's go inside."

"Not yet," she whispered. "It's too beautiful to leave."

He was too beautiful. A few precious minutes with Evan here and there were all she could ever have, and tonight she wanted those minutes to last a little while longer.

★ ★ ★

Snowflakes sparkled in Paige's hair, the porch light danced in her eyes, and her breath puffed in wisps from her parted lips. Behind them, the muted sounds of merriment slid through the window panes, but out here they were in a world of their own.

His fingers still rested on her jacket. He couldn't say how they'd come to stand so close. She'd been reaching for the snowflakes. He'd wanted to reach with her.

And something that was frozen inside him shifted toward her warmth.

He tried to make himself remember that she wasn't only his soon-to-be ex-wife's sister, she was also a good, honest, wonderful woman who deserved better than a man weighted down with all his baggage.

But the subtle perfume of her skin, her hair, and the succulent pink of her lips made it hard to give a damn about all the reasons he should keep his hands off her.

Lost in her chocolate eyes, he forgot who she was, forgot who *he* was. Beneath the night sky and the softly falling snow, they became two people without a history, without a past.

And with nothing between them but temptation.

The wind whipped up, and she leaned into him, close enough that he couldn't resist stealing the kiss he'd craved for what seemed like forever.

Her lips against his were light as a feather, testing, teasing, giving. But when he ran his tongue along her bottom lip, coaxing her to open, to let him in, her sweetness invaded him, took him over, made him greedy to feed his growing hunger. She pressed her hands to his chest as he cupped her cheeks and crushed her mouth beneath his.

God. He couldn't get enough of her taste, her heat, and the way she vibrated with need as she pressed her curves into him.

He groaned with need, intensifying the kiss, driving them deeper into sensation, passion, desire. Her hair was soft on the backs of his hands as he slid them down her shoulders, over her thick coat, to her waist, pulling her closer. She pushed her hands inside his jacket, her touch scorching him through his dress shirt.

He wanted nothing more than to drag her down to the deck, covering her with his body. Taking her. Filling her. Owning her.

Loving her.

Reality knocked him hard in the chest. He couldn't love another woman, couldn't risk giving his heart away to anyone ever again.

As he made himself draw back from her heat, her softness, the seductive pull of her mouth, he forcefully reminded himself how wrong this was. She was his sister-in-law—and they couldn't kiss like this, consumed by each other, dying for more, the next touch, the next taste. And certainly not when he wasn't even divorced yet. He needed to tell her that he was nowhere near ready to put himself out there for anyone. That he might never be again. That she deserved so much more than a few stolen, desperate kisses on a snowy night.

All he could get out was, "What are you doing to

me?" Even though he already knew. She was turning his battered and bruised heart inside out. No matter how hard he tried to fight it or ignore it, Paige wasn't afraid to get in his face and make him see the truth. Including the truth of his desire for her...

Before she could reply, the glass door slid open and Jeremy's excited tones tripped down the stairs. "Look at the snow falling, you guys. Let's go out and play!"

He grabbed Paige's hand and pulled her with him down the stairs onto the snow-covered lawn, with Noah right behind them, dashing into the snow, his glee lighting up the yard. Harper and Will joined them a few moments later, then Ari, scooping up Noah and saying, "Let's make a snow angel." Ari called out to Matt, "Come on down and make your own snow angel."

"I've already got two," he replied as he joined them in the fresh powder.

Charlie and Sebastian jumped into the snow along with Lyssa. Susan made a snowball she threw at Daniel. The yard was full of love and laughter. At the head of the steps, Bob smiled indulgently. Even Francine had wheeled her walker outside, the lines of her face creased into a big smile.

But at the center of them all was Paige.

She tipped her head back and stuck out her tongue to catch the snowflakes, and when she laughed, the joyful sound sent another deep pang of longing through Evan. Snow powdered her hair, and the porch light morphed her into something ethereal, a beautiful fairy with white crystals melting on her tongue.

Exactly the way he'd melted into her. No matter how wrong it might be.

Chapter Five

It was already the most beautiful wedding *ever*...and the bride hadn't even appeared yet.

The boys, as Susan lovingly called the Mavericks, had set up the latticed arbor, knotted with silk flowers, in front of the fireplace. The Christmas decorations had come down, and the room was now adorned with garlands and silver bells. The light dusting of snow outside the windows made the scene truly stunning.

The guest list wasn't large, just good friends. Noah Bryant, the Mavericks' lawyer, with his wife, Colbie. Cal Danniger, their business manager, who always seemed to be with a different woman. Award-winning vintner Marcus Sullivan and his rock star wife, Nicola. As well as movie star Smith Sullivan and his brilliant wife, Valentina. Paige found Marcus, Nicola, Smith, and Valentina to be totally down-to-earth. Fortunately, she was used to being around the Mavericks, who were regular people at heart, despite their enormous wealth and to-die-for good looks. Harper and Will could have gone for a huge wedding, but this understated affair was a much better fit than any glittering, lavish event would have been.

As the first bars of the *Wedding March* rang out, everyone stood—and gasped as Harper appeared on her brother Jeremy's arm. She was beyond beautiful in a gorgeous cream-colored suit edged with braid, a lacy blouse beneath. Paige loved that she hadn't chosen a traditional wedding dress, her blond hair pulled up in a classic knot with artful tendrils curling around her face.

Will's reaction was everything Paige had known it would be. So much love for his bride radiated from him that it stole Paige's breath.

She remembered the first time she'd met Harper and Jeremy. Paige had felt Will's deep love for Harper even then, the way his eyes followed her wherever she went. There'd also been a softening about him that she'd never seen before—not just for Harper, but for Harper's brother as well. Will had not only fallen in love with a kind beautiful woman, he'd fallen in love with her family too.

Will mouthed, *I love you*, to Harper, and Paige's heart flip-flopped in her chest. They were so adorable. So good to each other. The kind of couple who made you wish everyone could find a love like that. Paige certainly wished *she* could find the same beautiful love they shared.

Her gaze instinctively searched for Evan in the audience, one row up and to the right—only to find that he was looking at her too. For a long moment, their eyes held.

All night long, Paige had relived those sinfully sweet moments in Evan's arms, his taste on her tongue, his hands on her face, in her hair, his mouth taking hers with such passion. Such need. She could still hardly believe it had happened.

Evan had kissed her.

She knew no one had witnessed their kiss, because if they had, not one of the Mavericks or their significant others would have been able to hold back their questions and commentary.

Jeremy's voice pulled her attention back to where he and Harper now stood at the end of the aisle before Will. "I know my mom and dad would have loved Harper and Will getting married. And I love it too." Jeremy said his lines proudly, giving Harper into Will's care. "Did I do okay?" he whispered loudly to Will.

Chuckles spread through the audience, and Will smiled with deep affection at his almost brother-in-law. "You did great."

Jeremy flashed a huge grin at Will, then Harper, and finally took his seat in the front row, bursting with excitement and happiness.

Susan was beaming in the front row near Evan, a tissue in her hand as she dabbed at the corner of her eye, while Bob put his arm around her and smiled from cheek to cheek. Paige hadn't known Susan well when Whitney and Evan had their no-expense-spared wedding—one so grand it was featured in several major bridal and society magazines. But she was sure

Susan would have cried then too, hoping for their happiness. Happiness that never came to be.

"Dearly beloved," the officiant began, "we are gathered here today to celebrate the wedding of Harper Newman and Will Franconi." She smiled at the bride and groom. "I'm pleased to say that our celebrants have prepared their own vows."

Will curled his fingers around Harper's. "For so long, I didn't believe I would ever love anyone. I didn't believe I ever *could* love anyone. But then you and Jeremy came unexpectedly into my life, and I fell for both of you in an instant. One smile. One laugh. That was all it took. I will always love you, Harper. I will always love your family." Will looked fondly at Jeremy and smiled. "Your brother is my brother. My heart is your heart. My life is your life."

Paige's eyes misted at Will's beautiful words. She didn't want to sit here and compare this wedding with Whitney and Evan's, but it was impossible not to. When she glanced at Evan and saw him sitting ramrod straight, his expression tight and shuttered, she knew he must be remembering the vows he'd made to her sister.

Whitney had promised to love and honor Evan. But she never truly had.

And all the while her sister had been glowing in her ornate wedding gown, Paige had been standing beside her as maid of honor, wearing a pink dress that was too frilly and shiny. Dying inside.

Because Paige had loved Evan from the moment she'd walked into his classroom. She'd never admitted the truth to anyone—but that didn't make it any less real.

She'd been a teaching assistant, grading papers for him, helping him design student assignments. Sometimes he'd come to her campus apartment in the evening to discuss a particular student, their issues, good and bad. Then one night, Whitney blew into town for a visit. And as soon as Evan saw her sister, Paige had become all but invisible.

But she'd always wondered: Would he eventually have fallen for *her*, his friend and confidante, if he'd never met Whitney?

Some things were unknowable.

What she could hold on to now with all her might and all her heart was that last night, he'd finally kissed her. A kiss she had waited on for nine long years.

"You've made me whole again, healed me." Will raised Harper's hands to his lips. "Everything I have to give, I give to you. Please take my heart, my love. Because they are yours forever."

In the row ahead of Paige, Susan sniffled softly with Bob's arm around her. Sebastian looked tenderly at Charlie. While Evan stared ahead with fierce determination to appear completely normal.

Harper's voice trembled as she began her vows. "I will take your heart, your love, and give you mine. I never thought I could need anyone the way I need you.

I never thought I could *let* myself need anyone so much. But I also never thought I would meet someone I could trust with my life, with my brother's life. I trust you with all of that, Will, and more. You are the kindest, most loving man I know. You bring me light. You are mine," Harper declared as Will drew her closer. "And I am yours."

The audience gave a collective sigh of happiness at the romantic and heartfelt vows as the officiant collected the rings from Noah, who had to be the cutest ring bearer on the planet. After Harper and Will had slipped the bands onto each other's fingers, the officiant said, "I hereby pronounce you husband and wife. You may now kiss the bride."

Will cupped Harper's face in his palms, his gaze roaming her features as if he needed to map each beautiful contour he saw. Then he slowly lowered his mouth to hers. Paige held her breath for the perfect moment, the perfect kiss, and sighed when it finally came, the melding of their lips, their hearts, their souls. Harper's hands fluttered a moment, then settled on Will's forearms, holding him. Their kiss was almost too intimate to watch, yet too beautiful to turn away from. Then Will slid his big hands down her throat, skimmed her shoulders, and finally gathered her into him, their hearts touching. With one hand across her back, he dipped Harper low over his arm, kissing her with all the passion that always burned between them.

Paige flushed, unable to stop herself from looking

at Evan again. She swore she saw the same burn in his eyes as he looked right back at her, at least for a split second before he turned away, a muscle jumping in his jaw.

Finally, Will straightened with a grin, Harper laughed, her face glowing, and Jeremy jumped up from his seat to hug Will hard. Then he said in his best manly voice, "You better take care of my sister or else." He looked over at the other Mavericks and asked, "That's what they always say in the movies, right?"

Will laughed and group-hugged Jeremy and Harper. "Yep, that's what they always say. I will definitely take care of her, buddy."

"Just like we'll take care of Will," Harper said, then gave her new husband another very hot kiss.

Soon, everyone gathered around for hugs. Susan wiped tears from her face as she kissed Harper's cheek. This was family and love, close friends and best wishes. And when Smith Sullivan gave Harper a hug, Paige was sure millions of women would have died to be in her shoes.

Paige circled around, planning to offer her congratulations once the crush was over. On the far side of the room, Evan watched, the barest hint of a smile on his mouth.

"Great wedding, wasn't it?"

She turned at the sound of Daniel's deep voice.

"The perfect wedding for a perfect couple," he said. "Although I can see that you're worrying." Daniel nodded in Evan's direction.

Busted. Of course Daniel had noticed her scrutiny. The Mavericks didn't miss a thing. "I hate to think that he might be comparing his wedding to theirs."

"I'm sure he is. But he'll come through this."

"Of course he will." She gently nudged Daniel's ribs. "After all, he's got you guys to talk him down when he needs it."

"And he's got you too, Paige."

That was definitely true. Evan had always had her, whether he knew it or not. Yes, she'd put up with Whitney's behavior all those years because of her promise to their mother to look out for her. But Paige had also stayed for Evan—because she hadn't been able to bear the thought of walking out of his life if she'd walked out of Whitney's.

And now? Now that he and Whitney were done? Now that he and Paige had *kissed*?

She sighed, wishing she knew what to do, wishing she had all the answers. Her feelings for Evan were stronger than ever, but despite his passionate kiss last night, he was doing his damn level best to act as if it had never happened. She hoped he wasn't sorry, that he hadn't been about to apologize for kissing her when everyone burst out onto the porch to play in the snow. But given how raw and bruised inside he clearly was from her sister's betrayal, Paige knew that his regret for their kiss was a distinct—and awful—possibility.

"Anything else you want to talk about?" Daniel

asked. "Because that was a heck of a sigh." His eyes were warm and far too perceptive.

"It's been a busy holiday season," she said, even though they both knew the crux of her problems centered on her sister. "People needed lots of last-minute therapy sessions to make it through." She let out a small laugh, one without much humor. "I could have used some emergency sessions myself."

"We all could have," Daniel agreed. Again, she knew they were both talking about Whitney, even if they weren't saying her name aloud. "In fact, I'm pretty sure there's nothing that can't be cured with one of my signature Top-Notch cocktails."

Paige groaned, remembering the hangover she'd had the last time she let him make her one of his extremely potent concoctions. But maybe the alcohol would help. Maybe it would make her brave.

Brave enough to not only kiss Evan again...but to finally tell him what was deep inside her heart.

Chapter Six

Evan's hopes and dreams for happily ever after might have bitten the dust—but that didn't mean he believed the same was in store for Will. He'd seen the pure love in Harper's eyes. No one could fake that. He'd never doubted Harper, never doubted Will.

It was his own judgment he doubted.

The group of well-wishers around Will and Harper was still too large to wade into, so Evan watched from the side of the room. In the opposite corner of the living room, Daniel was mixing a drink for Paige. Probably his "famous" Top-Notch cocktail.

Despite knowing better, Evan couldn't stop his gaze from tracking the formfitting lines of the sea green dress Paige wore. Her natural beauty—especially when she laughed at something Daniel said to her—was enough to steal Evan's breath right out of his chest.

He'd forced himself to step away from her last night, but he hadn't been able to stop their intense and heated kiss from following him into his dreams. In the dark of his mind while he'd slept, he'd tasted her again, steeped himself in her scent and the seductive feel of her curves pressed against him.

Bob clapped him on the back, breaking Evan out of his forbidden longings. "Nifty wedding, wasn't it?"

Evan smiled. "Best Maverick wedding yet."

Bob didn't let go of Evan's shoulder as he turned serious. "I'm glad you apologized to your mom. I know things are rough on you right now, but she was real hurt when you didn't come home for Christmas."

Guilt twisted in Evan's belly. "I was wrong. She didn't deserve that. And neither did you."

"Takes a man to admit when he's wrong. We all love you, and we're rooting for you. Things are gonna work out in the long run. Don't let that bi—" Bob stopped himself before the word came out. "Sorry. Susan would let me have it for cussing on the wedding day. Just remember we've got your back."

All the Mavericks did. Just as he had theirs.

But what would they say if they'd seen his kiss with Paige last night out on the deck? Where would all their sympathy and understanding go if they'd witnessed him turning from his wife to her sister in barely the blink of an eye?

Surely, if anyone had caught so much as a whiff of the passionate kiss, they'd be all over him now. And he'd deserve every last ounce of their censure.

On the far side of the room, Matt and Ari joined Paige and Daniel. Noah held his arms out for Paige, and as she hauled him up, she whispered something that made the little boy laugh.

"He's a cutie, isn't he?" Bob observed. "That kid's the apple of his dad's eye. And he loves Ari to absolute pieces."

But Evan wasn't looking at Ari. He couldn't take his eyes off Paige. She was so good with Noah, with kids in general. She'd chosen family therapy because she loved bringing families back together. He had no doubt that she would make a wonderful mother one day. Unlike her sister…

"Looks like the throng is thinning out," Bob said, herding Evan to the arbor beneath which Harper and Will stood.

They looked so good together. He truly couldn't be happier for them.

"Harper." Evan enfolded Will's bride in his arms and hugged her hard. "There was never a prettier bride."

He shook hands with Will, then pulled him into a hug as well. "You done good. Real good. And Jeremy certainly approves."

Harper smiled with a fond look across the room at Jeremy, who was circling Noah, his arms out like airplane wings, making the boy giggle. "Jeremy had Will picked out even before I did."

"I've always said your brother's got damn good taste," Will said on a happy laugh.

The photographer signaled then, indicating it was time for family pictures. The slim gray-haired man arranged them all in front of the fireplace, with Will and Harper central in the arbor, Jeremy on Harper's right, and everyone else fanning out from there. Charlie and Sebastian stood hand in hand by Francine's walker. Matt and Ari surrounded Noah. Daniel and Lyssa stood next to their parents.

Evan tried not to feel like the odd man out.

"Paige, what are you doing back there?" Will called to her from across the room. "Get over here."

"But...it's just family."

Will gave her a look like she was nuts. "That's why we want you here."

Susan added, "Don't be silly, dear. You'll always be family."

They all joined in. The only one who couldn't find his voice was Evan.

Because he couldn't stop thinking about their kiss.

It hadn't been a kiss he'd give a sister. Instead, it had been like his first taste of water after years in a desert, and he hadn't been able to get enough, hadn't even come close to satisfying his thirst.

Before he realized what was happening, the photographer placed Paige next to him, probably because they were the lone man and woman in the group.

The silk of her dress brushed his hand—and just like that, he was back outside in the snow with her, the silk of her hair against his fingers as he kissed her, as he devoured her mouth.

He was desperate to feel and taste her all over again.

But he couldn't trust his judgment or his emotions anymore. He just plain couldn't trust, so he knew he had to stay away from Paige until he had himself totally under control again. Especially given that Whitney had left his bed cold since her last fake miscarriage as the distance between them grew into a deep chasm.

Last night's kiss with Paige had stirred up not only emotional longings, but physical ones too. Yes, he desperately needed to blow off some sexual steam with someone, but he knew damn well that the worst woman he could do that with was Paige. She was kind, giving, caring. And he wouldn't just end up hurting her badly.

He'd lose her friendship forever.

Yet he still couldn't stop reliving their wild, insane, sexy, mind-altering kiss.

The photographer took dozens of pictures, then rearranged them all again for more shots from different angles. "You two here," he said, pointing in front of the arbor.

Before he, or Paige, could explain that they weren't a couple, they were moved into position by the assistant, and more pictures were snapped.

Lyssa stepped between them as soon as the photographer finished and linked elbows with them. "What do you say the three of us get some champagne and start ringing in the New Year?"

Evan looked at his watch. "It's only four o'clock."

Lyssa rolled her eyes at him. "It's never too early to celebrate a new marriage *and* a new year."

He should be grateful for the way Lyssa had just separated him from Paige. Had it not been for her interruption, who knew what he might have said? Or done.

Because the kiss he and Paige shared had not only scrambled his brain, it had made it nearly impossible to remember who he was. Who Paige was.

But no matter how much he wanted to kiss her again, forgetting wasn't something he could allow himself to do. Not ever again. For both their sakes.

Especially hers.

Chapter Seven

Evan left Chicago right after ringing in the New Year with his family. He justified his early departure with the fact that he'd been gone from the San Francisco headquarters of The Collins Group, for over a month. He'd been in contact with his hundreds of traders, financial analysts, planners, and market analysts while he was gone, but there was still plenty for him to personally catch up on.

But it was more than work that had him flying out early on January first. All evening at Will and Harper's wedding reception, it had taken every ounce of will-power he'd had not to grab Paige's hand and pull her away from the crowds to a quiet, secluded spot where he could devour her mouth again.

Somewhere he could devour *all* of her this time.

She had been far too gorgeous in her dress, the silky fabric caressing each and every one of her curves. When she laughed, he'd not only picked out the sound above everything else, he'd felt her laughter deep inside.

Had it not been for the family and friends who'd

somehow managed to keep the two of them on opposite sides of the room the whole night, he might have slipped. He'd wanted to hold Paige close, bury his face in her hair and drink in the scents that had driven him nuts the night before. He'd wanted to bust past everything he knew to be wrong...and take the hot night of pleasure that Paige's kiss had promised.

But she was the opposite of her sister. She wasn't hard or conniving. Paige was sweet and guileless. She was giving and selfless. She cared for others above herself, thought of everyone's well-being before her own. She gave too much of herself already, and he simply could not take anything more from her. The best way he could look out for her now was by *not* dragging her into his mess of a life.

Because he would never forgive himself if he hurt her.

Which meant it had to stop. All of it—especially the erotic dreams of her at night. They needed to get back to the place they'd been, where they used to laugh and talk without tension, just like when they'd been friends in college and everything had seemed so much easier.

In San Francisco, Evan's driver met him at the airport. "It's good to have you back, sir," said Mortimer, holding open the door of the roomy town car.

"It's good to be back."

Mortimer had been with Evan for five years, and though Evan insisted there was no need for *sir*, Mortimer preferred the formality, along with a black suit, chauffeur's cap, and shiny black boots.

For once, traffic was light, and the drive down the Peninsula to his home in Atherton seemed to flash by as he buried himself in more of the work he'd been doing on his plane.

Mrs. Mortimer opened the front door as soon as they arrived. The Mortimers had come as a package deal—housekeeper/cook and driver/property manager—and lived in a cottage on Evan's property, with a tidy little garden. Mrs. Mortimer was as tiny as Mortimer was tall, with white hair as thick as her husband was bald.

"It's wonderful to see you, Mr. Collins. I hope you had a good trip."

"It was good, Mrs. M, and I'm happy to be home."

"In your absence, Mrs. Collins has been here several times. She—" Mrs. M pursed her lips, breathing out with a long sigh. "—took things."

He'd expected as much. "Don't worry about it, Mrs. M. I'll take care of it."

She frowned, but nodded without pressing any further. "Shall I make you a spot of lunch?"

"I ate on the plane. Just some coffee in the office, please."

Her footsteps had barely faded down the hallway to the kitchen when Evan noticed the first missing item, a large porcelain jar, Ming dynasty, that had stood on a pedestal in the corner of the entry hall.

Directly across, the living room wall was empty where the Salvador Dali had hung. He'd liked that painting, his choice rather than hers. Whitney had allowed it in the house only because it was worth a fortune. He would have to take inventory. Whitney should know he had every valuable documented. At the same time, however, he found he was numb to the loss of his possessions. The lawyers could hash it out.

Honestly, the more he looked around his home, the less he cared for any of it. It was way too large for him. This was Whitney's showpiece, a twelve-bedroom monstrosity with Italian marble in the large foyer, a curving staircase like something out of *Gone With the Wind*, and a tub in the master suite that rivaled the Roman baths. The house included a formal dining room and living room, an actual ballroom, a somewhat cozier family room, a library, and the gym. There was a large home office, plus an enormous kitchen and informal dining room used for private meals. The outdoor pool, Jacuzzi, and tennis courts were just beyond the formal garden, which included every flowering bush imaginable and exquisite roses his gardener tended daily. Of course, Whitney had spared no expense in furnishings and artwork, which she now seemed to think she was entitled to take. At least he could be reasonably assured she wouldn't make a grab for the first editions in his collection, since she'd never entered the library.

Evan had always spent the bulk of his free time in

the library. He'd enjoyed many evenings in that quiet, comfortable room discussing books with Paige over an excellent bottle of wine. He'd enjoyed those nights far more, in fact, than the galas Whitney had insisted they attend—and throw.

Now that Whitney was gone, he didn't need twelve bedrooms or elaborate grounds. What he needed was a change. A new start. He should sell the damn thing and buy a flat in San Francisco where he wouldn't have to commute to his headquarters.

But if he did that, he'd be too far away from Paige, who lived just a few miles away in Menlo Park. There would be no late-night discussions about books, no shared bottle of wine, no more spontaneous weekend visits.

And no more kisses.

Damn it, he needed to stop thinking like this. Needed to stop *wanting* like this.

When the doorbell rang, his immediate thought was that he'd conjured Paige, wishing it were true, even as wrong and crazy as that was.

A beat later, a worse thought hit. One far more likely since Paige was probably still back in Chicago. It had to be Whitney, here to whisk away another priceless piece of art—and fan the flames of anger and betrayal.

Never seeing his soon-to-be ex-wife again would be too soon. They could hash out the divorce through their lawyers. But he didn't want Mrs. M to answer the door and end up in the middle of something ugly between him and Whitney. That wouldn't be fair to the woman who had gone out of her way to take care of Evan all these years.

He steeled himself against the fury of seeing Whitney again, but when he opened the door, he instead found a young man and woman on his front porch.

Their hair was a matching shade of light brown—though the woman's was streaked with blond. They looked to be somewhere in their mid-twenties, and judging by the similarities of their features, they were obviously related.

"Hi," the man said. "We're looking for Evan Collins. And I'm pretty sure you're him."

A slight movement behind them made Evan realize they weren't alone. An older woman stood in the background.

Despite the years and the lines on her skin, despite the gray in her brown hair, he knew that face, even though he hadn't seen it in twenty-five years.

His mother was back.

Chapter Eight

The silence was so deep it had no bottom.

Evan's mother looked at him with the same expression she'd worn whenever his father had started to rage. Eyes narrowed with fear, brow furrowed, worry etched into the lines at her mouth. With a clench of his gut, he was right back in their dilapidated Chicago apartment, trying to dodge his father's fists.

"You're Evan Collins, right?" the stranger repeated, while the young woman stepped back to flank his mother, hovering by her protectively. Only, Evan's mother hung back as if ready to bolt. "Aren't you?" he said again in a surprisingly tough voice. Or maybe it was desperation that made him think he had the right to get up in Evan's face like this.

"Yes," he finally replied, "I'm Evan Collins."

That was all it took for his mother to break down, tears all but spurting from her eyes like a broken water line. "I'm so sorry," she sobbed. "I'm so proud of you." She put her hand to her mouth and kept repeating the words. "I'm so sorry. I'm so proud of you. I'm so sorry." Over and over again.

The young woman, slightly taller than his mother, drew her close. "It's okay, Mom. Everything's gonna be okay."

"She's your mom?" The question escaped before Evan could stop it. This young woman was his half sister? "What the hell?"

The guy put the flat of his hand to his chest. "I'm Tony." He hooked a thumb over his shoulder. "That's my sister, Kelsey. We only recently learned that you're our brother."

Shock wasn't the right word for what Evan was feeling. It was more like a bowling ball had just slammed into his head at top speed, leaving his brain cells scattered like bowling pins at the end of the alley after a strike.

Maybe he was dreaming. Maybe, from the moment Whitney had told him she'd lied about being pregnant, putting him through the grief of those faked miscarriages, never even wanting his kid in the first place— maybe it had all just been a nightmare. Sure, why not add in his long-lost mother walking back into his life, the woman who'd abandoned him to a child-beater? Returning with two grown kids, no less, who were his brother and sister.

Twenty-five years. That's how long she'd waited to come find him.

He hadn't been able to hold back his surprise, but he'd be damned if he'd let her see he was still hurting over her desertion. He'd gotten over it a long time ago.

"What are you doing here?"

His question was deliberately cool. Calm, despite the fact that his mother continued to bury her face against Kelsey's shoulder while the younger woman stroked her hair, murmuring to her. Evan had let his emotions get the best of him one too many times during the past month. He wouldn't make that mistake again, no matter the provocation.

"We didn't want to freak you out, but we worried that if we called your headquarters, we'd never get through to you. And if we did, you probably wouldn't believe we were actually related to you."

Hell, he could hardly believe it now, even though he could see with his own eyes that this was his mother—and knew he shared more than one physical feature with Tony and Kelsey.

"We aren't here for your money, if that's what you're thinking."

His thoughts hadn't had a chance to get that far, not when seeing his mother again after all these years had jumbled his brain so badly.

Evan raised an eyebrow, taking Tony's measure. They were the same height, with the same hair color and hazel eyes. Tony had a strong chin, a sturdy stance, and an intelligent gaze he didn't drop. He looked to be about a decade younger than Evan.

It hit him then—his mother had left when he was nine. One day she was there, the next she was gone. His father had told Evan she obviously didn't want to take care of him, or the husband she "owed everything" to, anymore.

That had been a brutal night for Evan. One that had played out in his nightmares for years. He hadn't been able to avoid his father's fists that night. And finally, alone in his bed, his body aching, Evan had given in to tears for the mother who hadn't loved him enough to take him with her.

"How old are you?" he asked almost roughly.

"Twenty-five," Tony answered.

He glanced at Kelsey and she answered his unspoken question. "We're twins."

Maybe he should ask their birthday, work out the exact date. But he didn't need to ask for any more confirmation. Not when he already knew by looking at them that these two weren't his half siblings. They were full-blood siblings.

It wasn't difficult for Evan to put two and two together. His mother must have found out she was pregnant and decided to get the hell out. Obviously, taking a nine-year-old on the run would have been too hard.

So she'd left him in hell.

Tony lifted his chin and looked Evan straight in the eye. "Can we come in?"

Jesus, how had his life come to this, screwed up beyond all comprehension? His wife had lied to him for years. He'd kissed his sister-in-law breathless. And now good old Mom was back, accompanied by two siblings who wanted God only knew what.

He could kick them off his property and file a re-straining order against them to ensure they never got within a hundred feet again. But Susan always said it was better to face the devil you knew. And his foster mother—the woman who'd saved him from the brutal pit his birth mother had left him in—was always right.

"You might as well come in."

* * *

Mrs. M made coffee and brought out pastries and coffee cake to go with it, as if this were a social call. They sat in the formal living room furnished with expensive chairs and sofas that Evan had always found uncomfortable.

Tony's sister—Evan's sister too—sat on the sofa next to their mother. Kelsey had produced tissues from her bag and given them to their mother, who was now dabbing her nose and eyes, sniffling. Tony sat in the chair on her other side, as if he and Kelsey were sentinels protecting her.

Evan poured coffee for everyone. Really, at this point, why the hell not? He pushed the sugar and cream their way across the glass tabletop. When his mother said, "Thank you," her voice was soft.

He remembered that voice. Remembered her sing-ing to him when he had trouble falling asleep at night. And he remembered her crying too. Remembered the sounds of breaking glass and slamming doors, the smell of mold in the hallways of their tenement. He remembered the bitter cold in the winters, his gloves, coat, and shoes too worn and too small to keep it out.

Kelsey fixed two cups with milk and sugar. Tony took his black, just like Evan. Despite the crazy situation, he couldn't help but be impressed by the twins so far. They were dressed as impeccably as any of the Mavericks and they were straight-forward and polite. They both obviously cared a great deal for their mother. And why wouldn't they, when she'd chosen their welfare over Evan's?

"So what's your story?" he asked Tony, planning to get as much information as possible out of them in the shortest amount of time. That way he'd have the ammo he needed to protect himself going forward. Evan had let people get the best of him one too many times. That stopped *now*.

"It was Mom's birthday a couple of weeks ago."

December fifteenth. He hadn't forgotten the date.

"We were watching TV, one of those houses-of-the-rich-and-famous shows. It was your home. Nice place, by the way."

Evan had completely forgotten about that interview. It was something Whitney had set up back in October. Before everything went to hell.

Although that wasn't true, was it? Because their marriage had gone bad long before she admitted her lies. Long before she'd lied about the pregnancies, if he was perfectly honest.

The shine had worn off almost right from the start, in fact, if it had ever truly been there at all.

"We saw the resemblance between you and Tony," Kelsey put in. "It was unbelievable."

His mother—no, Susan was his mother now. This woman didn't deserve the title anymore. *Theresa* sipped her coffee, looking at him over the rim, then held the cup between her hands as if she needed warmth.

Once upon a time, he'd been desperate for warmth. And she hadn't been there to give it to him. He was supposed to be getting answers from his long-lost siblings, but his fury couldn't be contained another minute longer.

"Did she tell you why she left me behind?" Bubbling, boiling rage rose up in him. "Did she tell you about the hell she left me in?" He had to put his coffee down before he broke the delicate china.

"She hasn't really talked about any of that," Tony admitted as Theresa broke down in renewed sobs. "We thought it would be better if we were all here. Then we could work it out together."

Evan drew on every ounce of self-control he possessed to ratchet down his breathing as he curled his fingers around the dainty, carved-wood arms of the chair, digging in like he had talons.

He didn't need to listen to this crap. He should toss them out on their asses.

But he couldn't. Not when he was desperate for answers to questions that had haunted him for years.

Why had she left? Where had she gone?

And why hadn't she taken him?

"What's your last name?" His voice sounded like gravel.

"Collins, same as yours," Tony said. "She didn't change her name."

With all the resources he had, he could have found her. But he hadn't tried. Because he'd sworn to himself that he'd moved on.

She beseeched him with her eyes, begging piteously for his understanding. Looking at her made his head whirl, sending his emotions tumbling. His knee jerked involuntarily, knocking the table, spilling coffee from his cup.

There were so many things he needed to understand, yet he couldn't get the questions out. Not when he was falling into the same pit Whitney had dropped him into a month ago. Going dark, going deep, silent—shutting down.

Get a grip. Pull it together.

He would, damn it. He'd draw deep from his well of self-control. But he couldn't stop wishing for Paige. She was a family psychologist. She could walk him through this minefield, which felt even more dangerous than anything he'd experienced with Whitney.

He needed Paige before he went off half-cocked on two people who'd possibly been as damaged by what their parents had done as he was. Paige would know how to straighten out this massively messed-up situation with her level-headed advice, her calm voice, her gentle smiles.

Because he sure as hell didn't know what to say.

But Paige wasn't here. And Evan wasn't a kid anymore, afraid of his father's fists, hiding under his covers, praying to someone who didn't listen. Crying for a woman who'd left him.

He was a powerful man, both in body and position. He was a billionaire. He'd overcome. He'd moved the hell on. So he would control his emotions. He would not sound like a raving madman.

"Let's talk about you two first. Tell me about yourselves." He was actually amazed at how calm and rational he sounded despite everything roiling inside him.

They blinked in duplicate, like the twins they were, obviously surprised by his abrupt switch.

"Well," Tony said, using the word like he needed a second to change gears. "I'm working on my graduate degree in engineering at UCSF."

"Impressive." UC San Francisco was a great school. Expensive too. He wondered if Tony had gotten some sort of scholarship, or if he was bogged down with student loans. Evan turned to Kelsey. "And you?"

"I'm a CPA. I work for a firm in San Francisco."

"Equally impressive. You like numbers, I take it?" Like him.

She smiled, nodded. He saw his mother's—no, Theresa's smile in her. The rare smiles from his youth, when his father hadn't been around.

"I'm so proud of them." It was the first full sentence Theresa had spoken since her litany on the front porch: *I'm so sorry. I'm so proud of you.*

The calm he'd exerted started to desert him again. He felt the mushroom cloud of anger welling up from his gut.

Yet again, he wished for Paige, for her common sense, her unruffled feathers, her expertise, her reassuring influence. She gave too much already, and he had no right to ask for more. But she would know exactly how to handle this, how to put them all at ease, get them talking without Evan clenching his fists at every word out of that woman's mouth. Paige would get the answers to all the questions he couldn't seem to ask.

Just as he was balling his fists, straining for the control to keep from shouting—or, at this point, just plain losing his mind—his doorbell rang again.

He didn't give Mrs. M a chance to answer. It was an excuse to get out of that room. To breathe for a few precious moments. Even if it was Whitney on the other side of the door, right now she seemed like the lesser of two evils.

But evil wasn't waiting at his front door.

Paige was.

The woman he'd been dreaming about.

The woman his muddled mind had been begging for.

He practically yanked her off her feet as he pulled

her inside. He hugged her before he could remember why that wasn't a good idea. The press of her gorgeous curves against him and her scent filling his head simply scrambled whatever was left of his senses, and he blurted out, "My long-lost mother is here. Along with the brother and sister I never knew I had."

Chapter Nine

Paige would have dropped her purse if the strap hadn't been slung crosswise over her shoulder.

She'd been nervous about coming here today, especially after Evan had gone out of his way to avoid her at the wedding reception. But she couldn't possibly pretend she hadn't loved kissing him, hadn't reveled in his body against hers. Or that she didn't want more.

Even if she was setting herself up for a terrible fall, she still had to know what their kiss meant to him. What *she* meant to him.

Only, instead of finding him alone...he suddenly had a mother, a brother, and a sister?

In the face of this astonishing news, her nerves, her questions about what the two of them were to each other—all of that disappeared. At least for now. Although, the heat his greeting hug had flooded her with wasn't going anywhere.

Paige knew the bare bones of his past. Evan had never hidden where he came from, but he didn't talk about it much either. She knew that his mother had abandoned him, leaving him with an abusive, alcoholic father. The Spencers had rescued him by taking him off his father's hands, which probably had felt like another abandonment for a preteen boy, even though his dad was violent. Then Susan and Bob had worked their loving magic, and Evan had grown into an amazing man despite his difficult youth.

"I know," Evan said, reading her expression. "It's a shocker."

Shocker was the understatement of the century. It felt more like the first enormous hill on the Giant Dipper roller coaster out at Santa Cruz Beach Boardwalk, when your stomach flew up into your throat and a scream was wrenched right out of you.

And it wasn't just the shock of his family that knocked her off balance. It was how hard she'd worked to gather the courage to confront him today…only to have to stuff it away again. Because she certainly couldn't talk to him about their kiss now.

She looked into his eyes. Beautiful hazel-green eyes that couldn't hide his anger, bewilderment, denial, confusion, or even his curiosity. No, her needs had to be set aside when, for Evan, seeing his mother would inevitably be a monumental trigger for all his childhood traumas.

Nothing was simple between Paige and Evan. After that kiss, their relationship had never been more complicated. But in this moment, the only thing that mattered was standing beside him and making sure he didn't go through this alone.

"How can I help?"

He grabbed her hands. "I shouldn't ask, because you do too much already," he said. "But you're here. So please. Come meet them. Talk to them."

Mrs. Mortimer poked her head out of the kitchen hallway. "Hello, Paige, it's lovely to see you again. I'll bring another cup for you."

"Thank you, Mrs. M."

As Evan ushered Paige into the formal living room, she wasn't surprised that he was treating them like guests rather than family, holding them at arm's length.

The three of them were clustered on the sofa and chair, talking in furious whispers. Well, at least his brother and sister were talking. Evan's mother was silent.

"This is my sister-in-law, Paige."

Sister-in-law. She'd always had a designation—never just Paige, never just his friend. Always an extension of Whitney.

She'd hoped their kiss had changed everything. But had anything changed at all?

Only, now wasn't the time to think about that, so she stuffed her own needs away—just for the time being, she told herself—as she smiled kindly. "It's nice to meet all of you."

"This is Kelsey and Tony," Evan said. "And Theresa."

She couldn't miss how he'd used her name, rather

than *Mom* or *Mother*. And she nearly shivered at the cool, unforgiving tone, so unlike him.

"Have a seat." It warmed her that he gestured to the spot beside him on the couch.

In the few moments it took to get her coffee, add milk and sugar, and fend off the pastries, she surreptitiously observed Evan's newly materialized family. Tony was a duplicate of Evan, though not quite as tall or broad. Kelsey looked remarkably like her brother, but Paige could also see a strong resemblance to their mother.

At the door, Evan had said he'd had no idea his siblings even existed until today, but it was clear Tony and Kelsey shared the same mother and father as he did. Where could they have been all these years?

The questions mounted.

"So," she said after she'd taken a sip from her coffee cup, "where are you from?" It was only the tip of the huge morass of questions she had for them, but at least it was a start.

"Modesto," Kelsey said. "Mom still lives there, but Tony and I are in the city now."

Mom. Theresa Collins looked to be mid-fifty to sixty, her face and neck weathered by the years, though her hair wasn't completely gray. She avoided meeting anyone's eye, concentrating on the tissues clasped in her lap. She added nothing to the conversation as she sat on the couch, shoulders hunched, and sniffled occasionally into the wad of tissues in her hands.

"Tony's at UCSF," Evan said. "And Kelsey's a CPA in San Francisco."

"We showed up on his doorstep just a few minutes ago," Tony offered without being asked, his smile very much like Evan's. At least when Evan actually used to smile.

Kelsey shot her brother a quick look, and when he nodded, she turned back to Evan and said, "Is there somewhere you and I could talk privately?"

Beside her, Paige felt Evan practically vibrating. For anyone else, anger and frustration would have won out over curiosity by now. But he'd always possessed tremendous control, so she wasn't surprised when he nodded and stood.

"Follow me." He reached out a hand for Paige. "I'd appreciate it if you'd join us."

She put her hand in his, even knowing the effect his touch would have on her. Like fireworks going off along her skin, inside her chest, deep in her belly. From nothing more than the connection of fingers and palms.

All her yearning flowed into that touch, the need to comfort, the desire for him. If only they'd had time to talk about that wonderful, beautiful, stupendous kiss. If only she could comfort him now. Wrap her arms around him. Protect him, heal him.

But all she could do at the moment was walk with him and Kelsey toward the great room at the far back of the house.

"Like Tony said," Kelsey began as soon as they were out of hearing distance, "we don't want your money." Paige was impressed with the strength she saw in the tall, lovely woman. Her back was straight, her long hair falling over her shoulders. "We just want you to help us with Mom."

"If you don't want money, how am I supposed to help?"

Paige hated how Evan said it, like he didn't have anything else to offer, that his only worth was his wealth.

"Why don't you sit down and help us understand?" Paige suggested. A discussion would be easier if they weren't facing off like opponents in a boxing ring.

Kelsey tucked herself into a comfortable leather chair while Paige took the corner sofa seat. Evan remained standing.

Paige patted the cushion beside her. "Sit down." With his combative façade, he would only make Kelsey nervous. Fortunately, he did as she asked, although he kept his arms crossed over his chest.

Despite the circumstances, Paige relished his body heat so close to her, his scent intoxicating her. But his maleness was a beautiful distraction she couldn't afford right now, and she did her level best to stay on point. "Please tell us the whole story, starting with how you learned that Evan was your brother. Then we'll see how we can help you." Next to her, Evan was rigid. She wanted to touch him, ease his tension, but she had to be content simply to lead the discussion.

"Okay." Kelsey nodded, looking briefly down at her hands, as if trying to decide where to begin. "You see, it was Mom's birthday, a Sunday. And her boyfriend was already halfway to drunk by the time Tony and I got there."

The situation had already been tense, but as soon as the words *boyfriend* and *drunk* left Kelsey's lips, you could have cut through the air with a knife. If Paige had thought seeing his mom was a trigger, then this would be like a shotgun blast.

One that made Evan's hands clench into fists...and renewed fury flare in his eyes.

Chapter Ten

"Theresa has a boyfriend who drinks." Evan's words were ground out through gritted teeth.

"Yes."

Paige squeezed his arm, softly saying, "Go on," to Kelsey. "Was he harming her?"

"No. He was complaining that the game had started and Mom wouldn't change the channel because she was watching an entertainment show." She looked at Evan. "It was you and your wife giving a tour of this home."

"She's not my wife anymore," Evan revealed flatly. "We're getting divorced."

Kelsey's face dropped. "Oh, I'm so sorry."

"Don't be." His voice was hard and emotionless.

Yet Paige saw through the walls he'd put up and knew that, right now, the best thing would be to move past his troubles with Whitney and stay focused on his three family members who had so suddenly appeared. "Did your mother say something about Evan?"

"It was *him*." Kelsey almost snarled the last word. "Greg—that's her boyfriend—claimed Tony was a dead ringer for the guy on the TV." She looked at Evan. "For you."

"Your mother didn't deny it?"

"Tony and I, we were just going to laugh it off. But she got this look on her face when Greg started in on her."

"Tell us about it," Paige urged her. "Was it shock? Guilt?"

"Fear," Kelsey said softly. "She looked absolutely terrified. She hadn't thought any of us would pick up on the similarities, but Greg immediately got in her face. Asking stuff like 'What's going on?' and 'Who is he?' and 'He's even got the same last name.'"

"It doesn't appear you like this Greg very much," Paige noted, just as she would have with one of her patients.

Kelsey shook her head, her hair falling across her face for a moment. "He's horrible."

"How long has she been seeing him?" Evan's words were barely more than a growl.

"About a year." His sister sagged back slightly in the chair. "When we were growing up, she never dated anyone. She didn't start until after we graduated high school. And she's only had maybe two or three boyfriends since then. But they're always a little—" She made a face. "—off, I guess. Rougher kinds of guys. But Greg." She narrowed her eyes. "He's just plain mean."

Evan's expression turned stony. If they'd been alone, Paige would have talked him down from the ledge, helped him face the emotions assaulting him as he was forced to acknowledge the parallels to his own life with his mom and dad. Unfortunately, it would have to come later, when they were alone. Because she wasn't leaving until they talked things through. Not about the kiss—that would have to wait for another day. But she wouldn't let his emotions about his parents fester inside him, especially piling on top of Whitney's betrayal. He must feel like he'd been hit by a tire iron right about now.

"So he was getting up in your mom's face," she pressed Kelsey. "And then?"

"She caved." Kelsey's eyes went soft with apology. "She admitted you were her son from before Tony and I were born. I swear she'd never talked about you before. All she'd ever said was that our father was a bad man and we were way better off without him."

Evan's nostrils flared. "He *was* a bad man."

God, to hear his existence and his childhood written off so flatly. Maybe she'd been wrong to press for all the information. Maybe they should wait for a better time, a calmer moment.

But before she could hit the pause button, Evan asked, "Did Greg hit her?"

"No. But he grabbed her arm and held on really tight, saying she had to contact you. The dollar signs were flashing in his eyes." Kelsey's hands were the ones fisting now. "Tony kicked him out when we saw the red marks on her arm. They turned into bruises later.

We told him not to come back."

"Good for you," Evan said softly, with something close to relish. He leaned forward, putting his elbows on his knees. "What do you need from me? It sounds like you and Tony took care of the issue."

"That's the problem. He didn't stay away." Kelsey grimaced in disgust. "He told Mom how sorry he was for his behavior, blamed it on the fact that he'd just gotten laid off and he was having a hard time."

"Just a bunch of excuses." Evan's voice had an edge of steel sharp enough to slice.

"No one should ever get physical," Paige agreed.

With a nod, Kelsey said, "Now that Tony and I are both living in San Francisco, we can't be around all the time to protect her. We've been doing our best to try to deal with Greg and the situation, but we can't help feeling we're in over our heads." Her eyes were beseeching. "She was terrified to come here. She thought you'd reject her. But I know how badly she wanted to see you, even though she was afraid."

The air was so thick, the silence so profound, that Paige swore she could actually hear the beating of Evan's heart.

Her heart tore open for him. Just as it hurt for Kelsey and Tony, who were desperate to save their mother. She ached to put her hand over his chest, to ease the furious throb of his pulse.

But despite the earth-shattering kiss they'd shared, for now she was merely his psychologist sister-in-law trying to get answers. And she wouldn't fail him.

★ ★ ★

Evan was swept up in a maelstrom of memory. His father's fists. The smell of his rancid whiskey breath. Hiding under the bed, making himself small so he wouldn't be noticed. His mother's cries. The bruises on her in the morning.

Once she was gone, all the bruises had become his.

Now his mother was at it again, choosing the wrong guy. Kelsey's story took him back to that grimy neighborhood and stinking tenement, a place he never wanted to see again in his life.

Damn straight, Theresa had to believe he would reject her. Sure, his father had been the abusive asshole. But his mother had been the sober one who made the decision to leave.

Without her son.

Without her *eldest* son, anyway.

It would have been so much easier if Kelsey and Tony had simply asked for money. What they wanted—for him to watch over their mother—was exponentially worse.

Even as his emotion threatened to choke him, it was Paige who calmed his raging blood enough to quell the explosion. If not for the sweet feel of Paige beside him, he might have detonated like a bomb.

She was the only one who knew exactly what to say and how to say it, even during the worst of times.

And she was the person he needed most on his side right now, warm, understanding, and nonjudgmental, despite the unbearable circumstances.

Level-headed Paige, the woman who could talk sense under pressure.

The woman he'd kissed with a depth of passion he hadn't felt in a very long time. Maybe ever.

The woman he felt next to him with every fiber of his being, her warmth, her gentle scent, the subtle movements of her body against his. During the past few minutes, he'd instinctively shifted closer. He honestly didn't know what he would have done without her. Nor did he know how he'd ever pay her back for her help.

Just the way he didn't have a clue how to deal with his brother and sister—and Theresa.

But a Maverick didn't waffle, damn it. He didn't hide. And he definitely didn't back down. He had to look Kelsey in the eye and make it clear that he was done with all these crazy turns his life had taken. That he was finally going to get things on track toward some semblance of normal.

Whatever the hell that was.

Only, just as he opened his mouth to lay it all out, his stomach growled. Loud enough that Paige's eyes widened.

As if a light bulb had flashed on over her head, she declared, "We should eat."

"Eat?" Evan and his sister spoke in surprise at the

same moment.

"Yes." Paige smiled at Kelsey, then turned her gaze on him. "And while we eat, we can get to know each other better."

Evan knew she was absolutely right. He was on overload. And he'd learned a long time ago not to make decisions in the heat of the moment.

"Let's do pizza so we don't put Mrs. M to a lot of trouble," Paige said.

Whitney had always treated the Mortimers like servants. They were paid generously, so she thought that meant they didn't need *please* and *thank you*. Paige, however, was never without a kind word. He'd been comparing the sisters damn near every minute since he'd returned. It struck him now that he always had.

"Anyone gluten-free, lactose intolerant, vegetarian, despise anchovies?"

Paige's laundry list of pizza no-no's brought a laugh from Kelsey. "We love pizza with everything on it except the anchovies."

Paige wrinkled her nose. "Nobody likes anchovies."

"I like them," Evan said.

"You do not," she scoffed.

"Yes, I do."

"Then why have we never once had anchovies on pizza?"

"Because Susan always said they smell up the whole room."

"Susan is a very wise woman," Paige said, her smile

so sweet, so all-encompassing that his heart actually melted. Just as it had two nights ago when he'd held her in his arms and kissed her with all the longing pent up inside of him.

As their back-and-forth about pizza toppings brought him down off the emotional tightrope, his gut feelings said that as long as Paige was here, he just might be able to get through this crazy day in one piece.

With Paige by his side, maybe he could handle just about anything.

Chapter Eleven

The pizza was gooey and good. Despite the growling of his stomach, Evan hadn't thought he'd be able to eat. But Paige somehow made it work, temporarily calming high emotions and defusing the biggest mines in the minefield.

No wonder Whitney had been so biting, so hurtful to her sister all these years. She'd been jealous.

"Why did you choose accounting, Kelsey?" Paige asked, keeping the conversation rolling, though tension still hung thick in the room.

"I was a bookkeeper for a local company when I was still in high school." Paige had already drawn out of them that both Kelsey and her brother had worked for their educations and received scholarships. Evan was glad they hadn't needed to resort to student loans, which could be crippling after graduation. "I like how numbers fit together," she continued. "If you're out of balance, there's always an answer. It's like piecing together a puzzle."

"She wants to be CFO of a big company someday." Theresa hadn't said much, but when she did speak, it was with pride for the twins. She finally looked up from her plate and into Evan's eyes. "Like you."

"Evan *owns* an investment company, Mom," Kelsey said. "I've got a lot more to learn at the CPA firm before I can move into industry."

"I know," Theresa answered softly, dropping her gaze again. "I just don't want you to underestimate yourself."

"We all have to start somewhere." Paige refilled her glass of ice water from the pitcher Mrs. M had put on the table. "What about you, Tony? What do you want to do once you finish your master's?"

Paige kept them talking, steering them past anything that had the potential for friction. She had a clear mission—for them to get to know one another—and she was sticking to it.

It was obvious why she made such a good psychologist. Evan had always known how smart, caring, and giving she was—but now there was a deep sensual awareness too. One he could no longer ignore.

The scent of apples in her silky hair, the sexy curves filling out her jeans, the softness of her skin beneath her clothes. Her eyelashes were long, sweeping down over her cheekbones every time she blinked. Her nose had the tiniest tilt to it, and her lips were lush and moist as she licked off a daub of pizza sauce.

Even in the middle of all this craziness, he couldn't turn off his reaction to her—and it was with no small amount of difficulty that he forced his attention back to his brother.

"I'm interested in building manufacturing equipment," Tony was saying. "Automation. I'm working on my master's thesis right now."

Evan immediately thought of Matt's robotics firm, Trebotics. There might be a fit there once Tony graduated.

Wait. What was he doing, making plans to bring Kelsey and Tony into the Maverick fold? Yes, he admired how they looked after their mother, and they were obviously intelligent. But he needed to slow way the hell down, even if a part of him wanted to relish the experience of having blood relations. Susan and Bob loved all the Mavericks equally, had turned them into family and taught them what they needed to know to become men—and he would always and forever be grateful to them. But he'd envied Daniel's blood tie.

It was, he had to acknowledge, a huge part of why he'd been so eager to have a family with Whitney. Not because he could see her as a mother, but because he'd longed so deeply for a child and a family all his own.

Now, suddenly, he had a ready-made family. But having been burned badly before, by his birth parents and by Whitney, he needed time to process the situation and keep his emotions in check. He couldn't let himself get entangled until he knew exactly what he was up against.

Which was particularly difficult to do when his mother finally spoke again and said, "Tell us about you, Evan." Her words came out slightly wooden and stilted, as though she'd rehearsed the question in her head before actually speaking.

"My name's all over the Internet, so you probably already know everything there is to know." He wasn't bragging. It was simply true. And he didn't want to talk about himself. Especially not with her.

"You and your wife have such a beautiful home." Her voice was less tentative this time, but still shaky.

Obviously, Kelsey hadn't yet told her brother and Theresa about his impending divorce. He didn't know why he felt compelled to explain, "My wife and I are getting divorced."

"I'm sorry, Evan."

His jaw clenched. He didn't want her pity. Or her apologies.

As if she saw everything going south, Paige jumped in. "Do you work outside the home, Theresa?"

"Yes." She crumpled her napkin. "I'm an accounts payable clerk. It's the same company that Kelsey did bookkeeping for. I've been there a long time."

When she looked back up, her eyes were watery. Evan knew what was coming—and he wanted to shove away from the table, forget any of these people had ever been here. Forget any of this had ever happened.

But a Maverick didn't run. And he sure as hell didn't forget.

"I'm sorry I left, Evan. I thought I had the stomach flu, one that wouldn't go away. I had some money saved in secret, so I went to a doctor. One your father didn't know about in a suburb of Chicago. That's when I found out I was pregnant. With twins." Her lips, her cheeks, her hands—they all shook. "Oh God, I was so scared. Two more children for him to hurt." Her breath was ragged.

Kelsey reached for her hand at the same time that Tony did.

Under the table, Paige curled her fingers around Evan's. He instinctively linked his with hers. She was the only thing keeping him grounded right now, the only reason he wasn't splintering into a million pieces right here in his dining room.

"I should have come here, should have said this a long time ago," Theresa said almost in a whisper, and Evan could see how hard it was for her to look him in the eye. But she did it. "I went a little crazy. I was so scared of what he would do. So I ran before he ever knew I was pregnant."

And left Evan behind.

"I got on a bus and rode west until I ran out of money. In Modesto. But I never forgot about you. I was going to come back for you as soon as I got settled somewhere." She swallowed. "It was two years later when a friend told me you were living with the Spencers. They were good people, and I knew they'd do better for you than I could. You'd get the best chance with them. And you did." It was almost as if she was trying to convince herself. "You really did."

Theresa was right, with two more mouths to feed, and two squalling babies in their cramped apartment, God only knew what his father would have done.

But Evan didn't want to understand, didn't want to trust her. And he didn't want to cool his jets. Not when the old man had lost it after she left, his drinking totally out of control—and Evan had paid the price every single day until the Spencers saved him.

It suddenly struck him then that Theresa probably didn't know what had become of her abuser. *Their* abuser.

"Did you ever hear what happened to the old man?"

When she shook her head, he couldn't miss the flash of fear in her eyes. Even after all this time, and all the miles she'd put between her and her husband, his power over her had barely seemed to lessen.

"He died when I was a sophomore in high school. Fell down in a drunken stupor and hit his head. I didn't live there anymore, thank God." She flinched at the reminder that she'd left him there to fend for himself. "The landlord found him when he didn't pay his rent."

Tears were welling in Theresa's eyes as she scooted back from the table. "Excuse me. I need to use the restroom. Kelsey, Tony, you stay here and finish eating." She was gone before any of them could follow.

Paige squeezed his hand again, hard enough that he had to look at her. From the moment she'd arrived on his doorstep this afternoon, her touch, her comfort, her caring had been the only things keeping him this side of sane. Now, he read the message in her eyes: *Everything is going to be okay, Evan. I promise.*

The craziest thing of all was that, even with his entire life in complete and utter disarray, he believed her. Because Paige never lied. She simply didn't have it in her.

Just as he had to face the reality that he didn't have it in him to turn his back on his mother if she was in danger, no matter what her mistakes had been.

"I can't do much if she really wants the loser she's dating," he finally said to his brother and sister, "but if you'll give me the guy's full name and address, I can at least keep an eye on him."

This time when Paige gripped his hand, it was more than a show of support. It was approval. That meant more to him than any compliment Whitney had ever paid him.

"Thank you," Kelsey said, beaming at him as if he were entirely responsible for the rising sun each morning.

But though Tony was clearly pleased with Evan's offer, it was obvious he had something more to say. "She shouldn't have left you, and I can't imagine what your childhood must have been like." As Tony paused and cleared his throat, Evan was suddenly certain his brother was about to make the biggest and most gut-wrenching request of all. "But if she could believe she was forgiven, then maybe she might not need assholes like Greg." Tony held up a hand, making it clear he didn't want Evan to respond too quickly. "I'm not asking you to give us your answer yet. All I'm asking, all we're saying—" He glanced at his sister before turning back to Evan. "—is that we hope you'll think about it."

Forgiveness?

The Mavericks had taught Evan how to fight a bully and make sure no one got up from his punch. He understood complicated mathematical theories. He had the vision to start an investment firm and build it into a billion-dollar powerhouse.

But forgiving his mother for abandoning him?

That would be impossible.

Chapter Twelve

Of all the things for Tony to ask Evan for, of all the things to even bring up today, Paige couldn't believe he'd chosen *forgiveness*.

It was too soon to even broach the idea. Evan was already on the edge dealing with the fact that his mother was back and in his house, topped with learning he had a brother and sister. He needed a heck of lot more time to consider forgiving his mother.

If that was even possible, given the hellish place she'd left him in.

A muscle was jumping in his jaw—and his siblings looked desperately hopeful. It was the worst possible scenario, certain to end in disappointment and deeply ravaged emotions for everyone involved.

Paige hoped she could do something, say something to salvage the tentative bond Evan and his brother and sister had begun to forge over pizza and conversation. He was clearly impressed with their smarts, their courage, and their fierce protection of their mother. She needed to remind him of all those things. Thank God she had several years of experience with family therapy to draw from.

"I'm really proud of the three of you." Every eye turned to her. "The way you've spoken so honestly with one another today isn't easy. Not even for family members who've known each other their whole lives."

Kelsey abruptly reached for Evan's hand. "I know this has all come as a huge shock, but I'm so happy to meet you. And to have another brother. One I already know I'm totally going to like."

Paige choked up as Tony nodded. "You could have kicked us to the curb and shut Mom down completely. But you haven't." He swallowed hard. "Whatever you decide from here on out, you're a good man. And I'm proud to know you're my brother."

For several long moments, Evan didn't speak. He was too good at burying his emotions. It wasn't his way to put his feelings out there for everyone to read, but since his return from his self-imposed exile in Europe, he'd armored up like every day was war. Even his apologies to Susan, Bob, and the Mavericks, though heartfelt, had still masked his deeper emotions.

The only time his guard had dropped was the moment he'd kissed her in Chicago, with snow falling all around them.

Finally, Evan said, "We should all exchange contact information." He reached for his cardholder in his pocket—like a true investment banker, he was never without it—and handed one to each of them.

Tony and Kelsey gave him their own cards with

huge smiles transforming their faces. Though there was no discernible change in his expression, Paige silently applauded this major step for Evan. She was proud of him for not cutting them off entirely. And her heart bubbled over with joy for him and these true blood relations who'd managed to find him.

Even if her own blood relation had proven herself beyond redemption.

As if she'd conjured Whitney up, Paige's phone suddenly jumped in her pocket. Her heart was in her throat as she slipped it out just far enough to see the name on the screen.

Whitney.

"How about we walk off some of this pizza in the garden while we wait for Theresa to come back out?" Evan suggested. "I'll have Mrs. M. bring her out to us when she's ready."

"Actually," Paige said, "I've got to deal with a quick phone call that just came in, so I'll wait for your mom inside."

As the three siblings headed outside, it struck Paige how they were not only similar in looks, they also moved with the same long-limbed grace and confidence that belied their humble childhoods.

Pulling the phone from her pocket, she saw that Whitney had left a message. Odds were her sister had finally returned from the south of France and was still hoping to convince Paige to change her mind about whose side she should choose.

Paige deleted the voice mail without even blinking. She couldn't talk to Whitney after Evan's kiss, couldn't bear to listen to her sister cajole and rationalize.

She stuffed the phone back in her pocket, metaphorically shoving her sister away too, then headed toward the guest bathroom to wait for Theresa to emerge.

When the door opened a short while later, Theresa's face was moist and shiny, as if she'd patted herself down with cool water.

"I wanted to make sure you were okay."

"That's very kind." Theresa clasped her hands tightly in front of her and studied the floor.

"I'm sure it must be a shock, seeing your son again and learning that your husband has been dead for many years," Paige said.

"It's a lot to take in," Theresa agreed, her voice the same soft, timid tone in which she'd spoken most of the afternoon. "But I'm not surprised about Evan's father." Not *her husband*, but *Evan's father*. "The drinking finally took its toll on him."

And talking about the drinking was the perfect segue for Paige. "I know this isn't my business." She fully intended to say it, however. "But your daughter told us about Greg, and I want you to know that you don't have to take abuse from anyone. If you ever need to talk things out, I'm a family therapist—you can call me anytime. I'll give you my number."

"Thank you. But it's really not as bad as the Kelsey

and Tony think. It's not like it was with…" She paused, breathed deeply, then finally looked Paige in the eye. "With Evan's father."

Who was the woman trying to convince, herself or Paige?

"The bruises Greg left weren't real?"

"They were," Theresa admitted. She looked back down at the floor before adding, "But he didn't mean to do it. He just got excited. And he apologized."

Paige dipped her head, trying to meet Theresa's gaze once more. "How many times did Evan's father apologize?"

Theresa laughed without a single trace of humor. "He never apologized. We got married when I got pregnant, and he was mad about the baby." Her voice dropped low. "We ruined his life."

"Those years must have been very hard on you." Paige sympathized with the choices a young woman had to make, feeling trapped and terrified and not knowing how to get out until the day she had to make a heart-wrenching choice.

Theresa bit her lip. "It was a very difficult time."

"I'm sure it was. But can you see how things escalate? You get a bruise, but there's an apology, and you think it will get better." She took a chance and reached out to squeeze Theresa's clasped hands. "You might think that because Greg apologized the way your husband never would, that the same bad things won't happen to you down the line."

"It was only the one time. Don't people deserve a second chance?"

Paige was a big believer in second chances. And forgiveness. But some things were unforgivable. Like what Whitney had done to Evan. And what Evan's father had done to *everyone*. "A real man never hurts a woman or a child. Has Greg ever yelled before? Gotten angrier than the situation warranted? Even if he didn't touch you."

"I—" Theresa shook her head, then straightened her back a moment later, once again meeting Paige's gaze. "He has. When he drinks too much."

"Then do you really want this person in your life? Because you deserve a man who treats you with respect. Men who are like your sons."

Theresa's lips pursed a moment, as if she was holding her breath. Then she said, "Do you think Evan believes that's what I deserve?"

"Of course he does. He would never want you to be with anyone who leaves bruises on you. What happened in the past doesn't make any difference to that."

"How can you be so sure?"

"I'm sure because I know your son. He's a caring, loyal man."

"But can he ever forgive me?"

Paige felt her heart contract—actually squeeze down tight behind her rib cage—with anguish for this woman, as well as for Evan. But she never lied to her patients, and though Theresa Collins wasn't her patient, she wouldn't lie to her either.

"Evan and I have been friends for almost ten years, and I do believe he's capable of forgiveness. But seeing you again has been very shocking and sudden for him. Whatever happens between the two of you, whatever hurdles you need to get past—it's going to take some time. And as much as I wish it were so, there are no guarantees when it comes to love."

It was something Paige knew all too well, given her decade of unrequited feelings for Evan.

"I knew it was too soon," Theresa lamented. "We should have written first. But Kelsey and Tony insisted we come today. They were convinced he'd understand. But how can he when I did the worst thing a mother could possibly do to a child? I abandoned him to a monster."

Paige rubbed Theresa's arm in comfort. "Today was just the first step. You were strong enough to take this one by coming to see Evan today. Which means you're strong enough to keep moving forward, no matter the obstacles." She paused to let the words sink in, then added the zinger. "But you need to make a decision about Greg right away. He doesn't sound like someone I'd want in my life, and though I don't know you very well yet, he's not someone I want in yours either."

With a sigh, Theresa finally whispered, "He's got issues. But without him—"

"You will find a man so much better for you."

"I'm too old."

"Never," Paige chided. "You underestimate your-self, how well you've raised your two wonderful children on your own, how you're absolutely capable of being independent again. And it sounds like you're also underestimating the wonderful person you could meet if you gave yourself a chance." Then she smiled. "So ditch the dirtbag."

She was more than a little surprised when Theresa smiled back, small and tentative, but a smile nonethe-less. "You're right. And I'm so glad Evan is with a wonderful woman like you."

The surprising statement knocked the smile right off Paige's face. "We're not together. We're just friends." *Friends who kissed each other breathless not forty-eight hours ago.* "He's married to my sister," she re-minded Theresa.

"But they're getting a divorce, aren't they?"

"They arc."

"Then why can't you be together?"

Paige wasn't used to people asking *her* the hard questions. Especially ones that tapped into every last one of her longings.

"It's complicated," was the best reply she could come up with.

This time, Theresa was the one reaching for Paige. One woman to another, both who loved the same man—one as a mother, one as so much more than *just* a friend.

★ ★ ★

As soon as Kelsey spotted Paige and Theresa entering the garden together, she made a beeline for them. "Are you okay, Mom?"

"I am." Theresa didn't look quite as pale or beaten down as she had when she left the dining room. "I know how worried you've been. So I've made the decision not to see Greg anymore."

Tony grinned wide as Kelsey covered her mother's hand with hers. Paige thought hope flashed in Evan's eyes, but it was gone before she could be certain.

"That's great, Mom. But you can't do it just so we don't worry about you." Kelsey faced her mother earnestly. "You have to do it for yourself."

Her mother nodded. "Paige asked me some questions I didn't like the answers to. And it makes me realize I need to make a change."

"Then I'm so glad." Kelsey's sigh of relief was loud and clear as she pulled her mother into a hug. With Theresa's face turned away, she mouthed, *Thank you*, to Paige.

"We've taken up enough of your time," Tony said to Evan. "And we've got a long drive back to Modesto. Plus, Kelsey has to work tomorrow. But I'll spend the night at Mom's since I don't have to get back until Tuesday."

Tony was giving them notice: They wouldn't be

leaving Theresa alone, at least not yet.

That was a good thing. Paige wasn't sure how long Theresa's resolve would last, especially if Greg showed up with more of his so-called apologies.

After a deep breath, Theresa turned to Evan, her smile tentative, her gaze still wary. "I've missed you."

Just as he had when his siblings said how happy they were to find him and how proud they were to have him as their brother, he seemed utterly lost for words. And as he had then, he reached for his cards and a small pen in his jacket.

"Write your phone number on the back of my card."

Though he hadn't said he'd missed her too, his mother looked ecstatic to give him her number, though her hand trembled as she wrote. When Theresa finally smiled, the expression transformed her face, momentarily revealing the beauty hidden beneath years of pain and abuse and guilt.

As Paige and Evan watched the three of them climb into their car and drive away a few minutes later, she wanted to believe this was a huge step for him. That change was in the air.

But the truth was that nothing was certain right now. Not how he felt about his mother or siblings.

And especially not how he felt about her.

Chapter Thirteen

Evan stood for a long moment, simply staring at the empty driveway, wondering how his brain could be simultaneously blank and full to the brim with a million questions—and brutally conflicted emotions roiling through him. Talking with Tony and Kelsey about their futures, their plans, learning more about who they were, that was fine. Good, even.

Rehashing ancient history with Theresa?

That sucked.

But it would have been unimaginably worse if Paige hadn't been here. Even now, she stood patiently beside him as he worked his thoughts into something resembling order. She'd always made him laugh. Today, she'd helped put everyone at ease.

And she did things to him inside that he couldn't allow himself to think about. Not now.

Not ever.

"Thank you, Paige," he said as they walked back into the house. "I couldn't have gotten through that without you."

Once they were back inside, Mrs. M. immediately

inquired, "Can I get you two anything else?"

"Thank you," Paige said, "but I'm stuffed from lunch."

"Why don't you and Mortimer take the rest of the day off?" Evan suggested.

The kind older woman studied his face. Obviously, she'd gathered some of what had happened this afternoon. "Are you sure you won't need us again? Will you be okay?"

The thought jumped into his head before he was aware it was coming: *I'll be okay, I have Paige.*

"I'm fine." His mantra. One he knew Paige could see straight through.

She wasn't the only one who could see through it now.

It was instinctive for them to make their way to the library, a warm room with comfortable chairs and light streaming in through the garden windows. They both sat on the worn, dark leather couch, and Paige kicked off her shoes, tucking her feet beneath her.

They'd often been alone in his library, talking about books or politics or a work problem that one of them was struggling with. But he'd never been this *aware* of being alone with her. Never so conscious of how her lips moved, how beautiful her smile was. How tempting.

"You must feel overwhelmed," she said in a voice as gentle as the smile she'd given him earlier. "I know I do, and they're not even my brother and sister." *And mother.* The two words she didn't say aloud echoed between them.

The easiest thing to say was, "Tony and Kelsey—I like them both."

"They're great. Do you want to get to know them better?"

"Yes." There was no hesitation when it came to his siblings. It was only the thought of their mother being a part of the group that made his gut clench.

"You like suddenly finding you have family, don't you?"

He leaned his chin on his hand and nodded, the smile he knew she was hoping to see finally finding its way to his mouth. "They're good people. Susan and Bob would like them." It was a massive understatement. Susan would *adore* them.

"But?" she asked.

"I didn't say *but.*"

"Sometimes silence is the loudest thing of all." She leaned closer, lowered her voice. "Talk to me, Evan. Tell me what you need. Let me help you."

Her eyes were bright, her skin glowed, and her mouth was so damned soft and sweet-looking. That was Paige—compassionate, wonderful, always taking care of others, taking care of *him.* And he was suddenly too freaking close to dragging her against him. Too damned close to tearing her clothes off and losing himself in her. Letting her help him forget, if only for a handful of naked, erotically charged moments, what a mess his life was, top to bottom.

That was his worst sin—wanting to take more from Paige, when all she'd ever done was give.

* * *

Paige couldn't breathe. Not when she felt as if they were on a precipice. With a looming fall whose consequences could be more beautiful than anything either of them had ever known.

Or utterly heartbreaking.

She'd meant to help him with words, with her skills at therapy, not with her body.

Yet if he'd asked, she would have given him her body, her pleasure, *everything*, if it would help ease his pain in any way.

A thousand times over she'd counseled her patients not to confuse sex with love—but knowing the rules didn't mean she could always follow them.

Especially not when she'd been in love with Evan for so long that she literally ached with it.

She was almost there, so close to offering her aid in a kiss, so close to reaching out the way her heart and body desperately wanted to.

But then Evan shifted back on the couch. Away from her. Deliberately putting space between them as he said, "What I really need is help with understanding why Theresa finally came back. She's obviously known where I've been all these years. So if not for money, then what's really going on?"

Disappointment that he'd chosen not to kiss her again was like a vise around her heart, but she pushed it down. Those emotions didn't have a place in this heavy discussion. Only the honest, but difficult, answer she knew she had to give him. "Forgiveness."

"Forgiveness?" Anguish—then fury—rippled across his face. "I remember the first time he hit me. I was six."

She tried not to wince. If she were closeted with a patient, she would ask questions, draw out feelings, impressions. With Evan, she could only bite her lip to keep from crying out.

If only she could cut off her emotions and listen with a purely psychological brain. That was how she got through her days of hearing things that curdled her soul. She listened, she offered aid, she encouraged healing, and she kept her emotions in check. She could do nothing for a patient if her emotions got in the way. It was how doctors and nurses were able to treat children with cancer. Empathy and sympathy without giving away their soul. Otherwise, the pain would kill them, and they would never cure anyone.

But this was Evan. And she had no guard against her emotions or his pain.

"He'd always grabbed and yanked and pulled and left bruises. And there was a lot of yelling, him at me, him at her. But when I was six, he just hauled off and backhanded me across the chest. The blow threw me across the room."

His eyes were bleak now, his voice devoid of emotion. Like an automaton repeating instructions. Her heart bled with the need to touch him. But if she did, neither of them would get through this, and he needed to get it out. She sure as hell didn't believe he'd ever shared any of this with Whitney. Because if he had, it surely would have changed her sister, made her into a better human being, more understanding. How could it not have?

"I'd stabbed one of his screwdrivers through a chair cushion. I was punching stars into a piece of paper. But it went right through the vinyl."

"It was just a mistake," she whispered. "An accident."

"That didn't matter. When she ran to me and said it was her fault for letting me play there, he smacked her across the face."

Paige put her hand over her mouth. She couldn't help the moan of pain.

"I don't think I'd ever actually seen him hit her before. I knew he did, because I saw marks, bruises on her. And because I could hear her crying in pain. But he'd never done it in front of me."

"*Evan*." Everything inside her wanted to touch him, wrap him in her arms, give him her warmth. But if she touched him, she knew he would stop talking. Stop unburdening himself the way he needed to exorcise his demons.

"After that, it was like he'd broken through some

barrier. We both turned into his punching bags whenever he got drunk or just plain pissed. If his boss yelled at him, or he had a run-in with a traffic cop. Hell, he didn't even need a reason. But she knew when it was coming, and she'd try to send me to my room. Or outside to play. Anywhere. So that she could take the beating, instead of me."

Paige thought about the way Theresa had been at the dinner table, keeping her mouth shut as much as possible and speaking very softly when she did talk. It was classic—make yourself quiet and invisible, don't say anything, don't draw attention to yourself.

"A few times I didn't move fast enough. But eventually I figured it out too. I called it his bullshit line. You'd think he was fine. Sometimes, he didn't even seem drunk. Then bam, he'd thunder out, *That's buullshhit.*" She could almost see his father's spittle flying. "Then you either ran or hid. Or you got it. She always got it."

Paige could no longer keep her mouth shut. "That's a terrible way for a woman and a child to live."

"Then she left." He kept speaking as if he hadn't heard her, lost in horrible memories. "I came home from fourth grade one day, and she was gone. He said she was sick of me. That she must have hated taking care of me so much she couldn't stay one more second."

He'd been nine years old. Abandoned to a monster. "Oh God, Evan. I'm so sorry."

"I can step back now and see what it was like. He was pissed about having to feed me, clothe me, pay for anything at school. And he'd made her life a living hell because of it." He shook his head as if to try to clear it. "I'm not heartless. I see how bad she had it." He stopped, a muscle jumping in his jaw. "But she rescued them."

The words he didn't say all but shouted into the room: *Why didn't she rescue me?*

"He went crazy after that. He didn't have anyone else to hit. Just me. I couldn't hide from him anymore. He sent a note to the school saying I was sickly and he refused to allow me in gym class anymore. So I never took my clothes off. I always wore long sleeves and long pants. Nobody ever saw."

No one ever saw him cry, never saw his pain. No one knew.

Until the Mavericks found him.

"How long did you live alone with him before you moved in with Susan and Bob?"

"A couple of years."

She couldn't make a sound. Not even a gasp of horror. Not now that she knew he'd endured seven hundred and thirty days in the worst kind of hell.

But then Evan laughed. Like he wasn't dying inside with all the memories. Memories she'd never be able to shake, though they weren't even hers.

"Susan and Bob. You had to love them. I came home with Daniel one day after school, and Susan and

Bob just gathered me right in. Like they did all the Mavericks. Sometimes I spent the night. One of those times, Susan made me take a bath, because I must have stunk the way only a dirty teenage boy can. I was standing there with a towel wrapped around my waist when she walked in to get my clothes so she could wash them."

He stopped, drew inside himself again.

"She saw the bruises?"

A barely there nod was his answer.

"Did they call child services?"

"They wanted to make sure I came to them, not shunted off into the system to end up with strangers, like what happened to Ari. They sat me down at the kitchen table and made me tell them my story." He huffed out a breath with the memory. "It was like pulling out every single one of my teeth."

It explained why he'd flown off to Europe last month. When under the strain of discovering Whitney's lies, he'd shut down, shut everyone out. He'd learned to do that in childhood.

"I remember them strategizing. Bob, he had it all figured out, what would get my dad to let me go."

"They're good people."

"The best," he agreed. "I wasn't with them when they approached him. They figured it would go better without me—and I was scared he'd demand to keep me around as his punching bag. They told him they sympathized with how much kids cost, the terrible financial burden." Evan dropped his voice to a gravelly note as if he were Bob. "Especially with his wife gone, all that responsibility, no one to take care of a kid during the day when he had to work. They understood how it was just too much. So they'd be happy to take me off his hands, relieve his burden." His face turned dark again, his tone suddenly hoarse. "Thankfully, he couldn't wait to get rid of the little guttersnipe. Said I was a pain in the ass, had always been a pain in the ass, and no amount of trying to fix me was ever going to do a damn bit of good."

She blinked back tears, but the crack in her heart was already wide open. "Susan and Bob wouldn't have told you any of that."

"It was a kid who lived across the hall in our tenement block. He overheard it all and wanted to make sure I knew all the reasons my dad didn't want me."

Kids could be brutal, especially if they'd been abused themselves. But Evan shrugged as if he hadn't cared. Even though his father's words must have felt like being abandoned all over again, no matter what the man had done to him. He'd still been unwanted.

"I'm so glad Susan and Bob opened up their hearts, and their home, to you."

"I wasn't a great houseguest."

"You weren't a houseguest at all. You were a son to them from the start."

"I know that now. But it took years. And a lot of acting out. And continued silence. Like you said, sometimes that's the worst. It must have hurt them that I couldn't let it all out. They must have felt like they weren't helping me. When the truth was that I would have died without them. I just didn't know how to show my gratitude."

Her chest was achy and tight for the boy he'd been, for the pain he'd felt, the agony, for the adult world he couldn't understand.

But he had learned in the end. To accept love. To trust. To discover people's true worth.

Until Whitney had destroyed him all over again.

Nothing and no one on earth could have stopped Paige from throwing her arms around him then. Holding him tight, giving him all her caring, her warmth, her sympathy, her comfort.

She'd done it for patients, when they were crying, when they needed an arm around them and a gentle voice to talk them through. That's all it was. It was all she intended it to be.

Until Evan's mouth met hers.

And it became so much more.

Chapter Fourteen

Evan sank into Paige, her taste, her scent. Her kiss was heady, and he lost himself in her, the feel of her smooth, soft skin beneath his hand where he reached up to cup her cheek, the sound of her breath as it hitched, the sexy little moan vibrating in her throat.

He'd been lost, wandering in the dark. Now, he let himself be found in Paige's light, her sweetness. Hauling her close, until there wasn't an inch left between them, he tunneled his fingers into her hair as he ravaged her lips. She surrounded him, with her arms, her warmth, her legs, her body. Straddling him, she took as much as he did, consuming him in equal measure.

Almost as if his hands didn't belong to him, they pulled open her shirt, the little buttons easily giving way beneath the force of his need. Her bra was next, the thin silk straps no barrier at all as he kissed his way down her neck to the hollow at her collarbone and along her shoulder. Her head fell back, giving him greater access, and she tantalized him with a moan of pleasure that thrummed through his body.

He dragged the silk, down, down, down...until the swells of her gorgeous breasts fell free.

He had to touch—*Lord*, she was beautiful—had to brush the pads of his thumbs over the taut peaks. And he had to taste. He would die if he didn't. His lips closed around her, sucking, laving her with his tongue, plumping her flesh. With his other hand, he cupped her butt through her jeans, his body rocking up to meet hers.

"Evan." His name came on a throaty groan of need. "It's so good. So perfect. Please. Don't stop."

God, he didn't ever want to stop. But her voice made it all real. What they were doing.

And how wrong it was.

He couldn't keep kissing her, couldn't touch her breasts again, couldn't taste her as if she were his.

Because she wasn't. She never could be. And not just because she was his sister-in-law.

He didn't deserve her light. Couldn't forget that he came from darkness. Couldn't forget that things were an even bigger mess now than ever before. Hauling her deeper into his screwed-up life would only get her hurt in the end. He owed her so much more than dragging her into all that trouble.

"Evan?"

She held him in her arms, and he wanted her so damn badly. His need, his longing, was an ache in every muscle, in every cell, his body crying out for her.

And his heart wanted her just as much.

More.

"This is wrong," he murmured, his arms still not willing to let her go even as his mind screamed out that he had to end it. He forced himself to shift back, to look her in the eye. "We can't do this."

"It's not wrong," she said softly, her lips so close he ached to taste them again. "And I'm not sorry for it."

He couldn't believe that the full-blown, no-holds-barred story of his childhood hadn't sent her running. Whitney had never wanted to hear it, preferring to think of the future and ignore the past as if it played no part in who they'd become as adults. And he'd been willing to go along with that, relieved to keep it all inside.

But it turned out that telling Paige had been an unburdening for him. He'd actually felt a fraction of the weight lifting off him as he'd talked.

Paige had offered to care, to listen. That was why she'd hugged him. But he'd taken so much more than that.

Because he was damaged goods.

God, she was so damned tempting. Intoxicating. Irresistible. He'd never wanted anyone more. *Never.*

But he couldn't have her. Couldn't make one more selfish, bad move. Not after Whitney's lies had sent him into hiding from the people who loved him. Not after the siblings he'd never known about had shown up on his doorstep asking not just for help, but for the simple chance to get to know him. Not after his mother had suddenly reappeared and all but begged for forgiveness.

"Why?"

The word was out before he could stop it. Everyone seemed to want something from him. Whitney had wanted him to live a life that was a lie. Tony and Kelsey wanted a big brother to help with their mother. Theresa wanted him to absolve her so that they could start again. But what did Paige want? He'd been so relieved when she'd appeared on his doorstep that he hadn't even thought to ask. But now that he was trying to get himself to think clearly again, it was imperative that he know.

"Why did you come here today? Why did you leave Chicago and the celebration so soon?"

"This is why." She looked down at her body draped over his, then shook her head as though realizing she'd said the wrong thing. "Not to jump you. But to talk with you." Her gaze lowered to his mouth again. "About our kiss in Chicago." She looked into his eyes. "And about why you avoided me after."

Suddenly, the air tightened around him, like a vacuum sucking all the breath out of him. He pulled her bra straps up, set them in place, then made himself lift her from his lap, setting her back on the couch.

"Kissing you..." *It's like being able to finally breathe again.* But he couldn't say that. It would only lead them deeper down the rabbit hole. "You're a beautiful woman, Paige. With a huge heart. I couldn't have done this today without you. Couldn't have gotten through so many things without you."

The hurt darkening her eyes made him cringe as he fumbled through. But he had to stop this thing growing between them. Now. Before he hurt her. He couldn't trust his own feelings anymore, his decisions, his emotions. And he couldn't let Paige pay the price for that.

"But we both know we can't do this."

He sounded like a broken record. But that was because there was nothing else to say.

"I don't know it." She was already buttoning up her shirt, her hands surprisingly steady when his felt like they were caught in a major aftershock. "But you've got your family to deal with right now. So I'll keep helping you with them." She stood, then added, "If you want me to."

Her gorgeous curves were backlit by the late afternoon sun streaming in through his library windows. Her lips were swollen from his kisses. Her hair was tangled from his hands.

God, the things he wanted. Things that might destroy her—that could destroy them both—if he actually took them.

Yet he couldn't stand the thought of pushing her away completely. "Yes, I still want that." *I still want you.* "Your help. I really need your help, Paige."

"All right, then." She didn't smile, but she met his gaze steadily. "Thank you for telling me about your father. I know it was hard, but I hope it helped you. And it explains so much if I'm to try to help you with your family."

For nearly a decade, he hadn't allowed himself to knowingly compare Paige to Whitney. But now he couldn't stop the thought that she outshone her sister by miles. Whitney's façade was indisputably gorgeous—but Paige was as beautiful inside as she was on the outside.

She walked away then.

Not only beautiful, but strong too.

★ ★ ★

Paige put a hand to her trembling lips as she drove.

She would have let him take her right there on the couch. She would have given him anything.

Everything.

She knew in every corner of her soul that what they'd just done wasn't wrong. Their passion had quickly flared out of control, but it had been perfect and beautiful.

Only the timing was wrong. As bad as it could be.

He'd been through so much in the last month with Whitney. Even more today with the surprise appearance of his siblings and the mother who had deserted him. He needed to deal with his family, find a resolution in his own heart. He had to find a way to come to terms with his past, his father, his mother, the things those two people had done to him.

Yet none of that changed her feelings. She'd never known how to make love easy. Or simple. And she sure didn't know how now.

All she knew was that with every kiss they shared—and with every part of his past that Evan revealed to her—she fell deeper. Harder.

And despite his insistence that what they were doing was wrong, those kisses—and the way he looked at her in those rare and precious moments when he dropped his guard—made her grow more hopeful that she might not be the only one falling.

Chapter Fifteen

Evan was strung out from four nights with hardly any sleep. He hadn't been able to keep from playing those moments with Paige on the sofa over and over in his head. How good her skin had felt beneath his hands. How perfect her lips had been beneath his. How much he'd wanted to tear off every last stitch of her clothing and take her.

Slow.

Fast.

Gentle.

Rough.

Any way he could.

Every way he could.

No matter how hard he'd tried to blank out his mind and fall asleep, he couldn't stop thinking about her. Until he was sure he'd go stark raving mad with need and desire.

But now it was Tuesday morning, and Evan was in the backseat finishing up his phone call with a florist as Mortimer maneuvered through traffic heading up to San Francisco. He needed to let Paige know how much he appreciated her help on Sunday. He wanted to say thank you with more than a bouquet of flowers. She deserved so much more for her unending support. But the flowers would at least brighten her day and make her smile, until he could come up with something more substantial.

Something he could do for her that didn't involve dragging her down into the muck of his life.

And now, regardless of how tired and distracted he was, it was time to make good on his promise to check in on Theresa. He pulled out the card on which she'd written her phone number. And was surprised by the twinge in his heart at seeing her familiar handwriting. Once upon a time, she used to write him funny notes to find in his lunchbox.

Shoving away the painful memories, he dialed. "Theresa, it's Evan."

"Evan." She sounded surprised to hear from him. "It's so nice of you to call."

"How are you doing today?" he asked politely, even though it felt like his tie was strangling him. He'd phoned because it was the right thing to do. It didn't mean he was going to start calling her Mom.

"I'm fine," she replied.

His catchphrase. He suddenly knew who he'd learned it from as memories hit him. All those times he'd rushed to his mother after his father had gone off on her. *I'm fine, Evan.* She'd repeated those words to him a hundred times. *Don't worry, I'm fine.*

"Just getting ready for work, Evan."

"Any problems yesterday?"

"No problems," she said in a low voice. And when she added, "It was lovely seeing you the other day," he thought he understood the nervousness in her tone. She was still afraid of rejection. And why wouldn't she be after what she'd done?

Still, he wanted her to know, "I'm glad you're doing okay." They were words that wouldn't get anyone's hopes up, but hopefully wouldn't do any more harm either. "I better let you finish getting ready." They'd exhausted any other conversation. At least, he had. "Is Tony there? I'd like a word with him."

"I'll get him." She called her other son's name, then said, "Evan?"

He tensed at whatever she might be about to add. "Yes?"

"Thank you for talking to me. On Sunday, I mean. And for calling today."

"You're welcome." His voice was stilted, his emotions deliberately blotted flat.

"Here's Tony."

Relief washed through him like fresh spring rain. Tony he could handle. "Just checking in, Tony. I figured you would have called if Greg showed up."

"Not a peep."

"Glad to hear it." He paused, before asking, "She didn't try to call him?"

"No. Mom made a promise, and she keeps her

promises."

Right. He knew just how well she kept promises. But revealing his story to Paige had made him realize he had to at least give his mother credit for trying to protect him, while she'd been there, from his father's abuse. It was her leaving without him that he couldn't forget. Or forgive.

"But since I have to get back to San Francisco this morning..." Tony's words already had a question in them. "Could you call her again sometime? I think she'll do better if you, me, and Kelsey are all checking in with her. Letting her know we're all available if anything happens."

Evan's knee-jerk *no* clenched tight in the pit of his stomach. He wanted to protect himself at all costs.

But honestly, a few phone calls wouldn't hurt him. They wouldn't mean he'd forgiven Theresa. Wouldn't mean he wanted her to be his mom again. But it was the right thing to do.

"I'll call."

"Thanks, bro."

Bro. The label took him by surprise. Especially how much he liked the sound of it coming from a man who was his biological brother.

Hanging up, he held the phone on his lap a moment, staring out at the buildings flashing by along Highway 101. He had a brother and a sister. Regardless of how it had come to be, there was something amazing about that. He suddenly had the urge to call Kelsey.

Just to check in and see how she was doing.

If Paige were here, she'd push him to do it. To step outside his comfort zone one more time by reaching out to his sister. Because Paige was all about connection, family, loyalty, love. Which was amazing, considering the way her sister always treated her.

But if Paige had actually been here with him, he knew what he'd be unable to stop himself from doing. And it wouldn't be making another phone call. He'd tell Mortimer to take them back to his house.

And then he'd finish what they'd started on the library couch the other night. It wouldn't end with a kiss this time. Not even close.

Mortimer pulled up in front of Sebastian's building, and Evan struggled to corral his focus. Sexy, forbidden daydreams about Paige couldn't be tolerated, especially during a business meeting with his fellow Mavericks.

The Maverick Group made their headquarters on Sebastian's twenty-ninth floor. Though each of them had their own enterprises, they came together for joint ventures, including real estate and other investment opportunities. Cal Danniger, as their business manager, handled daily operations on many of those ventures, but the five Mavericks made all the higher-level decisions as a group.

After telling Mortimer he'd walk to his own headquarters on Market Street when the meeting was done, Evan entered the lobby, passing Charlie's magnificent sculpture, *Chariot Race*.

Charlie Ballard was an extreme talent, her medium being metal. The sculpture of four racing horses dragging a broken chariot dominated Sebastian's lobby. It had become a tourist attraction all on its own, with people coming to admire the work of art, especially at noon when sunlight poured through the glass ceiling into the lobby, turning the metal into a blaze of glory. It was no wonder Sebastian had fallen for her.

Damned if Evan didn't think of Paige. *Again.*

And damned if he couldn't avoid the truth another second.

Because when Paige had been straddling him in his library, her arms and legs around him, her mouth pressed to his—all he could do, think, feel was *her.*

And in that moment, he'd never wanted anyone more.

Not even his wife.

Nine years ago, he'd been blinded by Whitney's seemingly brilliant charms. But holding Paige in his arms, kissing her, tasting her—he swore he'd felt their hearts touch.

And he'd never in his life experienced any emotion so powerful, so strong, so true.

Paige was his sister-in-law. One of his best friends. Too good, too sweet, to be dragged any deeper into the vortex his life had become. She was untouchable.

But, God help him, he wanted her anyway.

Chapter Sixteen

"Welcome back," Daniel said as Evan entered the conference room and took a seat at the table.

"Glad to see your seat filled again," Sebastian said with a smile. As a media mogul and self-help guru, he was beloved to millions of people around the world. Despite that, the guy was humble. He took neither his looks nor his fortune for granted. And he thanked his lucky stars for his fiancée, Charlie.

Matt leaned back in his chair. "Things haven't been the same without you." Like Sebastian—and unlike Daniel in his flannel shirt—Matt wore an impeccable suit. As head of a robotics conglomerate, he video conferenced with Japanese and Chinese colleagues regularly, and formality and proper attire were akin to respect.

Only Will wasn't here, as he and Harper were in Hawaii for their honeymoon. Evan hoped they were having a great time in the sand and sun—they both deserved it.

Looking at his friends, he realized how damn good it was to be home. "I have to admit I actually missed your ugly mugs."

The Mavericks had been together for twenty-five years, brothers without sharing blood. They fought for one another, stood up for one another. They were the men they'd become because of one another. Evan would do anything for these guys, and they had his back in return.

In the squalid Chicago neighborhood of their youth, they'd been on the cusp of manhood when they'd sworn a pact to get the hell out. And they had all succeeded. Evan with his investments. Daniel with his hands and craftsman's tools. Matt had employed his inventive mind. Sebastian had tapped into the perfect combination of charisma and empathy. And Will had turned his innate ability to recognize what people truly desired into an import-export empire.

Evan couldn't have done it without them. Or without Susan and Bob. Alone, he would still be in the old neighborhood, breathing the dirty air, cowering from the ghost of his father.

The Mavericks had saved him.

He felt doubly guilty for having gone dark on them the last month. He hadn't turned to the people who mattered to him most. He wouldn't allow himself to make that mistake again. Not even when keeping everything locked away inside seemed to be the far easier route.

In these meetings, they normally jumped right into a discussion of any business ventures with top priority.

But Evan's life had been anything but normal lately.

"I've got an announcement." He steeled himself to say the M-word. "My mother's returned." He paused to let that sink in before hitting them with the rest of the shocking news. "Along with a brother and sister I never knew about."

The jaws of each and every Maverick dropped.

"This has got to be a joke," Matt said. "You're trying to screw with us, right?"

"I wish I was."

"Your *mom*?" Daniel asked, his eyebrows rising almost to his hairline.

"The one who ran away?" Sebastian added with a glower.

"Yeah. Theresa."

"What about these two siblings you mentioned?" Daniel threw off his jacket as though the room and the conversation had suddenly gotten too hot. Which it most definitely had.

"They're twenty-five years old. Twins."

They all stared at him, barely blinking, obviously trying to take in what he was telling them.

"Did you even know she was pregnant when she left?" Matt looked dumbfounded.

"That was why she ran. She found out she was having two more babies." Evan hadn't been able to forget the way she'd said it at his house: *I was so scared. Two more children for him to hurt.*

Three pairs of penetrating eyes homed in on him as

they digested the shocking news.

"Are you sure they are who they say they are?" Daniel sounded as suspicious as Evan had initially felt.

"Tony looks like me at that age, and Kelsey isn't far off, just with longer hair and a heck of a lot prettier face. And their mother is definitely *her*." It still felt way too raw to call her his mom.

"What the hell do they want?" Matt asked.

Matt had been through something similar when Ari's long-lost brother, Gideon, had shown up. So far, Gideon hadn't appeared to want anything from either Matt or the other Mavericks. Although, given that he'd made contracting and home improvement his trade after getting out of the Army, it had made sense for him to take a job working for Daniel's company, Top-Notch DIY.

"They've said they're not after my money."

"Do you believe them?" Daniel wasn't generally as cynical as the rest of them, but he obviously didn't like the sound of three of Evan's relatives showing up out of the blue.

Evan didn't feel ready to jump in wholeheartedly either. "Paige thinks I should."

Their collective gazes settled on him like laser pointers. "Paige met them?" Sebastian asked.

Evan worked the hardest he ever had to school his expression into something normal. A countenance that wouldn't give away the two scandalously sexy kisses he and Paige had shared. Or the fact that he was fighting what might prove to be a losing battle against wanting even more from her. So much more.

"She came by the house after returning from Chicago."

"Probably wanting to check on you," Daniel mused.

Evan hoped he could get by with a nod. Because the truth was a million times more complicated. "She met the three of them. Liked them." Steering them away from Paige before they caught wind of anything, he quickly boiled the story down to the main points. Why Theresa left, how she got to Modesto, the TV show they'd seen him on, Tony and Kelsey wanting him to keep an eye on Theresa's abusive boyfriend. "She claims she's not going back to him."

"You want us to drive over to Modesto and take care of the guy, just in case she's tempted to go back?" Daniel rolled up his sleeves as if he was ready to go right now.

"We'll make sure he never comes back." Sebastian cracked his knuckles.

"Business can wait," Matt said, obviously in agreement with the others.

The Mavericks were always ready to jump in with their fists when it was required to protect one of the others. But this was Evan's problem. His brother and sister had come to him for help. And while he'd been the one who needed defending when he was a kid, now *he* was a defender of the weak.

And he realized he wanted to take on the guy. Not just for Theresa and for Kelsey and Tony. But for himself.

It was long past time to face down a few of his own demons—with men who bullied his mother sitting right at the top of the list.

"I've got it covered. I'll be taking a trip over there this afternoon." The Collins Group could go one more day without him.

He actually felt his blood heating, his ire rising, his muscles bunching for the fight. He'd never been a warrior like Will, but he suddenly itched for a shot at Greg.

It wasn't a shot at his father—but it was as close as he was going to get, so he'd take it.

Daniel looked at him pointedly. "Have you told Mom?"

Evan's stomach dropped. He hadn't called Susan, despite having all of yesterday to think about it. Any way he looked at it, allowing Theresa back into his life felt disloyal to everything Susan was to him. Yes, he knew that his foster mother would tell him that was absolute bull, but his insides were all tied up in knots right now.

Knots that were also tangled up with Paige. He'd touched her, kissed her, and now he couldn't get beyond the guilt of how badly he wanted to strip off the rest of her clothes, drag her beneath him, and take every ounce of pleasure she was willing to give.

What if he called Susan and she somehow figured out his emotions with her X-ray mom vision? What would he possibly say then?

But no matter how twisted up he felt inside, he owed her that call. "I'll take care of this guy in Modesto, then I'm on it."

★ ★ ★

After lunch, when Evan's meeting with the Mavericks ended, he picked up the car he kept at his headquarters, ready to head for Modesto. By the time he was passing over Highway 680 in Pleasanton, he had a ferocious need to hear Paige's voice. It would be wiser to keep his distance—given that every time he got close to her, his need for her only amplified—but the thought of never talking with Paige again, never laughing with her, never seeing her beautiful toffee-colored eyes, made his chest and his gut twist up tight.

But she beat him to the call. Just seeing her name on the screen in his car made his heart beat harder. Faster.

"Evan," she said once he picked up the call. "Thank you so much for the flowers. They're beautiful, and they smell so good."

The flowers weren't nearly enough to thank her for all she'd done on Sunday—for the support and comfort she *always* gave him—but he was glad she was enjoying them. His hands relaxed on the wheel, and he suddenly realized he hadn't been able to loosen up until the moment he heard her voice. "I'm the one who needs to say thank you to you again."

"Nonsense. It's what family does—be there for each other."

Hearing her talk of being *family* churned him up all over again. Because kissing her, needing her this badly, definitely wasn't the way he should treat his family.

"Peonies are my favorites. How did you know?"

Because I've never been able to stop noticing you.

But he couldn't admit that to her. Couldn't even fully admit it to himself.

"I'm glad you like them," was all he let himself say. To further throw her off the scent, he divulged, "I'm driving out to Modesto to see Theresa's boyfriend."

"Are you crazy?"

He sure as hell *was* crazy. And not just because he was going to battle with some guy who was abusing the birth mother he'd sworn he didn't even want anymore.

But also because he couldn't stop falling harder for Paige with each smile, each kind word. Each kiss.

"I thought you wanted me to get involved."

"I want you to get to know your family better. Not confront some creep."

"I can handle him."

"That's what I'm afraid of."

"Thanks for worrying about me."

"Evan," she said softly, her voice filling the car. Filling all of him, whether he wanted her to or not.

"Promise me you won't lose it."

Couldn't she see? He'd already lost it. He couldn't stop wanting her again. Wanting her *now*. No matter how certain he was that it would end badly.

"I won't do anything I can get arrested for," he promised.

"Good." But she didn't hang up. Unlike him, she wasn't someone who avoided the difficult conversations. "After you do this for Theresa, we need to talk. About what happened between us in the library."

"Yes," he said as visions of her gorgeous eyes, lush mouth, and silky skin landed one after the other, until he was damn near ready to turn the car around and drive straight to her. "We do need to talk." If only he could figure out how to discuss it without wanting *more* of her.

"Be careful, Evan."

"I'm always careful." Except with Paige, when he kept throwing caution off the highest skyscraper.

"Call me tonight and let me know how it goes."

Evan knew that if he called—*when* he called—he'd have no more excuses to avoid examining what was happening between them. Which meant he had until tonight to get his baser urges fully under control.

"I've got to go," she said. "I've got a patient now."

He wanted her to stay on the line, wanted to tell her that her voice centered him. That she made him feel like everything would be okay. And that somehow, in the very same breath, he was terrified by how much he was starting to need her.

Instead, he ended with, "I'll call you."

The GPS led him to Greg's front door. He'd imagined he'd have to worry about the Tesla getting stripped while it was parked, but the neighborhood was middle class, with kids riding bikes on the tree-lined street and the houses neatly kept. Even the car in the driveway wasn't the beater he'd expected.

It took two tries on the doorbell before anyone answered.

The man wasn't precisely what he'd expected either. He'd envisioned the guy drinking his way through daytime TV while sitting in a stained, threadbare lounger. But Greg Littman was dressed in brown slacks and a yellow polo shirt. His face was clean-shaven, his clothing uncreased and stain-free. He was fairly trim with only a slight beer gut, and at least ten years younger than Theresa.

But despite the clothes and the fresh shave this morning, he smelled like the inside of a brewery. His eyes were bloodshot, and his nose had the fine red lines of someone who drank too much. Or snorted too much cocaine.

"Who the hell are you?" His words ran slightly together. Drinking his way through daytime TV wasn't a bad guess after all.

"You recognized me easily enough on TV a couple of weeks ago."

Greg's bloodshot eyes widened with dawning realization, and Evan identified the meanness Kelsey had seen. "Mr. Money Bags," he drawled.

"Yeah. So invite me in," Evan said, like a vampire who needed an invitation before he took your soul. He intended to crush this guy if he ever went near Theresa again.

"Sure, why not?" Greg backed up and allowed his own personal devil into the living room.

The room had a big leather sofa and a large flat-screen TV, its volume muted on the replay of a hockey game.

"As I understand it, my mother—" Evan used the title only for effect. "—has ended her relationship with you."

"I apologized," Greg said with a shake of his head meant to correct Evan. "She forgave me."

"You apologized." Evan gave the appearance of mulling it over. "So you believe leaving bruises on a woman is fine as long as you apologize."

"It was an accident. Didn't realize my own strength." Greg puffed up his chest. "Told her it wouldn't happen again."

"You're right. It won't happen. Because you aren't seeing her again." He stared the guy down. "Ever."

Greg snorted, then bunched his fists and clenched his teeth with all the bravado he could muster. "That's up to her to say."

"She's already said it. You just don't listen well." Evan crowded a step closer. Greg stumbled a step back.

They were the same height, over six feet, but Greg was stooped, and Evan towered over the older man. "Don't go near her. Don't try to talk to her. And especially don't touch her."

"I didn't do anything." The skin beneath Greg's eyes sagged from the abuses to his body.

"Right. Her bruises just magically appeared." Evan took another step, until Greg backed into the coffee table. "I see who you are. A pathetic loser who takes his frustrations out on women. The only way you can feel like a big man is to rough up someone smaller than you."

"You don't know me. You don't know what I've been through. You're rich as Bill Gates, and you got no idea about having it tough." Spittle appeared at the corner of Greg's mouth, and his pupils had dilated with fury.

"I know exactly what it's like. And I know that only weak men hit women and children. Only weak men can't control their drinking or their anger. Only weak men have to use their fists on their wives and their kids." He pointed his finger in Greg's face. "You yell and you browbeat and you enjoy everyone's fear of you. It makes you feel big, like you're important. But inside you're just a scared little wuss who can't even handle his liquor."

"I'm not pathetic. I'm just having a hard time right now because I lost my job." The man's expression set sullenly. "So, fine, you want me to leave your ma alone. Then pay me to get out. Isn't that what rich guys do? They write checks to get rid of their problems. Write me a check, and I'll leave her alone."

The man actually had some balls left. But he used them in all the wrong ways.

"I'm not giving you a dime," Evan said, his voice terrifyingly soft. "But I am going to keep my eye on you. Someone will always be watching you, Greg. When you wake. When you sleep. When you go out. When you come home. Who you talk to. Who you piss off. If you make a move on her, I'll know." He paused to make sure the guy didn't miss a word. "And I'll grind you into pulp."

Greg swallowed, his Adam's apple struggling to get the spit down. A bead of sweat rolled down his temple. "You don't scare me." Even though Evan thought the guy might pee his pants in another second.

"Here's the truth, Greg," he said, his voice dripping with sarcasm. "You aren't worth scaring. But I will protect my family any way I have to. I don't give a crap if you drink yourself to death, but you're not going to take her down with you."

Greg's mouth opened, sucking in air. "I just need a little cash, that's all."

"Then get a job. Now repeat after me: *I will leave Theresa alone.*"

Greg's voice rose to a whine. "I already told you, I didn't mean to hurt her."

"All that matters is you *did* hurt her." He cupped

his ear and leaned closer. "I don't hear you repeating those five important words yet."

The beads of nervous sweat on Greg's forehead suddenly let loose, cascading down his face until one hung on the end of his nose. "I'll leave Theresa alone."

"Don't forget, I've got my eye on you." Evan picked up a half-full bottle of beer from the coffee table, two empties beside it. The rest of the six-pack was on the carpet by the sofa. "Maybe you oughta think about throwing the rest of these out. The beer is rotting your brain." Then he shoved it into the asshole's hand.

Evan left him in the living room, clutching the beer bottle to his chest as if it were an elixir to ward off evil.

★ ★ ★

Back in his Tesla, Evan contacted an acquaintance high up in the ranks of the San Francisco Police Department. With his help, it didn't take long to arrange for a Modesto patrol car to drive by Theresa's house occasionally. If there was any trouble, Evan would get an immediate call.

Once he hit the Bay Area again, the traffic stopped and started, but the Tesla zipped through every small break, easing ahead faster than the rest of the cars. And somehow, instead of ending up at home, he found himself outside Paige's condo.

Walking beneath an overhang of trees to her first-floor unit, he took in the little brook that babbled over river rocks. Ivy spread its fingers across the ground, and ferns sprouted. It was pleasant, calm, restful. While his house was a showplace, Paige's home was comforting. It showcased, yet again, the differences between the two sisters—ostentatious versus homey, gaudy versus warmhearted.

Climbing the wooden stairs to her front porch, he pushed the bell, the tinkling sound of it ringing through the interior. She opened the door, looking both beautiful and surprised to see him.

He didn't want to desire her. He didn't want to need her.

But, God help him, he did.

Chapter Seventeen

"Paige." Evan's voice was deep. Warm. Hearing him say her name with such feeling was nearly as good as his lips on hers. "I hope it's okay I didn't call first."

Between the flowers and this unexpected visit, Paige couldn't suppress her smile. Or the quickening of her breath, awareness tingling on her skin. No matter how tense things had been when she'd left his place on Sunday. "Of course it's okay. Come inside."

Her home was so small that the intimacy of having Evan in her living room was overwhelming. Yet she'd felt such a thrill the moment she found him standing at her door.

Paige truly believed there was nothing wrong with what she felt for him. Nothing sinful. Not when Whitney had thrown away her claim to Evan with the first lie she'd told—and all the lies after that. If only he'd see things the same way. Paige hoped he would one day soon. Maybe even tonight?

"Have you eaten?" There was so much they needed to talk about, but she wanted to give him a few minutes to settle in first. Especially after his long drive to and from Modesto. "I'm planning a stir fry."

"Actually—" With his hands shoved in his pockets, she could almost believe he was nervous. "—I'd like to take you out."

"Out?" Would this be a date? Or was she mistakenly attaching the label she wanted to what was, for him, nothing more than an impromptu dinner invitation?

He swallowed, gestured off toward the main drag of Menlo Park. "There's a great place just around the corner. The Grand Pacific. I know how much you love Pan-Asian food."

"I've always wanted to eat there." The Grand Pacific's menu wasn't just legendary, its prices were too. What's more, Whitney hated Chinese food, so they'd never been there as a group.

Yet again, Paige was amazed to realize he'd actually been paying attention to her all these years. To the flowers she preferred. To her favorite kind of food. And to the fact that she loved to try new places and things.

What else had he noticed?

"I'd love to. Just let me grab a sweater."

They could have driven. It was still early for dinner, and there were a few parking spots available as they approached downtown. But she enjoyed the walk, her shoulder brushing his occasionally, the backs of their hands bumping, his clean, masculine scent teasing her. The restaurant was full, but for Evan, an empty table magically appeared. A romantic spot in a candlelit corner.

Despite telling herself not to read too much into it, Paige's heart beat a little faster.

Everything on the menu looked amazing. They ordered salmon and avocado rolls dipped in wasabi, followed by a dumpling soup, then dishes with duck, filet mignon, and sea scallops, each prepared in divine sauces using ingredients like tamarind and coconut milk. They'd never eat it all, but she was dying to try every bite. A couple of glasses of Sullivan Cabernet complemented the food perfectly.

"So tell me," she said after the waiter left. "What happened with the boyfriend?"

"I told him not show his face again. Then I called the cops to have them do some drive-bys at Theresa's." He shrugged nonchalantly, as if it didn't mean much to him.

But she knew it did. And it was obvious she'd have to pull the details out of him. "Did he put up any sort of fight?"

"He asked for money." When she made a sound of disgust, he shook his head and said, "It could have been a bluff. A way to test my resolve. Who the hell knows? Just like an abusive, out-of-control drunk, he said he was sorry and it would never happen again."

"That's not what your father used to say, is it?" Though she was poking a raw nerve here, she wouldn't be timid with him. After all these years of holding her truest feelings, her most real emotions inside, she couldn't do it anymore. Not even when it came to his mother. "He never said he was sorry. Never said it wouldn't happen again."

Evan stared at the wine glasses the waiter had swooped in and deposited on the table. "You're right. We always knew it would happen again when he got mad or drunk. When he didn't have any reason at all, actually."

Abuse occurred at all socioeconomic levels, in all neighborhoods, even in Paige's neighborhood. It was committed by men, women, sometimes even teenagers. She'd heard the same tale so many times. She'd talked with abusers as well as the abused. She understood frustration and pain and anger and hopelessness and the need to lash out, yet there was always a part of her that absolutely could not fathom how anyone could ever strike a child. Or hit someone weaker and incapable of defending themselves.

But knowing Evan had been that child? It tore her up inside.

"How did you feel? Confronting him. Protecting your m—" She quickly changed the word to, "Theresa."

"In a way," he said slowly, "telling the asshole boyfriend to lay off was like telling my dad what I thought of him."

"That had to feel good."

"You know what?" His brow creased, and he looked pensively at the utensils in front of him on the table. Then he cocked his head slightly, his gaze rising to hers as a surprised smile took over his face. "It actually did feel good. Damn good."

It was a huge step for him. A ghost he could begin to lay to rest. She sensed the infinitesimal lifting of something dark off his shoulders, saw it leaving his eyes, making them a little brighter. Even when he clearly thought the safest thing was to keep his distance from his mother, he'd obviously found it impossible to stay away. Because he was a born protector.

She wanted to risk touching him, but didn't. Not yet. Not until she could believe he wouldn't beat himself up for his reaction to her. For wanting her the way she wanted him. As much as he would deny it if she asked him outright, it seemed that he was finding it impossible to stay away from her too.

"I'm so glad, Evan."

"I am too. It's good to have that duty out of the way."

"Duty?" The word bothered her. Was she seeing only what she wanted to see—healing that hadn't actually happened?

"I've done what I can for Theresa."

"What are you saying?" The waiter brought the salmon rolls and soup, and she waited until he'd left to add, "Now that you've dealt with her boyfriend, you don't want to see them again?"

Evan concentrated on the food. "I just mean that I've done what Tony and Kelsey wanted."

How could he not see that what they wanted most of all was to get to know their brother?

Before she could point that out, he told her, "They're good people. Responsible. Hardworking. I thought I could introduce Tony to Matt, since they're both into automation." He dipped a roll in the wasabi. "Kelsey might be interested in touring my headquarters."

He wanted contact. Future contact via businesses that meant so much to him. It was a *monumental* sign. One that made her heart swell with optimism for him and his family.

"It would be nice to invite them over again."

He shrugged to downplay the idea. "Maybe."

But she could see how much he wanted to. His desire was in the slight upturn of his lips, the overly casual tone of voice, the almost boyish way he talked of his brother and sister.

He loved the Mavericks, and Susan and Bob, but the twins were *his*.

She decided to go for the toughest issue. "You could invite Theresa too." She was careful not to say *your mom.*

He spooned soup into his mouth, probably so he didn't have to answer. But she didn't offer a single word once he'd swallowed, and he was forced to say, "They probably wouldn't come without her."

"Probably not." She let the thought hang a moment. "It would be good for you both if you could reach some sort of—" She searched for the most innocuous word. "—balance with her."

"I don't know if balance is even possible. She runs away because of all the crap my father did. Then she ends up with a sleazebag who's pulling the same kind of stuff." The set of his jaw said how much that pissed him off.

"People sometimes fall into a pattern. They don't always realize it until it's too late. But she did tell us she wanted to try."

He set his spoon down, put his elbows on the table, and looked at her over his laced fingers. "I don't trust her not to find another sleazebag even worse than this one. And I'm also not sure I trust her to slam the door in Greg's face if he comes back begging for another chance."

"I've seen it happen with a few of my patients."

"So you get my point."

"Yes." But this was about more than just his mother. It was about Whitney too, the damage she'd done. His mother and his wife had both betrayed him, committing horrendous acts against him. So he was no longer willing to trust. Not even Paige. Maybe because he saw her as just another woman wanting something from him. Whitney wanted his money, his contacts. Theresa wanted his forgiveness.

And Paige wanted the biggest thing anyone could ask for.

His love.

Chapter Eighteen

"Thank you for dinner," Paige said as they strolled back to her place. It was full dark now, and despite the fact that it had been a relatively warm day for January, the night had a definite chill. "It was even better than I imagined."

"It was my pleasure."

And it was true. Paige had asked tough questions and made him think about stuff he'd rather forget, but he liked that she wasn't afraid to challenge him. He liked that she cared enough to take the risk of pushing him past his comfort zone. He liked how comfortable it felt to walk beside her, even when they didn't say much at all. He liked her smile, her fragrance, the color of her eyes.

He couldn't think of a single thing he didn't like about her. Apart from her relation to his soon-to-be ex-wife, that was.

Noticing when she tucked her hands into the sleeves of her sweater, he asked, "Are you cold?"

"A little."

He reached out to touch her fingertips. "You're

freezing." Stopping, he slid both her hands between his palms and rubbed them for warmth.

Her chocolate eyes seemed to grow darker. "That feels nice." Her voice was low and husky. "Really nice."

Despite the danger that touching her posed to his self-control, he didn't let go of her hand as they started walking again.

He couldn't help but relish the feel of her so close to him, the sound of her voice as they small-talked about nothing earth-shattering or deep, the kinds of things they wouldn't even remember the next day. But he knew he would recall the peacefulness of it, even in the midst of the sparks that kept shooting off between them.

All too soon, they were back at her condo. He wasn't done yet. He wanted more. Being with Paige was so good. So right, despite everything.

She turned at her door and let go of his hand to take out her key and put it in the lock. She smiled at him. "Thank you again for dinner."

He wanted to beg her to let him in. Wanted to beg her to let him love her. Tonight. Tomorrow.

Forever.

Working to shake off the crazy thoughts, he said, "Good night," then forced himself to back up.

"Good night," she said, fluttering her fingers at him. The fingers he'd held in his. He couldn't take his eyes off her mouth, the lips he'd kissed.

What the hell would Susan think if she knew he was lusting after his sister-in-law when he'd split from Whitney only a month ago?

He turned, thinking it would be easier to leave if he couldn't see her anymore.

But nothing was easy about leaving her behind.

"Paige."

He reached for her, dragging her into his arms. Her lips opened under his, and he sank into her.

She was spicy and hot. Sexy and warm.

Perfect.

Their tongues met, toyed. He lost himself in her taste, her scent, the sensual feel of her in his arms. The kiss consumed him until he was completely lost in sensation. She'd been cold before, but now her hands were hot on him, sliding along the collar of his jacket, into his hair, holding his face close so that the kiss went deeper still.

There was no doubt. He wanted Paige.

Now.

Craziness didn't matter.

Right and wrong flew off into the night.

There was just her mouth beneath his, her body pressed so tightly against him that they were almost one.

"Come inside," she whispered when she backed off to drag in air.

There was nothing he wanted more. Go inside. Strip off her clothes. And love her until neither of them could remember why they shouldn't be naked and tangled together.

But her question, the sudden loss of contact, brought him back to who they were. To the night. To reality.

If he went inside with her, he would have her, probably right there on the floor of her living room.

And there would be no going back for either of them.

He couldn't do that to her. Couldn't take her without giving her anything but his body. It would destroy them.

Because whatever she wanted from him, he simply didn't have it in him to give. He was coming down off a bad marriage. And Whitney—her sister would punish Paige mercilessly.

Yet it still killed him to say, "I shouldn't." But Lord, how he wanted to.

"Why? You keep saying it's wrong, but it's not. We need to talk about this, Evan. What happened in the library. And the way you kissed me just now."

She'd promised him that discussion when they spoke earlier. He thought he'd avoided it with all the talk about Greg and Theresa and his feelings, which was bad enough. He should have known that wouldn't satisfy Paige. And he owed her *more*. He recognized that. An explanation. A reason. All the damn good reasons he'd been telling himself since he'd first kissed her.

He wanted to repay her for all her goodness, her kindness, all she'd done for him time and again. Staying away from her would be the best way to do that, wouldn't it? It could be the only way to protect her. From him. And from Whitney's wrath.

"I'm married to your sister," It was the easiest answer.

"And you're getting divorced because she treated you horribly," she reminded him. Just as he'd known she would, because Paige always saw right through the easy answers. Straight to the honest ones. "Tell me the real reason why."

So many reasons. Too many. Because he didn't deserve to be with her now after he'd been so stupid as to let Whitney turn his head nine years ago. Because risking his heart again seemed impossible when it was so badly bruised and battered. Because Paige deserved more than a man with such a complicated past *and* present.

And Paige would shoot down every one of them, because she didn't understand how irreversibly damaged he was.

All he could get out was, "It's just not possible."

She gazed at him for a long moment, her eyes tracking his face. Her lips were still wet and lush from his kiss. Slowly, she stepped back, leaving him feeling frozen all the way to his heart.

"Anything's possible, Evan. You just have to be willing."

Then she walked inside and shut the door behind her.

* * *

Paige sagged against the closed door, dropping her head into her hands.

She'd practically begged him to come in, to make love to her.

But he couldn't see past the other women in his life. Or the darkness that still haunted him.

Her phone rang, and when she dug it out of her purse, she saw that it was Whitney again.

It was just like her sister to choose the absolute perfect—or worst—moment to call. Frustrated, and angry, Paige swiped the call away. She would not let Whitney destroy the beautiful, hot memory of being in Evan's arms. It didn't matter that his almost ex-wife was her sister. Sure, it might be slightly awkward when they explained things to people. But it didn't *matter*, damn it! Whitney had given up her rights to him when she'd demolished him.

Paige put her hands to her cheeks. They were burning, and her lips were still tingling from his kiss.

Evan wanted her. She had no more doubts about that. If the door had been unlocked and she'd pulled him inside, they would have made love.

Only, instead of doing that, she'd stopped. Asked. Let him overthink and beat himself up for all the "wrong" things he thought he was doing. She'd let him walk away.

If he could, he'd stay away. Because that would be easier. Safer.

He'd lock himself away from all of them—not just her, but also his long-lost family—just as he'd tried to lock himself away from the foster family who took him in.

But Susan and Bob had fought for him, through difficult teenage years when he'd tried to stay inside his battered shell.

The Mavericks had fought for him, through thick and thin, profits and losses, personal hells and triumphs.

They'd all fought hard enough for him that he'd eventually had to accept their love as real. As strong. As lasting.

Now Paige would fight for him too. Because she'd loved Evan too long and loved him too deeply to walk away without a fight.

Chapter Nineteen

In his office the following day, with a rare thirty-minute break between meetings, Evan decided it was long past time to call Susan.

But even as he reached for his phone, he had a moment's trouble focusing. Yet again, Paige had consumed his thoughts last night, keeping him awake long past midnight. Not only the kiss they'd shared on her front step, but also how much he'd enjoyed their dinner, their walk together. When he'd finally slept, his dreams had been hot and wild—and full of joy.

Anything is possible, Evan. You just have to be willing.

Paige's voice had woven its way into his dreams. Had he been crazy for not carrying her inside and making love to her? For not discovering if waking up with her in his arms just might be the best thing he'd ever known?

Calling Susan when his insides felt this twisted was either a great idea, because she had a knack for finding the perfect words to say, or a terrible one, because she always saw right through to the heart of things. Even when Evan couldn't see them himself.

"Hey, lovely lady," he said when she answered.

"Evan." Her smile bubbled through in her voice. "I've missed your calls so much."

Guilt dealt him an uppercut, though Susan wouldn't have meant for that to happen. "And I've missed hearing your voice."

"How does it feel being back home?" He heard the two words she'd left out: *without Whitney.*

"It's good." Even if the house was way too big for just him. "But something huge happened on New Year's Day." There was no easy approach except saying it right out. "My mother came by to see me. To top it off, she has two adult children. My *real* brother and sister. Not half. Not step."

There was complete silence for two beats, then Susan's voice rushed out, "Oh Evan. Oh my God. I have to sit down." He heard the scrape of a chair. *"You tell me. Everything."*

He did, from start to finish. Except the part about kissing Paige. Or how exponentially his feelings had grown for her in the past week.

When he was finished, she said, "I'm just so glad Paige has been there for you. Just like she's always been."

Yes, without question, Paige had always been there when he needed her. He owed her so much. Flowers and an expensive dinner weren't enough. He just couldn't wrap his mind around anything that would actually show Paige how grateful he was. "I can tell,"

Susan continued, "how pleased you are to have met your brother and sister. But what about seeing your mom again?"

He stared out at San Francisco Bay, deciding he'd answer with the facts. "She obviously did a good job raising them. They got scholarships for college. Kelsey is a CPA. Tony is getting a master's degree."

"You're thinking that she did a lot better for them than she did for you." Though Susan spoke softly, she didn't hold anything back. She'd tried to teach all of the Mavericks to express what they felt, what they believed. Some of them had learned it better than others.

"It's not polite to read people's minds," he teased, in lieu of facing her statement head on.

She laughed before turning serious again. "Maybe she was trying to make up for what she did in the only way she could. What she was never able to do for you, she tried to do double for them."

He hadn't thought of it that way. But even though Susan made sense, it didn't lessen the ache inside him. "She did one thing right," he finally said. "She let me stay with you and Bob."

"I love you too, honey." Then she added the kicker. "I'm sure she's hoping she can rebuild her relationship with you. Any mother would want that."

Susan and Bob had taught him to always be honest. Even when it was difficult. And damn, it was hard to admit to her, "I don't know if I can do that."

"Evan, honey, have you ever thought that reconciling with your mother might be less about what she needs and more about what you need?"

"I don't need it." He had Susan. He had Bob and the Mavericks. Theresa had been gone so long that he couldn't even relate to her as a mother.

"When you didn't know where she was, you didn't have to think about it. But now she's brought back all the shadows. You can't have those shadows hanging over you if you're ever going to move on. Especially after what Whitney did."

He'd come home from Europe intending to move on, promising himself that he wouldn't let Whitney steal another moment of his life. But one of the reasons he hadn't gone into Paige's apartment last night was Whitney. If she'd ever found out, there would have been hell to pay. Which meant he was still giving his ex all the power she had never deserved.

"Just think about what I'm saying, okay?"

He smiled despite his dark mood. "I always think about everything you say."

"Sure you do," she teased. But then she gave an excited little yelp. "I just had the most marvelous idea. Why don't you fly the twins and your mom out here? Just for the weekend. So that Bob and I can get to know them too."

He pulled the phone away from his ear to stare at it. "This is a joke, right?"

"I'm totally serious. I'd love to meet your brother and sister. And our house is a nice, safe environment for everyone to get to know each other better. Plus, that would keep your mom away from the ex-boyfriend in Modesto for a couple of days. I'm sure this first weekend will be the worst for her, when she's alone in an empty house."

"This is crazy." Yet he felt an odd kick inside at the thought of a weekend to get to know his brother and sister better, especially with Susan and Bob there to keep Theresa busy.

"What do you think?" she pressed.

"If we did it," he said slowly, "there's not enough room for all of us at the house, so I'd book a hotel for myself."

"Of course there's room for everyone, but I get it. You want to make sure you have somewhere to go, if you need it." She barely paused before saying, "So, you'll ask them to come this weekend?"

He knew firsthand just how good Susan's intentions always were. But while Tony and Kelsey were great, Evan was wary about getting too close too fast, before he knew more about them. After all, that had been his problem with Whitney—he'd seen only what he'd wanted to see and had stupidly let her in. And of course, he wasn't interested in going out of his way to reconnect with Theresa.

Knowing him well enough to guess that his silence was a mask for his reluctance, Susan said, "What if Paige could come too?"

His heart stopped. Paige? God help him. He wanted a weekend with her so badly, he felt lightheaded. Wanted more time with her—talking, laughing, kissing—any way he could get it.

Hadn't he been thinking he needed to stay away from her for her own good? Yeah, right, like that was going to happen. Not when his heart jumped at the first opportunity to see her again.

"She's so good at smoothing over rough patches," Susan continued. "And I know how much you enjoy her company."

His heartbeat kicked up. *Does Susan know?* Could she read his feelings about Paige as easily as she could read everything else about him?

"She's been a good sister-in-law." He used the phrase deliberately, reminding Susan—and himself—exactly who Paige was. Whitney's off-limits sister.

"She's been a good *friend*," Susan corrected. "Through thick and thin, Paige has always been there for you." Now his foster mother was the one carefully reminding him that Paige, rather than his wife, was the one who had stuck by him in good times and bad. "She had such fun in the snow at the wedding, I'm sure she'd love to come back to a white winter for another couple of days."

If it was just a white winter that would make Paige happy, Evan could book her a weekend at a fancy spa resort in Lake Tahoe. But what Paige loved most of all—more than massages or fancy restaurants or impressive five-star resorts—was family. Paige would choose a weekend in Chicago with everyone over anything else he could offer. This trip was something he could give her, a small repayment for all she'd done.

Yeah, great rationalization.

Because the truth he didn't want to admit to anyone—especially himself—was that he wanted an entire weekend with Paige. Even if he couldn't kiss her, couldn't touch her when they were with his family, at least they would be together.

* * *

He called Kelsey, Tony, and Theresa first. Funny that calling Theresa felt easier than calling Paige. Probably because he knew where he and Theresa stood. Whereas with Paige…

Silently cursing his powerful desire for the one woman he could never have, Evan told his assistant to push back his next meeting, then dialed Theresa's number for the second time in as many days.

She answered on the first ring, her voice tentative as she said, "Evan?"

"There are a couple of things I wanted to check in with you about. First, I talked to Greg, and he won't be bothering you anymore."

"You talked to Greg?" She was clearly shocked, her voice suddenly higher than normal.

"He apologized for hurting you." He wouldn't tell her that Greg had asked for money. "But he was also on his third beer in the middle of the day."

"He has a problem with alcohol," she agreed softly.

Evan wanted to ask her how she could possibly pick yet another guy with a drinking problem after running away from her abusive, alcoholic husband. How could she be so blind? How could she make such bad decisions time and time again?

But he'd been blind with Whitney, hadn't he? Marrying her had been the worst decision he'd ever made. Though staying with her so long might have been even worse.

So he understood a thing or two about bad decisions. And turning his back on a woman in distress wasn't a consideration. He'd hold out his hand even to his worst enemy if he or she was drowning. Hell, he'd probably have given his hand to his father if he'd asked for help, even after everything. But his father had never asked.

"Greg's not your problem anymore. If he shows up, call me. A friend knows a guy in the Modesto Police Department who'll drive by your house occasionally.

"Thank you, Evan. You're too good to me."

Her words—and how hard they hit him—nearly had him hanging up before he got to the other reason he'd called. But he wouldn't disappoint Susan. Not when his foster mother had given so much of herself to him—even when he'd been a temperamental, hormonal teenager with a huge chip on his shoulder.

"Susan wants to meet you and the twins."

"Susan Spencer?" This time, her voice was darn near a squeal of shock. "The woman who took you in after…"

His chest, his gut, everything in him, tightened up as he said, "Yes, she'd like to meet you this weekend. We'd fly out on my plane Saturday morning to Chicago, if that works for you."

"Of course it does," she said, "but are you sure about this trip?"

He wasn't sure about *anything* right now.

"I'll check with Kelsey and Tony now, then confirm the travel details."

"I know they'll be thrilled to spend more time with their brother."

Brother. It was amazing how much that word meant to him. Even coming from her.

After they hung up, he called Tony.

"I knew we did the right thing coming to you," Tony said after Evan gave him the update on Theresa's ex-boyfriend. "Thanks a million." Then he laughed and changed it to, "Actually, thanks a billion."

Evan couldn't hold back a smile. Tony had charm to spare, even in the worst situations. "I just talked to your mom about a last-minute trip to Chicago." He explained about Susan—who she was and that she wanted to meet the three of them.

"Chicago sounds great," Tony said. And then, "She's your mom too."

"She is. But there's too much history to get into it

all."

"Okay." Tony obviously knew when to let something drop, at least for the time being. "Thanks again. Looking forward to hanging with you in Chicago, bro."

Evan's phone rang less than thirty seconds after they hung up.

"You are wonderful and marvelous and the absolute best," Kelsey gushed. "I'd love to go to Chicago to meet the couple who took such good care of you. And what you did for Mom today is *huge*. Thank you, thank you."

Kelsey's enthusiasm made his heart flip. She made him feel like a hero.

In business and finance, everyone demanded a piece of him. They either wanted his money, or they wanted him to tell them how to make money. But Kelsey was different. She'd asked him to help, out of the goodness of her heart. And somehow, he'd dredged up the goodness inside of him to do it.

"You're doing so much for us," she continued, "we've got to do something for you. I don't know what. But we'll think of something. Something huge, I swear."

"I don't need you to do anything, Kelsey."

"That's the whole point," she said, as if it should have been the most obvious thing in the world. "We want to do something because we don't *have* to. You're awesome, Evan Collins."

She hung up before he could set her straight. Before he could tell her he'd done only what he'd needed to, what any person with a soul would have done.

Before he could remind her that helping out her mom didn't mean he was ready to accept Theresa as *his* mom again.

★ ★ ★

So, really, how was she supposed to fight for Evan?

Paige finished the notes from her last session, then quickly checked her email while her mind mulled over what to do about Evan.

She was determined to fight for him. But how?

Evan had wanted her last night. His kiss, his touch, and the fire in his eyes had confirmed what her body knew. But she couldn't use his desire to bring him closer. Couldn't use it against him. That was Whitney's modus operandi—ensnaring men. As far as Paige was aware, Whitney had never cheated, but she still loved to gather men around her.

In any case, Whitney aside, Paige didn't want to fall into bed with Evan only to have him deny his feelings in the morning.

Because what Paige felt for him was so much deeper. On some level, she had to believe he knew it too. Their souls seemed to speak their own special language. She'd felt it all those evenings they'd talked for hours in his library about books, movies, politics, her work, his work. The connection had existed between them even in college, all the nights they discussed classes and students, science or high finance; daydreaming about how they would shape their futures; talking about their goals, what they wanted to accomplish and how; or even something as simple as what the best classic sci-fi movie was. They'd both chosen *The Day the Earth Stood Still*, with *Forbidden Planet* a close second. If she was going to fight for him, she had to do it by showing him how much more they had between them than desire.

Her eyes skimmed the headlines online and flitted over a sidebar without really seeing it.

She wanted to do something special, something that would help Evan see they were meant to be together, no matter how many obstacles stood in their way. But what could possibly convince him? What, what, *what*?

Suddenly, her gaze was snagged by a brief mention containing the words *science*, *fiction*, and *Mars*. Oh my God. It was the absolute best thing imaginable. It wasn't obviously romantic. It wasn't flashy and sexy. But it was so absolutely *them*. Grabbing her phone, she tapped in a quick text.

Andy Weir is speaking tonight at a bookstore down the street from your office. Do you want to go see him with me?

They'd both loved *The Martian*. They'd read it at the same time, marveled over it, dissected every chapter. And seeing the advertisement right on the heels of her thoughts about their favorite classic sci-fi movies had to have meaning. Evan answered almost immediately.

Sounds good. Mortimer can pick you up from your office and then we can come home from the city together.

Come home. Yes. The words were sublime, all she could ever have asked for. They made the rest of their arrangements through a few quick texts.

Mortimer picked her up for the ride to San Francisco, but the traffic was horrendous getting into the city despite it being a weeknight. She dashed into the bookstore with no time to spare as the emcee for the evening tested the microphone. It was standing room only, but Evan had saved her a seat, and she squeezed past an elderly couple to slip into the chair beside him.

"You're here." He reached out to squeeze her hand, and she wanted to hang on forever. He was scrumptious in his dashing dark gray suit and white shirt, his tie a shade of topaz and green that somehow emphasized the flecks of gold in his eyes. She wanted to eat him all up right then. But she'd promised herself this night wouldn't be about sex. Or desire. Or need. Or all the physical things she desperately wanted from him.

Before they could exchange another word, the bookstore owner introduced the author to a round of deafening applause. Andy Weir was an incredibly interesting guy. And his publishing story was amazing. When he talked about selling his AOL stock options at the absolute high after he was laid off, Evan gave her a thumbs-up and whispered, "This is my kinda guy." She loved that he could share this with her.

The talk was fascinating, even as Andy got technical. And yet, like his book, he presented the material in layman's terms she could easily understand. He was extremely self-deprecating, and when asked how he came up with the idea for *The Martian*, he said he was a geek who liked to sit around daydreaming about how it would be possible to accomplish this thing or that.

She nudged Evan and murmured, "Just like you."

And yet it was more. It was like all those nights in college discussing their plans for the future. Daydreaming. Evan had made all his dreams come true.

Except the one about a family and a loving wife.

The emcee opened the meeting up for questions, and the audience went wild with hands in the air. One man wanted to know why the main character in *The Martian* hadn't taken his situation more seriously, that he was actually a little flip, even sarcastic. And Andy said that he hadn't wanted to write a deep, dark character study, that it was more about figuring out how to solve a really big problem.

"His levity was what I liked best," Evan said to her softly. It was what they'd both liked best. You couldn't keep the hero down, no matter what nature threw at him. He always bounced back.

Like Evan? Would he eventually bounce back? She could only hope.

Some people got into the technical stuff. Others just wanted to know how much he sold his stock options for, or how much input he'd had in the movie, while still more questions delved into the book's themes.

To her, the biggest theme had been about never giving up. With each failure, the astronaut solved another problem. After each setback, he dove right back in. The same with NASA's efforts to save him. No one ever gave up.

And she wouldn't give up on Evan. She would keep on showing him how good they were together. No matter what.

If the applause had been deafening in the beginning, it brought the house down afterward. They got their autographed books, had a few words with the author while Evan complimented him on an amazing story. Andy probably didn't have a clue he was shaking the hand of a billionaire who'd waited in the same line as everyone else.

But that was Evan, equally as down-to-earth.

As they left the bookshop, Evan took her hands in his. "Thank you. I haven't enjoyed myself so much in..." He paused, his gaze roaming over her face, tracing the lines of her cheek, her nose, her mouth. As if he were memorizing her features. "Not since our last conversation in my library. Every conversation, in fact."

Her pulse beat harder in the tips of her fingers that he'd captured in his. "I'm glad you enjoyed it."

"You couldn't have chosen anything better." His eyes scorched her, suggesting there was something he might have enjoyed equally.

But she wasn't going to simply fall into bed with him. As badly as she wanted just that. Instead, she would show Evan that they weren't about the power of sex. They were about the power of connection.

Tonight had been the perfect start. And he had given her the perfect reaction, comparing this evening to all the nights they'd come together in his library. All the nights they'd shared their thoughts, their minds, their feelings.

She would not give up. Not on him. And not on herself.

And yet the pull of his body was magnetic, hers swaying into his as she drowned in his deep gaze. She might very well have kissed him if Mortimer hadn't pulled to the curb at that very moment.

"Your carriage awaits," Evan said as Mortimer hopped out to open the door.

She slid in, and Evan joined her. She wasn't sure whether she regretted the lost moment or not. But once they were rolling and they started discussing all the new things they'd learned about their favorite book, Paige found herself transported back to those magical evenings drinking a glass of wine and talking.

Tonight had been so right, without conflict or guilt, as they enjoyed each other's company.

They were exiting the freeway close to her condo when Evan said, "I finally called Susan and told her everything."

She could suddenly feel her heart banging right up against her chest. "*Everything?*"

Obviously recognizing that he needed to clarify what *everything* meant, he added, "About Theresa showing up again with Kelsey and Tony."

Disappointment did its best to lay her low, even though she knew better than to think he would have told Susan about their kisses. She mourned the sudden loss of the closeness they'd shared all evening, but she also realized this new discussion had a closeness all its own. So she shook off the slight ache, especially after their wonderful evening together. "I'll bet she's dying to meet your brother and sister."

"If we were on *Let's Make a Deal*, you would have just won the car behind Door Number Three." Despite his teasing tone, he drummed his fingers on the seat between them, drawing in a deep breath and blowing it out with obvious tension before he said, "She wants all of us to fly to Chicago this weekend."

Paige knew he wouldn't be this conflicted if *all of us* meant only his siblings. "She wants Theresa to come too, doesn't she?"

"She does. She thinks it will be a low-stress environment for everyone to get to know each other."

"She's right." Susan always was. "So are you going to do it?"

"Maybe."

"What's the deciding factor?"

He paused a long moment before saying, "You." But before she could respond to that stunning answer, he held up a hand. "You've already done so much to help me with my family. It's not fair to keep asking you for more."

"I already told you, this is what family does for one another. You'd do the same for me."

"But I didn't." Regret and guilt were clear in his voice. "So many times, Whitney lashed out at you. So many times, I let you be hurt by her."

"No." It was long past time for Paige to admit the truth. "*I* let myself be hurt by her." She ducked her head a moment, bracing herself. "I never told you. But when my mom was dying, I made a promise to take care of my dad as well as Whitney after Mom was gone." She still felt the anguish deep in her soul. "But I failed her. Dad went downhill, and I didn't stop it."

"Jesus, Paige." Evan took her hand in his and squeezed it tight, offering her his warmth. "Your dad's death wasn't your fault."

She wanted to fold herself into his arms, but she had to be strong enough to get through this. "I know in my head—" She tapped her temple. "—that he was lost and probably nothing could have brought him back, but..." She shrugged, and then she told him the bigger issue she needed him to know. "Whitney never let me forget it. She reminded me I was failing her whenever I didn't take her side."

"You weren't to blame for your father, and you weren't to blame for any of the lies Whitney told. And you've supported her in every way you possibly could. Until we both realized just how bad her lies really were." He kissed her knuckles so gently she wanted to melt into him. "God, I am so sorry for all her crap."

"Thank you for saying that. But don't you see? I've always *taken* her crap because it was easier than standing up, or pushing back, or going for the life and the love I truly wanted." She shook her head, feeling the weight of all the things she hadn't done. But that ended now. "I'm done with all that. I'm done letting fear and excuses and, most especially, guilt hold me back."

She wouldn't wimp out this time. Not if there was a chance that she and Evan could make things work.

She'd been a wimp nine years ago—and look how that had turned out.

It was finally time to be bold.

They'd pulled up to her condo by the time she looked him square in the eye and said, "I'd love to go to Chicago with you and your family."

"What did I do that was good enough to deserve you, Paige?"

She smiled then, despite the heavy tension of unrequited desire in the air between them. "Everything good, Evan. Everything."

Then she kissed him on the cheek and slipped out of the car before he could argue with her.

Her fight for his heart was definitely on.

A fight she hoped both of them would win in the end.

Chapter Twenty

They arrived at Susan and Bob's at two thirty Saturday afternoon. "How was the flight, dear?" Susan's smile was so bright it lit up the room.

"Good." Evan smiled, giving her a hug.

Theresa, Tony, and Kelsey had been utterly awed by his luxurious private plane stocked with gourmet food and drinks. Evan had done his best to make them all feel comfortable, but as he had an important Maverick contract the other guys were waiting on him to review, Paige was the one who truly smoothed the way for the three newcomers.

All the while, Evan had been almost painfully aware of Paige. How good she looked in her jeans and sweater. How soft her hair was when she flipped it over her shoulder, a few strands brushing his face. How beautiful her eyes were when she smiled. How lovely the sound of her laughter. On top of that, Paige's fragrance had been something new, light and fruity and more intoxicating than the champagne they were drinking.

Every time they'd been together since New Year's

was still fresh inside his head, his heart. It wasn't just their attraction that drew him to her. It was the way she made him think. It was how brave she was in facing up to her past mistakes with her sister and her father. It was how confident she was that anything truly was possible.

God, how she must have suffered over that promise she'd made to her mother. He should have known there'd been something like that in her past. But she was so strong, so courageous, so caring. Take the treat she'd planned in San Francisco, suggesting they see Andy Weir together. No one else would have known how much that would mean to him. But Paige did. She was everything a man could need.

But she needed a man who was worthy of her.

And now he needed to get it together. Especially when he was in the same room with Susan.

While Bob was hanging up coats and jackets, Evan made the introductions. "Meet my brother, Tony, and my sister, Kelsey." He felt proud saying it. Theresa had done a good job there.

"Oh my Lord." Susan grabbed Tony's arms, held on to him as she looked up into his face. "You're the spitting image of Evan." Then she took Kelsey's hand. "You're beautiful, honey."

Kelsey blushed. "Thank you."

"I can't wait to get to know you both better. Evan is so proud of the two of you." Then she passed them on to Bob, who gave them each a big bear hug. That was where Daniel had learned how to hug, from his dad.

"And Theresa." She'd hung back, still shy and hesitant, despite Paige's cheerful chatter on the flight. Susan took Theresa's hand in both of hers. "It is so lovely to finally meet you."

"Thank you. You too." But when Theresa's eyes met Evan's again, he read her clear confusion: *How can she think it's lovely to meet me when I abandoned my son to her?*

Though Theresa had heard of Susan back in the neighborhood and knew she was a good woman, she couldn't possibly comprehend Susan's amazing capacity to love, her willingness to forgive a wrong, her need to make things right. If it was in her power, Susan would make this right too. It was why they were here, after all.

Evan wasn't sure anyone had that power. Not Paige. Not even Susan. No matter how good their intentions.

"Paige, honey." Susan opened her arms again. "Come give me a hug. I haven't seen you since last year."

Paige laughed as they hugged. "Last year was only a week ago."

It seemed like a lifetime. A week ago, he hadn't kissed Paige, hadn't held her or tasted her skin, hadn't dreamed of her, hadn't needed to hear her laughter more than he needed food or water or air.

And he hadn't known he had a family besides the Mavericks.

Susan herded them into the great room. "Have you eaten?"

"You wouldn't believe the food they served on Evan's plane," Kelsey said with a smile that was still more than slightly awed. "And champagne too!"

He smiled indulgently, feeling a tug on his heart-strings. He still couldn't quite believe he had a sister. Or that she could be so fun, so smart, so pretty.

"If you get hungry again, I've put out a few snacks." Susan's version of *snacks* was a smorgasbord of guacamole and chips, spinach dip with French bread, a platter of shrimp, and bowls of nuts on the coffee table. She'd spent years feeding five hungry teenage boys, after all. "Now come in, make yourselves at home." The massive fireplace and brickwork filled one wall, and a blaze was pumping warmth into the room accompanied by the pleasant crackle of the fire.

Theresa sat on one end of the sectional sofa, and Susan took a place next to her. Tony relaxed into the couch on Susan's right. Bob had pulled chairs to the other side of the coffee table, but before Evan could take one of the seats, Bob sat with Kelsey beside him. That left a corner of the couch for Evan, with Paige next to him. Which, truthfully, was right where he wanted her to be.

"I want to hear all about raising twins," Susan said to Theresa. "I've always marveled at parents who manage such a feat." The way she said it, you wouldn't have thought she'd raised six kids herself.

Theresa smiled fondly at Kelsey and Tony. "They were easy babies. Great kids."

Paige shifted next to him, and between them, where no one could see, she squeezed his fingers. Even as wound up as he was over her, the gesture relaxed him.

"People were always so kind," Theresa continued, speaking more easily with Susan than she did with anyone but the twins. "Especially the man who gave me a job the first day I was in Modesto. I used the last of the money I had for one night at a cheap motel. There was a coffee shop across the street, and I went in to ask for work. The waitress said they weren't hiring. But there was a man eating at the counter. He said he needed a receptionist if I was interested. And even when I told him I was pregnant, he didn't retract the offer."

"You'd finally found a safe haven," Susan said in a gentle voice.

"It was a miracle," Theresa agreed.

Susan wasn't looking at Evan, nor had she been speaking directly to him, but her message was clear nonetheless. In the world of his childhood, kids were left alone for hours. They suffered abuse—physical, verbal, and more. But Susan and Bob's house hadn't just been a haven for Evan—it had been equally as miraculous as Modesto had been for Theresa.

Yes, she'd made a terrible choice between him and the twins, but if she'd come home for him first, would any of them have made it out? Or would they all have ended up rotting in that squalid neighborhood, buried by his father's fists?

★ ★ ★

Paige was impressed by Theresa's story. She'd beaten the odds, and the twins had grown into extraordinary people.

If only she hadn't left Evan behind.

"I've worked for Hugh Cramer's company ever since," Theresa was saying.

"He sounds like an amazing man," Susan said.

Beside Paige, Evan sat still as a stone. His expression was just as unreadable. Paige wondered if the thought of Theresa immediately getting a job in Modesto with an understanding boss bothered Evan. Because if she was settled, if she could easily have come back for him, why hadn't she?

"Hugh and his wife were wonderful," Theresa said softly. "They're both gone, and we all miss them so much."

"They were like our grandparents," Kelsey said with fondness brimming over. Tony agreed with just a smile.

"After the twins were born," Theresa went on, "they knew I was juggling the job and child care, so she would often babysit, and he let me bring the kids in with me. I also needed to keep borrowing money from them." She glanced at Tony and Kelsey, who smiled encouragingly. "But I paid it all back." She took a deep breath, one that didn't seem to do much to center her before she said, "I don't know how I can ever pay you both back for what you did for Evan." Her voice was watery, tears obviously close.

Paige felt Evan stiffen beside her. Aching for him, she gave the only thing she could with everyone around them—a gentle brush of his shoulder with hers.

Susan patted Theresa's leg. "My dear, we're the ones who have to thank you. It was a privilege to have him." She looked at Evan with deep emotion shining in her eyes. "We love him with all our hearts."

"We love all our boys," Bob said in agreement.

"Look at all those games on the shelf," Kelsey said, clearly afraid that they were about to degenerate into a tear-fest. "You must have a lot of grandchildren."

Evan tensed once more, and worry flickered on Susan's face as she glanced at him. Paige knew they were thinking about the same thing. Whitney and her pregnancy lies. All the grandchildren Susan *didn't* have.

Fortunately, Bob jumped in to save them all. "We have one wonderful grandchild from our foster son Matt. Noah is nearly six. We adore him. But Susan and I love to play games in the evening."

"When you're not bingeing on *Sons of Anarchy*," Paige teased, hoping to lighten the mood. "You even got me addicted to it."

"When you're done, you've got to try *The Walking Dead*," Susan said like an overexcited teenager.

Evan groaned like any son would when embarrassed by a parent, and everyone laughed. Everyone but Theresa, who was carefully watching the interaction between Susan and Evan. Not with jealousy, but with regret.

It was clear to Paige that Theresa wished she could have been the mother Evan needed. But could Evan understand that?

"Why don't we play a game?" Susan suggested. "How about Skip-Bo?"

"Do *not* let her con you into playing that," Bob said. "She wins every time."

Susan shrugged. "What can I say? I'm lucky at cards."

"How about Yahtzee?" Paige said, spying the game on the shelf.

"We used to play that a lot," Tony said.

Theresa smiled. "It was thrifty entertainment."

"And Tony liked it because he always won," Kelsey put in. "Even though I'm the numbers girl."

"Well, you'll all have some stiff competition with this one." Bob jerked his thumb at Susan. That was one of the things that Paige loved about the Spencers—the way they teased with such love in their eyes.

They cleared the food remainders off the table, and while everyone was preoccupied with carrying things to the kitchen or sifting through the games on the shelf, Paige drew Evan aside. "How are you doing?"

"I'm fine."

She growled at him, "You know I hate it when you say *fine* like that."

He laughed softly, and she felt a tingle low in her belly. "I'm not going to lie and say this is the easiest social gathering of my life. But it's a heck of a lot better than last Sunday."

She wanted to lay her head on his chest, as if listening to his heartbeat would confirm his feelings better than his words could.

"Did it bother you to hear about Theresa's experiences bringing up Kelsey and Tony in Modesto?"

"A little." She appreciated his honesty a great deal. Especially knowing what it cost him. "But it also cleared up a few things."

She smiled at him. "I'm so glad you feel that way."

When he returned the smile, she wanted so badly to kiss him. Right then and there in the middle of Susan and Bob's living room. With everyone watching. Soon, she hoped. Soon, leaning in to kiss him in front of everyone would be as natural as breathing.

"Thank you for coming here this weekend." He brushed a lock of hair from her cheek. "I can't imagine doing any of this without you." His fingertips lingered on her face. "I wouldn't want to."

She melted on the inside. Not just from his caress, but from the amazing things he'd said. His gaze on her burned with desire, tracing her face, sweeping down to her lips, as if he imagined putting his mouth on hers.

Before she could put voice to any of her swirling, growing feelings—or steal the kiss she could practically taste—Tony called out, "You any good at Yahtzee, Evan?"

"Wait and see," Evan said with a smirk.

"Sorry in advance when I crush you, bro."

By the grin that spread over Evan's face, Paige knew how much he liked it when his *bro* egged him on.

Still, Paige's stomach twisted. Because once she and Whitney had grown into teenagers, they'd *never* had that kind of relationship. And now they never would.

"Paige?" Looking back up into Evan's eyes, she saw concern deepening the hazel color. "Are you okay? You look upset."

He'd been honest with her. She could do no less with him. "I was thinking about Whitney. How we were never very good together as sisters."

"*You* were." His words were impassioned. "You were the best sister she could ever have hoped for. It's her fault she never knew how to love you the way you loved her."

With his heartfelt words, Paige felt a spell weaving itself around just the two of them, drawing them closer and deeper together.

"Time to get your caffeine fix," Susan called out, carrying two carafes while Bob carted a tray of mugs and cream and sugar. Theresa followed with a big plate of cookies.

Even then, the spell didn't break. Because Paige could still feel the threads of attraction—and strong emotion—connecting them.

★ ★ ★

The game was fabulous. They laughed and cursed and groaned and had a marvelous time with each roll of the dice.

"You can't use a calculator." Tony snorted at his sister when she fished one out of her purse.

"I'm an accountant. We do everything better with calculators."

"I'm not touching that one with a ten-foot pole." Bob's eyes widened to saucer size.

Everyone laughed. Even Theresa. And she wasn't the only one having a good time. At long last, something seemed to let loose in Evan too.

Was it spending time with his new siblings?

Was it realizing that the ghost of his mother wasn't nearly as horrible in real life as it had been in his head all these years?

Or was it the bond Paige felt growing moment by moment between herself and Evan?

He rolled and one of the dice fell off the table. He leaned down to get it, searching on the carpet, but somehow found her leg instead, his hand gliding up the half boots she wore, as if he hadn't been able to resist touching her.

Paige flushed, almost gasping out loud at the sensual touch.

When he finally came back up with the die, Susan pointed a finger at him and said, "You better watch out for him."

Paige's heart stopped beating. *Does Susan know?*

"He was always the quiet one, our Evan," Susan continued. "But then you'd find he'd done something tricky, like switching out the dice under the table."

Evan let his mouth drop open. "Me?"

"Yes, you." She was laughing as she said, "You were our little prankster. Remember that time you put a frog in my apron pocket?"

"That was because you made us all watch *The Sound of Music.*" He looked around the coffee table, grinning as he said, "Seriously. Five teenage boys watching Maria flirt with Captain von Trapp?"

"So you're saying Evan was incorrigible?" Kelsey asked.

Susan nodded happily. "Totally."

He looked at Paige. "You've known me all these years. You could defend me, you know."

"Actually," Paige said with a wicked little grin, "I'd rather Susan and Bob tell us more stories about their little prankster."

It turned out there was no end to the mischief Evan had caused.

There was the time he'd put the goldfish in the toilet while he cleaned the fishbowl. "How was I supposed to know Matt wasn't going to look down?"

And the time he painted the windows shut. "Daniel was the one who was good with his hands. No one told me I was supposed to tape first."

"And what about when you put the hammer through the wall while you were hanging a picture for me?" Susan's smile was fond with the memory.

"The walls were like tissue paper," Evan protested. "The hammer just followed the nail right through."

"And you didn't know your own strength," Bob added.

"Exactly. But how did you two know about that? Daniel helped me patch it up so it looked like new."

Susan laughed. "Lyssa."

"That little tattletale," Evan grumbled, but there was light in his eyes for the youngest Spencer. All the Mavericks had a soft spot for her.

Paige wondered if those small incidents had been Evan's way of acting out like a normal kid—especially considering he'd grown up with a father who wouldn't let the slightest transgression pass, even if it was an accident. If so, Susan and Bob had taken it all in stride. They told the vignettes with a smile, a laugh, and, from Susan, sometimes a little swat at Evan. Meanwhile, he and Tony kept racking up the points on their Yahtzee scorecards.

"I'm so glad Evan had such a wonderful family to live with." Theresa clutched the cup to her chest before she shook out the dice.

Susan's eyes softened with emotion. "We're so glad

to have you and Tony and Kelsey with us now too."

Susan had more than enough love to share. She would never be jealous of Theresa's sudden return.

As for Evan, he didn't seem to be as tense or upset. Paige wanted to believe he was enjoying this. But what did he truly feel?

She longed to get him alone to find out. Longed just to be alone with him. Even though that was bound to be impossible this weekend with family all around.

Still, she had faith that more magic would happen between them soon. Magic so powerful that he wouldn't be able to walk away this time.

In the meantime, she was delighting in all the things she was learning about him. With their score-cards almost filled and Evan neck and neck with Tony, the intensity of the game punched up. There was whooping and hollering with every throw.

"I've still got a really good chance against you two," Kelsey groused as she took her throw. And came up with zilch.

"Hah!" Tony crowed.

She leaned over to rap his arm lightly. "I'll get you next time." Paige sensed the love there, the deep twin bond.

Then it was Evan's turn. "You're going down, dude," he boasted to Tony as he shook and threw, then punched the air when he rolled four fives. "Gotcha."

"No way. I still beat you." Tony pointed to his scorecard, then Evan's, and punched the air too.

"Let me double-check." Kelsey grabbed the two cards.

"Now don't cheat just because he's your brother," Evan warned.

She wrinkled her nose at him. "You're my brother too."

Evan leaned in. "But he's your *twin*," he emphasized.

The three siblings were so easy with each other, as if they'd known one another for years. Evan laughed and joked and teased. God, it was so good to see him smile, especially with his family. Paige caught Susan's eye, and she was sure she saw the mist of happy tears there. This trip had truly been an engineering masterpiece. Even Theresa was smiling as she gazed at all three of her children.

"I declare it a tie," Kelsey said. "And we're going to need a rematch so I can beat the pants off both of you."

They were all competitive, but what Maverick wasn't? Tony and Kelsey clicked with Susan, Bob and Evan as if they'd been born Mavericks.

With the game finished, Susan announced, "I'm starving. Let's take a dinner break." Then she said that she and Bob were going to make grilled cheese sandwiches.

"My favorite," Evan said as he hugged her off her feet. "I'll help you."

As the two of them headed off to the kitchen, Paige watched Theresa, looking for signs of jealousy over

Evan's relationship with his foster mom. It would be natural, as much as it would be a consequence of her own actions.

"I'm very glad you and the twins came," Paige said as an icebreaker.

Theresa turned, a sheen in her eyes. "I am too. Susan and Bob took such good care of him. He obviously loves them very much."

"All the Mavericks do." Throughout the game, Susan had talked of her other foster sons and of her own children. "Susan and Bob have a lot of love to give."

"So does Evan," Theresa said in a soft voice, one that was filled with so much longing it nearly broke Paige's heart.

She wished she had the right words to make it better. Something more than, "This trip is a good start." One small step on what Paige hoped was the road to forgiveness.

Theresa clasped her hands, as if in prayer. "He seems to really be bonding with the twins. I'll be patient. It can't happen in one weekend."

Paige felt a great kinship with Theresa in that moment.

Because patience where Evan's heart was concerned was something Paige knew all too well.

★ ★ ★

After they'd eaten, Evan said, "It's been a great day, but I've got a few things to take care of before bed. I've got a room at a local hotel so I won't crowd anyone out. I'll see everyone in the morning for breakfast." He pulled Susan beneath his arm. "You haven't eaten breakfast until you've had Susan's eggs Benedict."

"Paige," Susan said suddenly, "it would probably be best if you stayed at the hotel too."

Paige couldn't hide her surprise at this suggestion. A beat later, however, she wondered if this was Susan's way of not only saying she approved of what might be going on between her and Evan, but also giving them a helping hand in making it happen.

Still looking at Susan as if she'd just lost her mind, Evan said, "There's always been plenty of room here for Paige before."

She wanted to smack him, even if he was running scared after the three deliriously glorious kisses they'd shared. But she wanted to hug Susan.

Especially when she said, "The bathrooms will be crowded when we're all trying to get ready in the morning. Not to mention the hot water with all those showers."

With that, Evan didn't have a single excuse left.

While everyone hugged Evan good-bye for the night—even Theresa, who, miracle of miracles, he didn't push away—Susan gave Paige a hug.

In a low voice, she said, "He needs to decompress and talk through the day's events. This has been a big step for him."

"I know." Paige nodded. "I'll make sure he doesn't

hold it all in."

"Thank you, honey. I can always trust you to take care of him. And I know he'll always be there for you too."

Susan could have simply been talking about their friendship. But Paige was certain that she heard something more in his foster mother's words.

Something that sounded a lot like *love*.

Chapter Twenty-One

Thank God the hotel had another room available. Because if they'd had to share a room…

Evan didn't have one damn ounce of willpower left after sitting next to Paige all day, surrounded by her fragrance, her heat, her voice, her laughter. Just the five-minute drive to the hotel had been almost more than he could bear.

"Let's have a drink in the bar," she said after the young man at reception had given them their room keys.

It wasn't a five-star hotel, but Evan had wanted to stay as close to Susan and Bob's as possible. This place was well-maintained, with soft music playing and modern decor. It had a bellhop, and he'd already sent their suitcases up to their rooms. The bar next to the restaurant was fairly full, populated by tourists and business people.

Having a drink with Paige? Not a good idea. She was too much temptation, her lips too kissable, her scent too mind-altering.

But how the hell could he possibly resist her invitation when what he wanted above anything was to spend more time with her? Exquisite, torturous, amazing time with her. "Sounds good."

Paige looped her arm through his. Her soft curves were tantalizing, making him recall his brief, accidental touch along her calf when he'd leaned down to find the fallen die.

Although he could have avoided touching her if he'd really wanted to. Evan Collins was a Maverick, after all. A master of control.

Except when it came to Paige.

Everything inside him ached with a desire he'd never known. It was like the warm waters of the bright blue Caribbean Sea, all-encompassing. It was more than want, more than desire. It was complete and total aching need. She was the only person who made him feel whole and good. The one person who made him feel like he had a prayer of figuring out his family, his failed marriage, his life, so that he could actually find true happiness one day.

And still, he knew he couldn't have her. Couldn't be with her. Knew it was impossible.

After they'd found a small table, he asked, "What would you like to drink?"

"Champagne."

He cocked a brow. "Are we celebrating?"

She smiled up at him, her face so beautiful and hopeful in the flickering light from the table's candle. She was one of the most direct people he'd ever known, which was why he wasn't surprised when she said, "I hope so."

He knew what she wanted to hear: that he'd forgiven Theresa and they would all live happily ever after. But he couldn't give her that.

Not when happily ever after had let him down so badly.

The waitress was inundated by the other tables—and he was in dire need of some space to get his head, and heart, back in rational, working order—so he went to the bar himself, returning a few minutes later with champagne and a beer. It wasn't that he didn't enjoy champagne. But drinking it *together* seemed so romantic. Too romantic, if he wanted even half a hope of resisting her.

Which he most certainly had to do.

However, considering the way Susan had all but forced Paige to come to the hotel with him, Evan wondered if that hurdle—the one where his family disapproved of him being with his soon-to-be ex-wife's sister—even existed anywhere but in his own mind.

Paige shot him a mock frown as he sat beside her. The chairs were close, his knee brushing hers as it had all afternoon while they played Yahtzee. He felt the headiness of her proximity like the bubbles in her champagne.

"You're not celebrating with me?"

"Beer has fizz." He clinked his mug against her glass, then drank, licked the foam off his lip, and noticed the way her gaze locked on his mouth.

Like she wanted to do the licking.

Jesus. She wasn't just invading his dreams, she was inside his head, his body, his heart, every second of the day.

"Today went extremely well, don't you think?" She looked at him over the rim of her glass as she sipped the champagne.

"It did," he agreed, even though he'd rather be leaning close and whispering hot nothings in her ear and closing his eyes to steep his senses in her.

"Are you going to give me two- and three-word answers all night?"

Kiss me. Those were the two words he wanted to give her. And then three more. *I want you.*

Instead, he said, "No." And thought, *I shouldn't be having these feelings for you.* "Tony and Kelsey are great." *But I can't stop thinking about you.*

"And what about your mom? Does her story help at all?"

"Some." *If I kiss you right now, you won't be able to ask a single other question. And you'll taste like heaven.* "If she'd tried to get me, if my dad had caught her trying to leave him, she might not have been able to run at all."

"Do you feel you could ever forgive her?"

One kiss is all it will take to clear your mind of everything but how good I can make you feel.

Before he could formulate a response to her extremely weighted question, her phone rang from the depths of her purse. Her pupils dilated slightly as she looked at him.

"Aren't you going to answer it?"

"No," she said flatly. Then she swallowed and said, "I'm sure it's Whitney."

Whitney. Always goddamned Whitney between them. "How can you be sure?"

Without taking her eyes off him, she fished out her phone and showed it to him. "I've been ignoring her calls."

"That'll come back to bite you." He knew that better than anyone.

"I don't care." Her gaze was militant. "She won't ever listen to reason or take responsibility. No matter what I say to her. No matter what *anyone* says. Like I told you before, I'm done with her games."

So was he. But would Whitney let either of them ever be done with her?

"This is why I don't see forgiveness in my future," he said, "because people never change, do they? Take Whitney. She was always a liar. And I was always the idiot who didn't know it."

Paige put her hand over his, and he realized his fist had clenched. "You weren't an idiot. She's just so good at—"

"Manipulating me."

"She manipulated me too." Her thumb stroked the back of his hand.

God, her touch. It made him insane. Filled him with so much desire that there was barely any room left in him to care about how bad his marriage had been. All he wanted was to drag Paige onto his lap and ravage her mouth until she forgot everything else. Until all that mattered was her, and him…and pleasure.

"Tomorrow." The word came out hard. Partly out of frustration over how badly she wanted him to forgive Theresa. But mostly because of the battle between his conscience and how much he wanted Paige, no matter the consequences. It was his mistakes with Whitney that made a relationship with Paige an impossible fantasy. "We can talk more about all of this tomorrow."

Her face dropped all expression, her eyes grew shuttered, and her hand slid from his. She pushed her drink away, picked up her purse, and headed for the elevator, Evan close at her heels.

The elevator door was closing as she said in a stilted voice, "The only thing I truly want is to help."

"I know that." He wouldn't let himself look away from her beautiful eyes. "But maybe I can't be fixed."

Chapter Twenty-Two

"You're wrong, Evan."

Nine years. She'd waited nine *years* for him to come around. Nearly an entire decade for him to look in the mirror and see what she did every time she looked at him.

Tonight, Paige was done with waiting.

Either he was willing to finally open his eyes to everything that she saw, everything she knew to be true.

Or he wasn't.

"I'm not trying to fix you." She refused to let her hands tremble. Wouldn't allow her stomach to twist. "You don't need anyone to do that. Can't you see that you're already perfect just the way you are?"

He stared at her for a long moment.

"No," he finally said, "you're the one who's perfect."

She didn't have time to breathe, or even to blink, before he was hauling her up the elevator wall and crushing his lips to hers. His kiss was brutal and beautiful.

And, *oh God*, he tasted like pure bliss.

Her mouth opened beneath his, and she wrapped her arms and her legs around him, holding him tight against her. He consumed her, testing every hollow and dip of her mouth, caressing her tongue with his, letting her feel all his heat, his muscles, his arousal against her.

The elevator dinged, and he lifted his mouth from hers. "Don't leave me."

"I never could. Not then. Not now."

She was still in his arms, still curled around him, as he strode out of the elevator and down the hall toward their rooms.

His defenses were down after the day he'd had, after all they'd talked about tonight. Any other night, she would have made absolutely sure she wasn't taking advantage of the situation, or of him.

But she couldn't stop now. Even if he decided in the morning that it was all a mistake. She wanted all of him now, so she wouldn't worry about the rest until later.

Paige had fallen head over heels for Evan when she was twenty-one. She couldn't wait another second to love him with every part of her body, heart, and soul.

At the door to his room, he held her up against the wall and took her mouth hungrily. No man had ever kissed her as if he needed to devour her, to make her his, to bind her to him.

Didn't he know that her heart was already bound

to him? That she had been his from the very first time she walked into his classroom and he'd smiled at her?

His breath brushed her lips, his forehead against hers. "Are you sure?"

"I've never been more sure." Even if there were regrets in the morning, she didn't care. Paige needed tonight. "I want you. I want to be with you."

He stared down at her, his gaze intense. And so hot with desire that it took her breath away. "I don't have any protection."

"I'm on the Pill. And there hasn't been anyone for months." There'd only ever been Evan in her heart.

He shoved the card key in and pushed the door open, pulling her inside with him. The lock clicked with finality behind them—and this time, she didn't wait for him to kiss her.

She was so done with waiting.

Pressing her lips to his, she reveled in his groan and in how badly he wanted her. She licked over his tongue once, then again. Slipping her hand beneath his open coat, she splayed her fingers over his chest, loving how his body pushed into hers almost involuntarily, tantalizing her with the feel of every one of his hard muscles.

All day and all evening, she'd been wholly aware of him, every move, every look. Now, her fantasies turned blissfully real as he lifted her in his arms and carried her to the bed.

He set her down and stepped back to look at her.

"Paige." His voice was a reverent whisper as he slid her coat down her arms and let it fall to the carpet. "You are so beautiful."

She pushed his jacket from his shoulders. "So are you. Not only beautiful, but a good man too. In every way."

"I'm not."

Her heart squeezed at the pain and guilt in his voice. "How can I make you see that you are?"

"If only I'd been able to not look at you," he said, almost to himself. "To not see how beautiful you are." He took her hand, lifted it to his chest, as though she could absolve him of his crimes if only he confessed. "The Halloween party. I saw you there." A muscle jumped in his jaw. "I wanted you there. Wanted you with everything I am."

"I felt your eyes on me." She put her hands to his face, made sure he was looking into her very soul. "I wanted you too. With all my heart. And I'm not sorry or guilty for the way I feel about you."

"Paige."

Her name was still on his lips as he gathered her close again and kissed her like he'd been waiting forever for her.

The way she'd been waiting forever for him.

He trailed his fingers down her face, along her throat, over her back to her hips. His fingertips played along the small bare patch of skin between her jeans and her sweater. A beat later, her sweater came off, her jeans quickly following, until she was in nothing but panties and bra.

"*God.*" His voice was reverent. And full of the most delicious lust. "Do you know how many times I've imagined you just like this?" He skimmed his hands over her body without actually touching, and yet electricity arced between them. "Today, on the plane, you were all I could think about. I wanted to kiss you. Touch you. Strip you bare and love every inch of you with my hands." He traced a finger along the sky-blue lace edge of her bra. "With my mouth." His lips dropped to swells of her breasts.

Paige threaded her fingers through his hair and arched up into him as he brushed the gentlest, the sweetest—and the *filthiest*—kisses along her flushed skin.

Her breath was coming in short pants when he finally lifted his head again. "You." It was all she could get out at the moment. "Naked."

Her hands trembled from the force of her need as she reached for his shirt and slipped the buttons free. She'd seen him without his shirt during pool parties and barbecues, but when she pushed the crisp blue cotton from his shoulders, she lost her breath.

Finally—*finally!*—she could touch him, run the flat of her hands over his warm, tanned skin, his corded arms, his broad shoulder muscles. At long last, she could lean in and brush her lips over his chest. Kiss the hot flesh over his beating heart.

The more she touched, the more she tasted, the more she wanted. And her hands no longer shook as she undid the top button of his slacks, then slid the zipper down.

"I want to touch you." She licked her lips, watched as his eyes moved to her mouth, his gaze hungry. "I *need* to touch you."

"What are you waiting for?"

He was right. She was done waiting.

They both were.

She wrapped her arms around his neck and pressed herself flush to him. Skin to skin, chest to chest, heart to heart.

She tilted her head back so she could see his face. So he could see the flush of desire on hers. "Love me, Evan. I don't want to wait any longer."

Her words galvanized him. After tossing the covers back, he picked her up and almost tossed her onto the bed, climbing up over her. Then he slowed everything down, trailing his hands up her stomach, making her quiver. "So much pretty lace." He edged her bra with his finger, dipping inside to caress her nipple. Dragging the lace down a centimeter at a time, he leaned in to take her aroused flesh between his lips.

His mouth. God, it was good. *So* good. Better than anything else had ever felt.

She arched against him, holding his hips down to her, rubbing herself against him as he tasted her.

He snapped the front clasp of her bra and pushed

the cups aside. "You're so soft, so perfect." He traced his tongue between the two peaks, and she cried out, sensation streaking down to her center, out to her limbs, making her fingers and toes tingle.

He slid the straps down her arms and pulled the bra from beneath her, tossing it away. Then he brushed down her belly again, until he reached the lace panties. With the tip of one finger, he traced the line of her sex. She shivered, moaned, as he leaned into her, sucking on her throat, licking her.

Then he slid inside the panties and found her center.

"*Jesus.* You're so wet, so ready for me." He kissed her hard, stroking again, just barely touching her overheated skin as she shook with need. "I need to be inside you." His fingers delved deep, and she gasped.

"Yes." She was almost incoherent as she pressed hard into his hand. She had just enough brainpower left to tug his boxers down. With her feet, she kicked them off his legs. And then she did what she'd long dreamed of, curling her fingers into a fist around him and stroking.

"Sweetheart, you're killing me."

"Then take me, Evan. *Now.*"

"I need to taste you first." He hauled her up the bed until her head was on the pillow and kissed her lips, tasting deep. "Every inch of you." He trailed his tongue around the shell of her ear, and she dug her fingers into his arms. "I can't get enough of you." He kissed down her throat, her chest, lavishing her with tongue and mouth, teasing her breasts.

She writhed beneath him. "Evan, please."

She was begging him for all of it—his mouth between her legs, his body inside her, his heart open to hers. She'd dreamed of him for too long, watched him for too many years, knowing he would never be hers, never touch her, never kiss her. Yet he'd owned her soul almost from the moment she'd seen him.

And now they were here. Together. Loving each other.

At last.

But he didn't rush as he layered kisses down her stomach. And he was right, the extra little bit of anticipation only made it better. Hotter.

She rubbed her hands up and down his arms, over his back, ran her fingers through his hair, growing desperate as he reached for her panties and slowly stripped them down her thighs. She was going to burst, was going to explode if she had to wait one more sec—

He swiped over her with his tongue, and she nearly came off the bed, almost shattered into a million little pieces with just that one small wet lick over her most sensitive flesh.

"*More,*" she whispered, the word close to a sob.

He twirled around her with his tongue, excited all her cells into wild, crazy motion. Suckling and licking and tantalizing and turning her into a mindless creature that couldn't think, only feel. And beg.

"Please, Evan. *Please.*"

Her hips moved beneath him, pushing him. She climbed higher, reaching for the fire in the sky. He clamped his hands on her hips and held her tighter, so close that she couldn't feel any space between them.

Then he slid his fingers inside, and she lost conscious thought, lost everything but the ability to scream, losing herself completely to him.

The same way she had so very long ago, from nothing more than his smile.

* * *

Evan had never known lovemaking could be like this.

There was so much joy in touching Paige, so much wonder in kissing her, so much beauty in tasting her. He loved her voice, loved her abandon, loved that she seemed to crave the things he did to her.

He'd needed her for so long and never known it.

No, that wasn't true. He'd just never wanted to *admit* it. He'd been able to admit only that he enjoyed being with her, talking to her, listening to her, exploring her mind, sharing books and laughter with her.

He'd never let himself question why she brought him so much happiness, because questioning would have destroyed the life he'd so carefully built.

Only to have it implode anyway.

Tonight he was asking only for a few precious hours of joy. A few stolen moments with a woman who had never hurt him, could never hurt him. All he wanted was the chance to hear Paige's cries of ecstasy…and to forget everything but her, for one perfect night.

"Show me," he whispered. Her reaction to his caresses had been an epiphany. "Show me how to do that. How to let go of everything and just feel."

"You already know how." She took his arms in her hands, drew him up until he hovered over her.

He looked into her eyes and realized she was right. "I do."

But only with her.

Everything he was, everything he ever wanted, everything he ever needed, came down her. To this moment when he moved inside her. To the heat of her slick skin around him. To the breathless press of his body deep into hers. To the heady sound of her gasps, her moans, her long, low sigh, as if she was finally exactly where she was meant to be.

Evan closed his eyes to feel her fully, shifting so that he grazed the spot inside that made her shiver and quake. Then her muscles contracted around him in pure heaven, and he had to see her again. Had to look into her eyes as her pupils dilated and his name fell from her lips.

His body ached for faster, harder. But he wanted to hear her scream again, to know he could make her as happy as she'd always made him.

She panted as he thrust deep, dug her fingers into his arms, rolled with his body. The muscles of his arms quivered and strained as he held them straight to drive slowly, deeply again, to caress her inside and out.

She pulled her legs up to his waist and threw her head back. "Evan," she cried out, her body spasming around him, her nails scoring the skin on his arms.

Her pleasure broke him apart, stole the last of his self-control as her climax exploded around them both.

He saw stars. He felt bliss. He reached heaven.

All because she took him there with her.

Chapter Twenty-Three

"I can't believe I actually screamed." Paige laughed, her entire body brimming with joy. With ecstasy. With *love*. "Twice."

Evan's chest rose and fell beneath her ear as he cuddled her close. He'd pulled the covers over them, and his body was deliciously warm and hard against hers.

"You did scream. And I loved it. My fantasy finally came true."

Paige knew what that meant, that Whitney had never screamed. Likely because her sister was always so worried about looking and sounding good, even during sex.

No. Paige wouldn't let Whitney intrude on this precious moment. Wouldn't ruin everything by comparing herself to her sister.

He pushed the tangled hair back from her face. "I want to hear you scream my name again." He rolled her beneath him. "I want to exhaust you so that you fall asleep in my arms, and then I get to wake you up in the middle of the night and do it all over again."

Her heart melted like a chocolate bar in the sun, and she felt positively gooey inside. For nine years, she'd dreamed of hearing Evan say words like these. Dreamed of finally telling him her feelings for just as long.

I love you.

For the first time, she thought it might almost be possible to say it.

"I want you to do that," she said in a low voice, "but first I want to do it to *you*."

Surprise had only just registered on his gorgeous face when she pushed at his chest. "Lie back." She shoved the covers aside, and in the city lights through the window, he was so magnificent, it was hard to draw breath. "I can hardly believe it," she found herself whispering. "That you're here with me. That I'm here with you."

He was already aroused again, and as she stroked his body, gliding her palm lightly over his skin from chest to abdomen, then skimming down to his thighs, he grew harder still.

"Look what you do to me." His voice was rough. Raw. As full of need as she was.

She reveled in her joy. In the knowledge that he wanted her, *really* wanted her. She wasn't just a fill-in for someone else.

He wanted her for herself.

"I want to lick you like an ice cream cone."

His breath rushed out. "Jesus, Paige. Just hearing

you say that…" She trailed her fingers up his thighs. "Have me. I'm yours." The need—the emotion— threading through his voice was another miracle.

They'd had friendship, common interests, and like minds. Now they had this aching desire too…and a connection that ran so deep she swore it touched not just her heart, but her soul too.

His words—*I'm yours*—resonated through every part of her as she put her mouth on him.

"*Paige.*" Then he swore, and even those four letters were music.

She took all of him then, and his body quaked, his groans growing hoarse and guttural. His hips rose to meet her as she took him deeper.

Then he tangled his hands in her hair, his body moving to meet her lips as he called out her name. Shouted it. *Her* name, no one else's by mistake. She was the only woman in this room with him, the only one he wanted.

And he was the only man she'd ever needed like this.

After, she climbed his body, felt his arms close around her. Then he raised a hand to take her chin in his fingers and kissed her so deeply that the room spun around her.

She smiled against his lips. "I made you shout."

"Hell yes, you did." He pulled the covers over their cooling bodies and drew her closer against him.

She'd never seen him this relaxed. This *satisfied*.

And, oh, was she ever satisfied too.

"I've dreamed of this," he murmured in a low voice. "Needed this. Needed you."

"It's all I've ever wanted," she said, but when he didn't respond, she wondered if he'd spoken from near-sleep. A place where the truth could finally come out, where his subconscious mind could finally take control for a few hours.

"You're so sweet in my arms. So soft. So warm. I don't want you to go."

"I won't." Leaving was the very last thing she wanted.

"Just a little while longer."

Paige was almost asleep now too. She tried to rouse, to listen to what he was saying, but it was impossible when she was exhausted not only from their beautiful lovemaking, but from the emotional angst of the preceding week.

"Just until morning."

Morning. He was saying something about the morning. But she refused to allow real life to steal so much as one moment of the night's fantasy. Instead, there was only this, his body against hers as he moved to his side, shifting her until her back was to his chest, one hand over her heart.

A heart that beat only for him.

★ ★ ★

He was doing it again, making her wild and crazy with

his large, talented hands roaming over her body.

The morning sun tapped at her eyelids, but she didn't want to know what time it was. Didn't want to face what "morning" might mean.

She wanted *this*. His hands on her, his lips, his warmth. Wanted all the beautiful, heartfelt things he'd said last night.

I'm yours.

He skimmed his fingers across her breasts, exciting the peaks to tight buds, then down her belly and over her sex. Gently—hungrily—he pulled her leg up over his, opening her to his touch.

It was pure instinct to put her hand over his, guiding him. She loved the feel of their linked fingers, the combination of both his caress and her own.

He pressed a hot kiss to her neck. "Good morning."

"*So* good," she said. More like moaned as he nipped at her neck, sending tantalizing shivers through her body.

A kernel of fear tried to bubble up, worry that this would be the last time, and she needed everything before it all went away. But she knew better. Lovemaking based on fear held no love at all. So she shoved that darkness away as she turned in his arms, wrapped hers around his neck, and kissed him deeply.

They rolled together on the bed, a passionate tangle of arms and legs, until he was sitting up in bed and her legs were wrapped around him, her arms curled at his neck.

She looked deep into his eyes and then, holding his heated gaze, she took him inside. All of him in one gloriously slick, hot thrust that stole her breath. And made everything inside her melt again.

Together they began to move, her body slowly rising on him, stroking all the nerves on the inside. His tongue entered her mouth as his body plundered hers, the pace deliciously, agonizingly slow. They rocked and rolled together, their mouths feasting on each other, arms tight, bodies fitting together like a hand and glove.

She rode him, and he took her, her breath quick as they writhed and undulated sinuously, their bodies growing slippery. Until finally the pleasure was too great, and she had to move faster, matching the rhythm of her hips to the rapid beat of her heart.

She threw her head back, dragging in air, and he bit down lightly on the soft skin between her shoulder and neck, marking her.

"*Evan.*" His name falling from her lips sounded wild, sexy, sultry, crazy, and so unlike her. So unlike the woman she used to be, before the greatest pleasure she'd ever known.

She heard him cry out her name, and he sounded just as raw, just as desperate as she had. Then she was beyond thinking, could feel only a million bursts of pleasure multiplying, spreading, shooting throughout her body until they became a wondrous cataclysm of ecstasy.

Until the only sound she could make was the three words she'd been holding back for what seemed like forever. They could no longer stay locked inside as she leaped from the peak and tumbled down into bliss.

"I love you."

Chapter Twenty-Four

I love you.

They were the most beautiful words Evan had ever heard.

And the most terrifying.

He tightened his hold on Paige, their limbs still fused as they breathed with what felt like one breath.

There was no question, no doubt that what they'd shared had been so far beyond *just* sex. It was communion, connection, total intimacy.

But was it love?

Even as Paige lay in his arms—the one woman who would never lie to him, who simply didn't have it in her to do so—he couldn't shake away all the lies he'd been told too many times before in his life. Couldn't forget how badly love could go wrong. That the people who said they loved him might eventually change their minds...and abandon him.

"It's not a bad thing." Her whisper was like a soft caress inside and outside. "I've always loved you. Since forever."

He felt her words, felt *her*, in the very place he

knew better than to let himself feel. No one knew better than he did that it was so much smarter, so much safer to keep the walls around his heart.

She lifted her face to his and cupped his jaw with warm hands. "I'm not asking for anything." She stroked her thumb over his bottom lip, and he had to open his eyes to the beauty of her gaze as she opened her soul to him. "I know your world is upside down right now. I know you probably think this, us, is crazy. And I know you need time to process."

She sounded like the psychologist she was. Except that she'd also said she loved him.

Since forever.

"I know what I feel." Her words were soft, but steady, the way she always was. Even now, as she did the most frightening thing in the world by laying her heart on the line for him. "My love for you is steadfast. It's not some transient thing that will be gone tomorrow. You can believe in that, even though trusting anything or anyone is hard right now."

He should move away from her, unwrap his arms, disengage in some way.

But he couldn't do it.

Her lips lifted in the faintest of smiles. "I'm not going to push, no matter how much I might want to. And the truth is," she admitted, "that I do want to push. Because I've waited so long for you." She shook her head. "But none of that changes the truth. Or the facts." She held his gaze. Unwavering. "I'm here, Evan.

And I love you. Always."

His brain and his heart were both whirling. He couldn't remember ever feeling this way before—full of so much longing, pleasure, and confusion all at the same time.

All he could latch on to was that tonight, this morning, Paige had fused all the cracks in him, stopped all his leaks. For a few precious hours, she'd made him whole again.

And when she pressed a kiss to his lips, she filled him up completely, in ways he hadn't known anyone could. In the light, easy parts—but also down in the deepest and darkest.

"What we did was the most beautiful thing in the world." Her lips curved, a smile of reassurance this time. For both of them. "So let's just leave it at that for now."

Her kisses, her body against his, her undemanding words stole all the fight out of him. He couldn't pull away. Couldn't block his longing, his desperate need.

"One more time," he said. Any other words were more than he could manage. He couldn't commit, but he couldn't hurt her either. "Make love with me one more time before we go."

Then he rolled on the bed with her, pinning her beneath him.

And they did the most beautiful thing in the world. Again.

★ ★ ★

Susan and Bob's house was redolent with the scent of bacon and eggs and Susan's special sweet milk pancakes. Tony and Kelsey were chattering away in the dining room as they set the table. Paige left Evan's side immediately to talk to them, giving them both hugs.

He'd made love to Paige again in the shower. He couldn't keep his hands off her. And he didn't have a clue how the scene would play out this morning when all he wanted to do was drag her back to the hotel and taste every delicious inch of her again. But somehow, just the act of getting in the car and driving over here had shoved a wedge between them that he couldn't pry out. And now they were walking around each other like the floor beneath their feet was made of glass.

She'd said she loved him.

But he hadn't said it back.

She'd said she didn't want to pressure him. And she was certainly following through with that by keeping her distance this morning.

Even as he desperately wanted the closeness they'd shared in the hotel room.

"Hey, big brother." Kelsey hugged him. Tony clapped him on the back.

It felt good. Real. He liked them. And his gut said they liked him too. How had it happened? That he could suddenly feel like these two *were* family?

Yet at the same he was still so conflicted about the woman who had given birth to him. He couldn't reconcile the two feelings.

Just like he couldn't reconcile his need for Paige, his complete and utter desire for her, with the certainty that he should stay away for her own good.

God, how he wanted to touch her, hold her, kiss her. Right there in front of his brother and sister. In front of all his family. No matter how wrong it was. No matter how badly he could hurt her in the end. She deserved a guy who hadn't left her hanging for nine years. A man who hadn't picked the wrong sister. Someone whose life wasn't a minefield littered with an almost-ex-wife—her sister, no less—and a long-lost family popping up out of the past.

"Where's your mom?" Paige asked.

Tony hooked a thumb over his shoulder. "Just packing up. She'll be out in a minute. Susan and Bob are cooking."

"They wouldn't let us help," Kelsey said, "but we can at least set the table."

"I better say hello." Evan skirted around Paige to get to the kitchen door.

She didn't look at him, but he caught her scent, the shampoo he'd washed into her hair this morning. He'd touched all those curves, tasted all that delicious skin, reveled in the feel of her. And he wanted more. Wanted to wrap his hand around the nape of her neck and drag her in for a long, drugging kiss of need and ownership.

Heading into the kitchen felt almost like running away.

"I thought you were going to make eggs Benedict," he said, swaying with Susan in a big hug, the spatula in her hand dripping with batter.

Bob swiped the spatula out of her grip before the batter could hit the floor. "The kids wanted her special pancakes after I raved about them."

The kids. Like they were part of the family now. He didn't feel an ounce of resentment, only a strange mixture of amazement and pleasure.

"Let me help with that, Bob." Paige suddenly materialized beside them and grabbed a potholder for the hot plate Bob was flipping the pancakes onto.

Evan looked at Paige, couldn't help himself. Couldn't help loving the smile on her face as she bantered with Bob. Or remembering the feel of her in his arms, the taste of her in his mouth. Her gaze flitted to him, held like the brief flutter of a butterfly, then flicked away again. Yet in that quick glance, he read her need, her love. And her desire to give him the space she'd promised. She was so damned loving. So beautiful, sexy. So…

He snapped back to Susan, knowing she would see the look in his eye, the way his gaze followed Paige like she was the magnet to his compass. Bracing for her censure, his gut churning—Jesus, he was lusting after his sister-in-law—all he saw were Susan's kind, understanding eyes.

And she smiled. A smile that said she knew what he'd done with Paige last night. That she approved. Maybe even that she'd sent Paige with him last night hoping it would happen.

Where his family was concerned, it seemed he had worried for nothing. Like when he was a little boy hiding under his bed, curled in a tense, tight ball, his muscles aching, terrified of the monster who might find him that night. The fear of the beating had sometimes been worse than the beating itself.

His own fears and guilt could actually be worse than anything Susan and Bob—or any of the Mavericks—might think.

Yet did it change what was right for Paige? Did it change how badly he could still hurt her?

"Have you said hi to your mom yet this morning?" While Paige referred to her as Theresa, same as he did, Susan wasn't afraid of calling her what she was.

"Tony said she's packing up."

Susan pushed him toward the door. "Why don't you go tell her breakfast is almost ready?" Then she called, "Tony, you have dibs on the first batch. Get in here. And bring your sister with you."

Susan. God, she made him smile. She always knew what was best. And never failed to let her brood know what they needed to do.

Tony practically galloped past him, Kelsey close behind.

And he found himself alone in the dining room with Theresa, who had emerged from her bedroom.

Susan might have engineered it, but he still could have turned around and followed everyone right back into the kitchen. Yet there was a part of him that acknowledged it was time.

He rested a hand on the back of a chair and said, "Have you enjoyed yourself this weekend?"

Theresa looked more than a little surprised by this, as if she hadn't expected Evan to seek her out. But it wasn't just Susan's push. It was the things Paige had reminded him of last night in the bar. That Theresa had *had* to make a choice. If she'd tried to take him, his father would have made sure none of them escaped. In making him acknowledge that out loud, Paige had opened something up inside of him. Something small, perhaps, but it was a widening crack nonetheless.

"I have. Susan and Bob—they're wonderful."

"They are." Theresa couldn't know the half of it.

"And so is Paige. You seem so happy when you're with her. She makes you smile."

She almost sounded like a mother, telling him she approved of the girl he had a crush on. It was instinctual for his ruff to go up—she had no right to act "motherly."

But how could he deny the way Paige made him feel? She *was* wonderful.

And he was so damned happy when he was with her, even if there were a million reasons he should keep his distance.

"Paige has always made me smile." He couldn't stop his gaze from gravitating to her through the kitchen door, and his heart flipped in his chest when she laughed. He'd never felt anything like this before, not with anyone. Only her. He forced his attention back to Theresa. "I'm glad we did this trip. It was great that you could meet Susan and Bob."

Her eyes went misty with pleasure at his words— and an obvious longing for more. He knew what she wanted, for him to say he understood her choices. That he forgave her.

Words he wasn't sure he could ever say. Just as he wasn't sure he could say *I love you* to Paige.

The growing tension broke when Tony walked into the dining room with a stack of pancakes that rivaled the leaning tower of Pisa.

"Better get in there," Evan said, "before they're all gone." And then he held an arm out, showing Theresa the way.

Somehow, it seemed symbolic.

The meal, as usual, was fabulous. After the lacking in their past, when they'd struggled to put enough food on the table for all the growing boys they'd lovingly invited to share their home, Susan and Bob now made sure everyone's plates were always full.

"These pancakes are to die for," Kelsey enthused. "How do you make them so light and fluffy?"

Susan whispered the secret recipe. Even Paige

leaned in to hear.

She hadn't taken the seat next to his. Which was probably a good thing because he'd never be able to keep his hands to himself. She could have pushed him, used his desire against him, but that was never Paige's way. And yet, even on the other side of the table, his fingers actually tingled with the memory of how soft her skin was. With each bite of pancake smothered in syrup, he tasted Paige's sweet lips.

And the war raged on inside him. All the things he wanted from her, wanted to give her. Versus the insurmountable reasons why he couldn't have her. If he hurt her—*when* he hurt her—he'd never be able to live with himself.

"We'll help you with the dishes," Tony said when they were all stuffed.

"We won't hear of it." Susan flapped her hand. "You've got a plane to catch."

Kelsey shot a glance at Evan. "I'm pretty sure that Evan's plane can take off whenever he wants."

Susan tutted and wouldn't be talked into any help. "Take your coffee into the living room. Evan, can I have a quick word with you before I let you all go?"

Uh-oh.

His stomach actually fell. Then he glanced at Paige. Found her gaze on him. And somehow, everything settled inside him. They might be walking on glass, but she was so very there for him exactly when he needed her.

"I have something for you," Susan said as she led him down the hall to her sewing room, where she retrieved a box from the closet, set it on a dresser, then pulled the lid off. "Do you remember this?"

A small plastic dinosaur sat on her palm. It was something Noah, Matt's son, would have loved. A T-Rex, its jaws open in a big roar.

"I remember," he said, his voice so soft he wasn't sure he'd spoken aloud.

"You brought it with you when you came to us. You didn't bring any other toys, just this."

He hadn't had any other toys. And the dinosaur wasn't a toy. It was a memory. He felt a tightness in his chest. "I'd forgotten about it."

"I always thought it had something special to do with your mom. Maybe it's time for you to take it back."

He wasn't ready for it. Wasn't ready for the memories. But he took it anyway, slipping the small dinosaur into his pocket.

"You can talk about it whenever you're ready, honey."

"Thanks," he said too quickly, almost as if he had to cut her off.

"I also wanted to say something else."

He laughed, maybe a bit too loudly. "You always have something else to say." And what she said was always spot on.

"Paige is good for you. Really good. And I know

you." She poked his chest. "You've been telling your-self that you've somehow stepped over to the dark side. The wrong side of right and wrong."

"Mom," he said, trying to head her off.

But Susan headed exactly where she wanted to go. "I've got eyes in my head, honey. I see the way you look at her. And the way she looks at you. Especially after last night."

God. She wasn't going to talk about sex. Please, no. And yet what he'd done with Paige was *not* just sex. It was so much more.

"I know I don't need to have this talk with Paige. You're the one who needs to hear what I have to say. I see how much you're struggling. You can't look at her, but you can't look away either."

"Mom," he said again.

"Paige is such a wonderful woman, in every way. You had your eyes set on the wrong sister from the very beginning."

How utterly right she was. And the words just seemed to burst right out of him. "I never felt like that with Whitney. Last night was…" He didn't have adequate words to explain the full joy of having Paige lying so close to him, her heart beating against his. Of being with her at last. Even the simple act of holding her. "Nothing has ever meant so much."

Susan touched his arm. "I know. It was written all over you when you walked in this morning."

"But it can't be right." His voice felt harsh in his

throat. "She's my sister-in-law. I'm not even divorced yet."

Susan laid her hand on his chest. "You're divorced in here." She patted right over his heart. "Nothing you feel for Paige is wrong. You aren't cheating."

"The world isn't going to see it that way. And I've got too much freaking baggage to dump on Paige."

"You know I believe in second chances. But they're not always easy. Sometimes, taking the risk for that second chance seems impossible."

Evan wondered if she was talking only about his falling for Paige—or also about second chances with his birth mom. He thought of the small dinosaur in his pocket.

"And sometimes," she continued, "it's the hardest road you'll ever walk. Hard, but worth it. Of all my boys, you're one of the strongest, Evan."

Evan was surprised at that. He'd never been the Maverick who had his fists raised.

She tapped her hand over his heart again. "Here. You were so tough that it took us years to get through, to prove to you that we loved you. So tough you refused to give up on your marriage when anyone else would have walked out long ago. And you've always been toughest on yourself, even now, when you're thinking about giving up the best thing that's ever happened to you."

"You and Bob are the best thing. And the Mavericks."

"We were," she agreed. "But now you have a chance for even more." She didn't add *for true love with Paige*, but he heard the words as clearly as if she'd shouted them through a megaphone.

Chapter Twenty-Five

It was still early afternoon on the West Coast when Evan's plane landed in San Francisco.

They all stood out on the tarmac saying their thank-yous and good-byes. Evan had hired a car to take Tony, Kelsey, and their mother back to Modesto. The twins intended to stay for the evening and return to San Francisco later that night.

"It was so good getting to know you better." Paige gave Theresa a heartfelt hug. Then the twins.

Evan's hug for his siblings was easy. He clapped Tony on the back and actually placed a little kiss on the top of Kelsey's head. It was so darn adorable, Paige's heart felt a huge tug. But Theresa? Paige had witnessed their conversation in the dining room, and though she hadn't been able to hear it, she'd known instinctively that it was a start. And now Evan hugged Theresa, though their arms were wide, as if to keep contact to the bare minimum. But Paige wasn't about to get picky on the kind of hug, because at least there *was* one.

Shoulder to shoulder, they waved as the car carrying his siblings and mother pulled away.

So what now?

Her heart was screaming to know.

They'd made beautiful love over and over at the hotel. But she'd promised herself she wouldn't be a pushy female who kept asking, *When will you call?* And most of all, *When will you finally realize you love me too?* She hadn't clung to him, hadn't tried to lay claim to him in front of his family, hadn't pressured. In fact, she'd tried almost too hard, to the point of practically ignoring him from the moment they'd arrived at Susan and Bob's until now. But she also hadn't missed a single one of the looks he sent her, looks that told her he wanted to touch her, kiss her too.

But was that enough?

She'd laid her heart on the line last night. She hadn't expected him to say he loved her back. In fact, she would have been shocked if he had. But there was a part of her deep inside that had hoped. And that was terrified of having her heart trampled if Evan never came around. If he couldn't let go of his fears or his past enough to actually figure out that they were meant to be together for more than a night. For more than lovemaking. She wanted a lifetime.

"Well," he said in the deep voice that always made her feel hot all over. "That went just fine." He smiled when she shot him a look. "I know. You hate that word." And finally, he laced his fingers through hers. "I was wondering if you've got the next few hours free."

Her heart soared off into the sky. "I do."

"Then let's take another flight." He turned, leading her back onto the plane.

"Another flight? Where are we going?"

He helped her into the seat she'd occupied on the way back from Chicago. "It's a surprise." He put a finger to her lips as she opened her mouth to ask more questions. Taking the seat beside her, he said, "I want to do something special for you after all you've done to help me."

"You don't need to do anything for me."

"I do." He poured more champagne. "Last night was beautiful. But I need to do something just for you. I *want* to do something for you. Take you to a very special place."

She wanted to cry. She wanted to throw herself at him. She wanted to forget every single one of the worries that had been running through her mind all morning. He wasn't saying he loved her. But he was giving her something wonderful—a few more precious hours with him.

They landed in Monterey, only half an hour's flight time from San Francisco. She smiled, laughter lacing her words. "What are we doing here?"

"Hush," he said, his finger on her lips again, as if he needed an excuse to touch her. "Let me surprise you. Let me give you something for all you've done."

Then he ushered her into a waiting limousine, sitting close, her hand clasped in his.

Her heart was fluttery with emotion, with need.

She wanted to cup his cheek, turn his face to hers, and kiss him until he couldn't deny that what he felt for her was as momentous as her own feelings. And yet she wanted simply *this*, her hand in his, a surprise awaiting her.

After leaving the airport, they headed south on Highway 1. The weather was gorgeous, the sun bright, the sky clear, and the temperature in the low sixties. January could be a rainy month, broken up by gloriously sunny, relatively warm days. Vastly different than Chicago, though that certainly had its own appeal too. South of Carmel, their driver took a private road out to the coastline.

"What are you planning?" Her smile bubbled through.

"Something you've always said you wanted to do."

The limo stopped at the end of the road, and Evan took her hand as she climbed out. The driver came around the hood and handed him a small package. "Per your instructions, sir."

Evan smiled his thanks, then said, "Down here," pulling her through a couple of fence posts and out onto a dirt path they followed to the cliff edge.

"What *is* this place?"

Hand in hand, they descended a few steps cut into the rock until they reached a bench on a small plateau to the left of the path. "A friend of mine owns the land." He waved south. "There's a cottage over there." Then he pointed down to the ocean below. "And these stairs lead down to a private beach."

It had been windy up on the cliff, but the bench they sat on was sheltered in the cleft of the rocks, and the heat of the sun warmed her through her jacket. Evan warmed her hands. And her heart.

"It's beautiful. And peaceful." The sun sparkled on the ocean, and the sound of the waves drifted up to them. Seagulls squawked overhead, diving down to the beachhead below.

"I knew you'd like it."

"It's perfect, Evan. Thank you."

He unwrapped the package the driver had handed him. She was stunned to see a pair of binoculars.

"You always said you wanted to go whale watching. But you never have. And this is the perfect time of year. The gray whales are heading down to Mexico to calve."

"Oh my God, Evan." Without the aid of the binoculars, she stared out to sea. Then she saw it, a spout of water high into the air. Then another and another, like the bursts of a string of steam engines cruising by. "Look! They're out there." She could make out their dark shapes in the ocean, beyond the waves.

"Try the glasses."

She could barely suppress her eagerness as she grabbed the binoculars from his hand. The ocean was the deepest blue-green, the whales like a cavalcade through the waves. "Oh Evan, this is so amazing. They're gorgeous. And so mighty. So powerful and perfect." They seemed close enough to touch through the lenses.

"We'll come again toward the end of February, when they're heading north again with their calves. They swim much closer to shore then to protect their young from the sharks, and they're slower too, because of the babies."

"Yes, oh yes. We have to." She hugged the binoculars to her chest, watching the procession with the naked eye, overcome by the beauty of nature right before her. "This is so much better than being on a boat with a bunch of strangers. We've got our own private overlook."

Then she looked at him and felt the immensity of what he'd done for her, the tenderness in his gaze, the joy of having his body so close to hers, sharing this moment with her. "Thank you so much. You didn't need to do this for me, but I'm so glad you did."

"I needed to do something for *you*, just you. Remember that special we watched on PBS? You said you'd never made it down here to watch the migration, but that it was just as good to watch it on TV."

"I was wrong. It is so much more magnificent out here." When had they watched that show? It had to have been years ago. Maybe three or four. Yet again he'd been listening to her, storing up her likes and preferences. "You couldn't have given me anything better." In a way, it was like telling her he loved her. Just without the words. And it renewed all her hope that he could eventually say them.

"Here." She shoved the glasses at him. "You have to look too."

They sat there for an hour, maybe more, exclaiming every time there was a huge spout, pointing out new sights to each other. "Oh look," she cried out. "There's a school of dolphins too." She had never felt so special. Or so appreciated.

"Are you hungry?"

"Not if I have to miss a moment of this." A moment of sitting here beside him, sharing this special event he'd planned just for her.

He laughed. "You can have both." Fishing his cell phone out, he made a call.

Minutes later, their driver, carrying a big basket, passed their little nook in the rocks. He disappeared down toward the beach below them.

"What have you arranged now?" Her heart raced just contemplating his next revelation.

"Another surprise."

She adored his surprises.

He'd gone to so much trouble. And when had he organized it all? Yes, she'd seen him on the phone during the flight, but she'd thought that was work. She didn't ask, though. It was somehow more special to simply accept that he'd been thinking of her all day.

On the way back up, the limo driver saluted them.

"It's all ready." Taking her hand, Evan helped her down the rock steps cut into the cliff face.

Down on the beach, it was cooler and slightly windier. She was glad she'd worn jeans and her jacket. A blanket was spread out on the sand, its corners anchored. A bottle of champagne chilled in a bucket, and the basket sat in the middle along with two extra blankets. The waves crashed on the shore, the sun heated the sand, birds flew overhead, and the whales frolicked with dolphins out in the ocean. It was perfection.

"You're amazing."

"I thought the whales were the most amazing thing."

She grabbed his face in her hands and kissed him quickly. Then she flopped down beside the basket. "What have we got here?"

He sat beside her, spreading one of the blankets over her legs. "To keep you warm." He uncorked the champagne, poured some into two crystal glasses, and handed her one. Then he clinked with her. "To making sure you don't get thirsty." Finally, he opened the basket. "Brie and crackers. And spring rolls. And this tub looks like spinach dip." He moved things around in the basket. "And cold, roasted chicken. Along with fruit."

All her favorite picnic things. He'd thought of everything.

"Look at this." He flourished a plate of chocolate-covered strawberries. "Where do you want to start?"

With him feeding her the strawberries. Her licking

the chocolate off his fingers. Then he could lick it off her lips.

But as much as she wanted his touch and his kiss, this was too perfect to rush into anything physical. Just as it wasn't the time to talk about his mother or his siblings or Whitney or his past.

She didn't want anything bad or difficult to intrude in this special place. Only good things. Only the romance of being here with him. Only love.

"First a spring roll. Then some brie."

He served her on china packed in the lid of the basket, with cloth napkins to wipe their fingers. She dipped a chocolate-covered strawberry in her champagne, relishing the fizz. They ate all the food out of order, talking, laughing, jumping up when they saw a whale spout above the waves. Everything was delicious.

Just being with Evan was delicious.

"So I want to know more about the crazy things you and the Mavericks did when you were teenagers. I loved hearing Susan and Bob's stories this weekend."

Evan dipped a bit of French bread in the scrumptious spinach dip and handed her the piece, their fingers brushing with a zing of sensual awareness. "I wouldn't call us crazy. We were...boisterous." He cleaned a bit of dip from the side of her mouth and licked it off his finger. Just as if he were licking her.

She laughed to cover the surge of heat through her body. "Come on. Spill."

"Well, there was the time we were hot-rodding in Will's souped-up Chevy. The cop barely caught us."

"Oh no." She put a hand over her mouth. "Don't tell me you got arrested."

"Not with Sebastian in the backseat. The glib SOB told the officer we'd just spent a year fixing up this baby, and we'd gotten carried away with our triumph. If anyone else said a word, the cop would probably have hauled us off to the pokey, but Sebastian had noticed the look in his eye. And the policeman simply ran his hand over the paint, said, 'Good job, boys. I had one of these beauties when I was sixteen. But slow it down, ya hear?' And he let us go."

Paige shook her head, laughing. It was so like Sebastian to figure out exactly the right thing to say to get them off the hook. "More," she said, wanting everything from him. All the good things. He gave her a sliver of melt-in-your-mouth chicken. "The food is delicious, but I meant more stories."

"Have you ever tried peppermint schnapps?" His lips curving in a smile, he caressed her cheek, pushing a stray lock of hair behind her ear.

She almost purred into his touch. "Can't say I have."

"Well, you won't ever get the chance if you're around a Maverick."

She pushed his shoulder. "What did you all do?"

"Matt got hold of a bottle, and we all got drunk. The next morning all I could smell was peppermint.

And even now, put some peppermint schnapps in front of me, in front of *any* of us, and we all get a little queasy."

"I bet Susan thought overindulgence was the best cure."

"Of course." He stood, held out his hand. "Come on, let's got for a walk. We can finish the strawberries when we get back."

She let him pull her to her feet, holding his hand as they strolled, the sun warming half of her, his body warming the rest.

"And we can't forget Daniel. He had the hots for this girl who lived a couple of blocks over. So we boosted him up her fire escape to get to her window."

"Like in *West Side Story*?"

"Yeah." He laughed. "Susan made us watch that musical too. But Daniel never got inside her window. Someone saw him out there and called the cops, thinking he was a peeping Tom. We had to head off the patrol car and keep them busy so he could climb down before they saw him."

She hugged his arm, wishing she'd known him then. Parts of his life had been so terrible. But he had so many good memories too. Susan and Bob had given him that. Thank God they had rescued him.

She wanted to remind him of something good they had shared too. "Do you remember how we used to sneak into the library after it was closed?"

He laughed. "Most college students would be

sneaking a joint. But we had to sneak into the library."

"Yes, but all those books." She made a happy sound of remembered delight. But it had been about more than just the books. It had been about being with him. "We had to read by flashlight."

"And the security guard almost caught us."

"Right. We had to keep scurrying down different aisles to avoid him."

She'd fallen irrevocably in love with him on all those stolen nights.

He stuck his hand in his pocket, his other still firmly clasped around hers, and went silent. Against her side, she felt him tense. But just when she was expecting him to tell her a bad story about his mom or his dad, he pulled something out, holding it in the palm of his hand.

A small plastic dinosaur. A T-Rex.

"Susan gave this back to me this morning."

Paige gazed up at him, waiting.

"My mom took me to The Field Museum in Chicago. I was probably six or seven. And she got me this little dinosaur."

Her heart trembled for him. But she steeled herself for the worst.

"It was one of the best days I ever remember."

★ ★ ★

Paige curled his fingers around the small memento. "I'm so glad you have this as a reminder." Then she tucked the dinosaur back in his pocket. "Tell me all about that day."

"I'd forgotten about it till Susan gave me this." Susan had known the perfect moment to return the plastic T-Rex. And Evan suddenly needed to share his memory with Paige. Their afternoon together at the seaside had been so perfect. She'd loved his surprise trip. Of all the people in the world, Paige would appreciate this memory the most.

"We spent hours in the museum. We saw everything. It was near to closing time, and I wanted to see one last room before we had to go." He remembered his excitement like a rush of adrenaline through his veins. *Just one more, Mom, just one more.* "I ran down the stairs so fast she couldn't keep up. Then all of sudden she was sliding down the banister right past me. A guard stood at the bottom, and I was sure he was going to yell at her." He'd actually been petrified for a moment, frozen to the spot. "But he high-fived her. Then he let her steady me while I slid down the banister too." The guard had winked, put a finger to his lips, and whispered, *Don't tell.*

Leaning against him as they walked, Paige squeezed his arm. "I love this story."

"I do too." He laid his hand over hers. "I remember how she looked. Happy. Even joyful. I'd forgotten all that." There had been joyful times with his mother. But after she'd gone, he'd pushed them all deep inside, too busy demonizing her, blaming her for leaving him.

"Sometimes we were so happy."

He felt that happiness now. It seemed to blossom in his belly. Not *everything* had been bad. There had been moments of great joy. "Thank you for reminding me of all the good things." There was so much he was so damn grateful to this gorgeous woman for.

He'd loved her pure and simple pleasure in watching the whales. Loved the way she closed her eyes and moaned as she savored every morsel of their meal. It had been so like her moans of pleasure as he'd made love to her.

She laid her head against his shoulder. "There are so many wonderful memories just waiting out there for us."

Most of all, he loved that she could share this moment, this memory, and make him see that it was priceless. "Tell me one of your best moments."

"We had a big creek out back of our house when we were kids. And my dad hung a thick rope with a knot at the end for us to swing on."

Us. Paige and Whitney. As children.

"We used to swing out over the creek as far as we could. Then we'd let go, flying into the water. It was like we were working together. I'd push Whitney and she'd push me, and we'd see how far we could get."

"Who got the farthest?"

"I usually did. But it was like we both won because we were a team."

In the halcyon days when there'd been no competition between them. "It sounds like fun."

"It was," she agreed. Then she stopped, tipping her head back to look at him. "But it was also the last really good summer for us. We always forget the good stuff when things go bad, don't we?"

"Yes." Just as he'd forgotten—or buried—his mother's joy. "But I'm so glad we've remembered."

He turned her in his arms and raised her hand to his face, placing her cold fingers on his hot skin. "Your hands are freezing. I better get you out of here."

"I'm not cold with your arms around me."

He hadn't kissed her since they'd left the hotel this morning. And as much as he'd wanted to make love to her again, he hadn't touched her. This day, this trip, the whale watching, the picnic on the beach, even the memories, were all about her happiness. And his need to give her something as exquisite as all she'd given him.

She couldn't know, couldn't possibly fathom what she'd done for him. Even today, drawing out the joy from his past. Replacing the dark with light.

"Thank you," he whispered.

Whether he moved or she did, their mouths touched. Her kiss was perfect for its very purity. Their breaths mingled, and her hands warmed against his chest. He licked the seam of her lips, and she opened for him, tasting of chocolate and champagne and beautiful woman. She gave him the sweetness of her soul in that kiss. And he gave her the depths of his.

The sea surged beyond them, crashing on the shore, and the wind surrounded them, blowing the silk of her hair across his cheeks. His blood was high, screaming for him to pull her down to the sand with him, to show her all the fury of his desire. Yet his heart wanted nothing more than her taste on his lips, her arms around him.

And in that kiss, he gave her everything he was, everything he couldn't say, everything he wanted her to have.

Chapter Twenty-Six

It was dark as Evan walked Paige up to the front door of her condo. Susan's words echoed in his mind as she turned her key in the lock and set her bag and purse just inside the door. *You had your eyes set on the wrong sister from the very beginning.*

He looked at Paige beside him. Sweet Paige. Hot, sexy, wild Paige.

Loving Paige.

She tipped her chin up to smile at him. "Thank you for a lovely weekend. And for that wonderful trip down the coast."

That wonderful trip? It had been so much more. Standing out there on the beach with her in his arms, her lips open beneath his, he had never felt such passion. And yet ending with only that kiss had been its own perfection in that beautiful moment.

He'd spent nearly every second of the past two days with her, yet he wasn't even close to being ready to let her go.

"You're welcome." It sounded so freaking inadequate for all the emotions churning inside him.

When she smiled again, his hands flexed with the need to haul her into his arms and kiss her senseless.

To *love* her senseless.

Susan was right, he *had* chosen the wrong sister. He recalled all those nights in Paige's dorm room or sneaking into the university library, talking until he was hoarse, delving into her mind, relishing the way she did the same to him, the brilliant way she helped him shape his plans.

Then he'd seen Whitney. And he'd grabbed on to her because she made it easy for him. With Whitney, he didn't have to really look inside himself and decide whether or not he was worthy of a truly good woman. He'd always felt good enough for Whitney, because deep in his heart, no matter what he told himself and everyone else, he'd known she wanted him for the money he'd make, for the things he would eventually be able to buy her.

Whereas Paige had never wanted those things. All Paige had ever wanted was to love a man with a true heart. A good man. A worthy man.

And he'd never felt worthy of Paige.

He still didn't. Especially when he couldn't erase his marriage to Whitney. When Paige would never be able to forget that he'd slept in Whitney's bed, tried to have children with her sister. That Whitney was the sister he'd chosen back then, even if he chose her for all the wrong reasons. He worried that his past and the terrible choice he'd made would forever stand between them like a living, breathing human being.

And yet...

He couldn't turn away from Paige. Couldn't shut down this need, this attraction, this *connection*. Maybe it was the revelation of what he'd been running from all those years ago. Her beautiful, caring nature. Her pure love. His own feelings of unworthiness.

But even as he lowered his mouth to hers for a good-bye kiss, his gut cried out that it couldn't be good-bye. He needed her, wanted her. Last night and this morning would never be enough. He wanted more beautiful days on the beach with her. More long conversations in his library. More nights in her bed. More of *her*.

In an instant, the good-bye kiss stopped being sweet or nice...or good-bye. He held her face in his hands and plundered her gorgeous lips. She opened with hunger, taking him with the same desperation he felt, a moan purring in her throat.

Not enough, never enough.

He devoured her. Consumed the air right out of her lungs. And they still weren't close enough.

Bending, he hauled her up against his body, her legs rising to his waist. He cupped her, held her tight, her center hot against all his hardness. She shoved the door all the way open, and with his hands under her butt and her arms anchoring him to her, he carried her inside.

He'd barely kicked the door closed behind them

when she tore at his clothes, their lips still locked together. First his jacket, then the buttons of his shirt. He let her feet slide to the entry floor. He heard the suitcase fall on its side as his foot knocked it out of the way.

He threw her coat somewhere, heard the zipper thwack the wall. Then he whipped her sweater over her head. "You are so beautiful." He cupped each gorgeous breast, feasting on them.

"Shoes," she said. "Everything. Please. I want it all off. *Now.*"

Then there were just hands, mouths, gasped breaths, and the rustle of clothing as they ripped and tore and tossed. Something fell off a table and rolled across the carpet as he dragged her down to the floor in her living room. Her scent was a mixture of sea air and chocolate. He buried his face between her breasts and gloried in her moan as he took a tight peak into his mouth.

"Evan. Oh God." She arched against him, riding him.

Never enough. He tore off her panties, the last scrap of fabric between them, needing his hands on her, in her. She was so wet, so hot, and he couldn't think, couldn't breathe with the want so tight in his gut. He crawled down her body until finally he could taste her. Her cries filled the room, filled his head, and she tangled her fingers in his hair, tugging him closer, needing, wanting as urgently as he did.

Her explosion rocked them both, and she was still

high when he plunged deep inside her, her body still contracting as he hit home. But he needed so much more, and she urged him on with her hands, her lips, her tongue. Begging wordlessly.

He took her hard, driving their bodies across the carpet, and yet she clung to him, crying out his name, pleading for more, higher, harder, deeper. He lost his mind, he was simply sensation and desire, his need so powerful that it roared in his ears. They were one body, one mind, one heartbeat, one being, and together they flew to the highest peak and flung themselves off, falling into endless pleasure and bottomless bliss.

He held her tight. She was such perfection in his arms. But then thought returned. Realization.

"Did I hurt you?" He remembered the carpet against her soft skin.

She stroked his cheek. "You could never hurt me."

But he could. So badly. "I didn't mean to do that." His words were hoarse, raw from pleasure. And the guilt germinating inside him. He never wanted to hurt her, not physically, not emotionally. "I didn't intend to drag you inside and devour you in your entryway."

"I loved being devoured. And we both did the dragging inside." She kissed the tip of his nose. "But I think we also both need some time and space to process."

His chest tightened. Terror, that's what it was. Terror that she'd think and process...and end up choosing a life without him. She'd promised him otherwise at the hotel, said she'd always be there. But his mother had promised always to be there for him—and she'd vanished like a ghost.

When Paige looked into his eyes, he swore she could read his thoughts—even as mangled and twisted as they were. "Don't overthink it, okay? You. Me. Together. We're beautiful. Remember that."

"I can't forget it."

She touched her lips to his, then started to pull away, but he wrapped his hand around her nape, taking her lips in a long, decadent sip. She opened to him again, so beautiful, so trusting despite everything. And he wanted them to stay here, just like this, forever.

But in the end, though it felt like the hardest thing he'd ever done, he let her go. Rolling to his feet, he put his clothes on. She was dressed too by the time he opened the door, and she went up on her toes, kissing him once more. His heart ached with the gentleness of it, but he didn't beg her to let him stay.

Because he had to let her go. They needed time, just like she said. He'd hurt her all those years ago, and he could so easily hurt her again.

Because Paige loved him.

He hadn't been worthy of her love nine years ago.

Was there any chance that he could be worthy of her now?

★ ★ ★

Paige closed her door and leaned against it. Nothing was certain with Evan, but she still felt dreamy and sexy and giddy—all the things that people in love felt. She could have gotten him to stay the night. She certainly could have lured him into making love to her again.

But where the lovemaking they'd just shared had been instinctive—utterly impossible to resist on both their parts—if she'd angled for the whole night, that would have been manipulation. And though her heart was on the line, she refused to be like her sister, manipulating Evan to her advantage, wheedling to get what she wanted.

He needed time to build his trust—anyone in his situation would. It might take months, maybe even until after the divorce was final. And after he'd worked out his feelings for his mother.

He hadn't said he loved her. And she hadn't expected it.

But she had *hoped* for it. For Evan to look at her and see everything he'd ever wanted. To tell her she was the woman who had been in his heart all along.

She was lost in her turbulent thoughts when her doorbell rang. She jumped away from the door, joy infusing every cell of her body at the thought that Evan had already done his thinking. That he was back to say he wanted to be with her. That he might even be here to say that he loved her.

She jerked the door open, breathless, excited, hopeful.

And found Whitney standing there instead.

Chapter Twenty-Seven

Paige's blood roared in her ears like the engines of Evan's jet.

"Aren't you going to invite me in?" Whitney's voice was nauseatingly sweet.

Paige couldn't reply. Couldn't get her lips or her voice to work. Not when all her joy in the weekend, in the perfect beach date today, in every beautiful moment she and Evan had shared together, was dying a nasty, brutal death beneath her sister's gaze. But though her tongue couldn't move, her legs did what they always had before—stepped back to let Whitney in.

Her sister wore an elegant black dress with gold trim. Her auburn hair caught the light, her brows were perfectly arched, and her lipstick was an exact match to her red-tipped nails. In her stiletto heels, she towered over Paige in her bare feet.

Whitney was glamorous, Paige wasn't. Just like usual.

And yet an insistent voice inside her head cried out that it was *her* body, *her* skin, and *her* heart that still sang from Evan's kisses, his caresses. From his total possession.

"You've been ignoring my calls since I returned from the south of France."

"I've been busy." She'd ignored Whitney's calls since that first glorious, wonderful kiss with Evan in Chicago before the wedding.

The kiss from her sister's husband who was an ex in every way but the legal one.

"Where have you been?" Whitney drawled, looking pointedly at the small suitcase on the floor. The one Evan had kicked on its side before he'd ripped Paige's clothes off.

Her purse lay beside the case, and her jacket was still on the floor where Evan had thrown it. A bowl on the living room side table had fallen, rolling across the carpet. Her lips were swollen from his kisses. Paige could only hope Whitney was too busy drilling her about why she hadn't taken her calls to notice.

She barely avoided putting a hand to her hair to straighten the locks Evan had run his fingers through. "I just returned from a trip to see Susan and Bob."

"Weren't you just there for the wedding?" Whitney widened her eyes beneath her perfect makeup.

Paige's mind strove furiously for an explanation. The same way she always reacted to Whitney, defending, rationalizing. But that voice inside her was louder now.

You don't have to do this anymore. You never did.

Paige stood taller, her shoulders straighter. "Why I went there isn't your business."

Instead of unleashing her wrath, Whitney smiled as if she'd just reeled in a fish who hadn't put up much of a fight. "But it is my business why you were with my husband, isn't it?" She batted her thick, false eyelashes.

Whitney paused. Waited for Paige to understand her true meaning.

Like an ice pick to the heart, the realization hit Paige that her sister must have seen their tumble through her door. And then, a good while later, she'd watched Evan leave, his clothes hastily donned, his hair a mess after their lovemaking.

Just as Paige's was. Whitney had seen everything, from the suitcase tipped sideways, to the jacket, to the bowl in the middle of the living room floor.

No. God, no. It was the very last thing Paige and Evan needed, for Whitney to plunk herself down right in the middle of what was already such a complicated—and tentative—new relationship.

"You're screwing him." Whitney's voice turned malicious, her face lined with rage. "Aren't you, you dirty little slut?"

Paige's fierce response was instinctive. "Don't call me that." Her legs might have stepped aside to let her sister in…but her heart refused to do the same.

Whitney wasn't listening. She'd never listened to anyone.

"How could you betray me like this? Your own sister." Moisture glittered in Whitney's eyes. On anyone else, Paige might have thought the tears were real, but she knew her sister too well. The tears were designed to make Paige feel guilty, to drive home the guilt as Whitney injected a pathetic wobble into her voice. "I've needed you so badly since he left me." She pointed her finger in Paige's face, all pretense of tears vanishing. "But you. Weren't. There." She punctuated every word with fury. "Instead, you were off screwing my husband." Venom smeared every syllable. "What would Mom think of that after you promised her you'd take care of Daddy and me?" Then she hit Paige with her worst. "But you let Daddy die. And now you've stolen Evan from me."

Paige knew exactly what Whitney was doing. Her sister was a master at making a person squirm, at pushing just the right button to make her opponent cry or scream or give in. Paige *knew*.

Yet the accusations still cut her to ribbons. Her heart felt raw and bleeding, flayed open as if Whitney had the skill of Jack the Ripper.

Paige *had* failed her mother. She'd failed her father. She'd even failed Evan, because she'd never told him what Whitney was like beneath all the glitter and elegance and lies.

But her parents were dead. Evan wasn't. He deserved another chance at happiness.

And—*goddammit!*—Paige deserved to be happy too.

Nine years had been way too long to wait for Evan.

But *thirty* years had been an absolute eternity of being Whitney's emotional slave. That story she'd told Evan about the rope swing had been one tiny glimmer of decency in years of bondage. And Paige wouldn't let one more second pass playing the role of protector that her mother had given her. Just as Evan had to deal with the bad choices his mother had made, so did Paige with her own mother.

Guilt and duty had been her constant companions all these years. This moment brought righteous anger. Hopefully, the future would bring forgiveness.

But it was anger that gave her the strength to hold her own and say, "What would Mom think of what *you* did, Whitney?"

Whitney sniffed haughtily. "You mean be the best wife I could to Evan and still keep my sanity?"

"No." Paige's voice was sharp enough to cut through Whitney's smugness, her eyebrows rising in surprise. "What you did to Evan was horrible. Unthinkable. Unforgivable. You lied, not just once, but three times." She held up a finger when Whitney opened her mouth. "Oh wait, four times, when we count the tubal ligation you never told him about."

"It's my body. I can do what I want with it."

"Except lie about it to your husband." She advanced a step and Whitney actually backed up. Paige had never challenged her sister before. Never gone head to head like this. It was so hard. But so incredibly satisfying. To finally speak up with a voice that she'd held in for far too long. "Mom would have been really upset by what you did."

"She would have supported me because she loved me."

"You're right. She would have pretended you made a mistake and told herself that what you did wasn't deliberate. But I know it was." Paige steeled everything deep inside and said the things she should have said years ago. "I don't support you. I don't support what you did. And I'm not giving you any sympathy. Unless you can admit how wrong you were and ask Evan's forgiveness, I'm not taking your calls, and I don't want to see you."

Whitney stared as if Paige were ready for the asylum, all wrapped up in a straitjacket. "You don't mean that." Shock threaded her words.

"I do." Paige crossed her arms. "Every word."

The storm built on Whitney's features, her cheekbones reddening, her eyes narrowing, and her lips pursing into a thin, ugly line.

"You bitch." A tiny fleck of spittle flew out of her mouth. She crowded Paige, backing her into the living room. "He might enjoy screwing you. He might have fun being worshipped by poor little Paige who always wanted him but couldn't have him. But do you actually think he could ever love you? Because he'll never stop loving me." Whitney stabbed a finger into her breastbone with an audible thud. "You're a fool if you let yourself forget that the moment he saw me that first day, he forgot all about you. It was so damn easy to take him away from you. But you still hung around all these years, begging for scraps, always underfoot, always hoping he'd notice you. It would actually be funny if it wasn't so pathetic. My friends and I used to laugh about it all the time." Her voice dripped with sarcasm. "Poor Paige, the pathetic little puppy dog drooling after my husband. Did you really think you could steal him away from me? I can have him back with a simple snap of my fingers. I just haven't tried. But now you've given me a reason to do it."

Whitney's gaze was rabid, her features a mottled blue-red with her rage.

But Paige's rage was just as potent. "You knew how I felt about Evan back then?"

Whitney rolled her eyes. "I know everything about you. How you think. What you'll do. You're so pitifully transparent."

Whitney had used Paige to prop up her own ego, to make herself feel superior. She'd taken Evan simply because she could. Because Paige wanted him, and Whitney couldn't stand to let her sister win. "You never really loved him, did you?"

Whitney waved that away, as if the whole question of love was preposterous. "You didn't deserve him. You were too weak. He needed me to push him. To help him become the billionaire he was supposed to be. Lord knows if he'd ended up with you, he'd probably be tossing a baseball to a snotty-nosed kid in a little yard somewhere." She looked disgusted by the image. "He was meant for bigger things than just being a father."

Paige had always known about Whitney's ugly traits, that she could trample people like they were ants in her path. But this was diabolical.

Purely malicious.

As a psychologist, Paige should have seen it. That was part of the reason she'd chosen her career, to figure it all out. But she never had, not truly. She hadn't been able to see the truth right in front of her. Hadn't wanted to see, because the truth was too close. It was too difficult to admit that the monster was real, that her sister was a sociopath who had never loved anyone but herself.

Until Whitney shined a spotlight and forced her to see.

"You've lost him," Paige told the woman who was no longer her family. Blood had bound them together...until poison destroyed that bond. "Not because of me, but because he finally sees what you really are." She looked at Whitney in her designer dress and towering high heels. Really looked for the first time. "He won't ever be back."

Whitney laughed, a hollow, grating sound. Like the wicked witch. Then she snapped her fingers. "That's how easy it'll be to get him back." She shrugged, a rude and careless shift of her shoulders. "Or maybe I'll just take every penny he has after I prove he was screwing my very own sister behind my back."

"Then all your friends will call *you* the drooling idiot, won't they, Whitney? You wouldn't want them to know your pathetic, puppy-dog sister stole him away from you, would you?"

Whitney growled, tossed her hair over her shoulder, opened the front door, and slammed it on the way out, shaking the whole building.

Paige looked at the door, feeling like an earthquake had just rumbled through her. Or a tornado had snapped her up and spun her hard and fast.

And yet, she was lighter too.

For her whole life she'd kowtowed to her sister. But she never would again.

Paige's career was helping people achieve freedom after years of emotional oppression. Finally, she'd done it for herself.

She wanted to call Evan to tell him her news, her epiphany, her breakthrough. And she needed him to know that Whitney was going to mess with the divorce in any way she could.

Determination—and that growing lightness within her—made her hand surprisingly steady as she fished her phone out of her purse and dialed his cell phone.

"Paige." She loved the sound of her name on his lips, soft and low and full of need. "I was just thinking about you. It seems like I can't stop."

She wanted to tell him the same, to talk as lovers did. But she needed him to know, "Whitney was just here."

He cursed, four letters that crudely, and accurately, summed up the situation.

"She saw us kiss at the door and disappear inside." Her heart raced as she remembered the beauty, the passion of their connection. "She was still watching when you come back out. After." Heat infused Paige head to toes with the pleasure, the joy, and the love still tingling deep inside her. "After we made love."

Again, he swore, fury—and frustration—underlying the short word.

"She's going to use it against you in the settlement. Use *me* against you. She wants to destroy you."

"She won't." His tone was hard. All the warmth with which he'd said her name was gone now. "I won't let her, damn it."

Paige was suddenly holding a phone full of dead air. And wondering if, like an emotional vampire, Whitney had just sucked away everything that was good.

No. That was the past talking. No matter what Whitney said with that snap of her fingers, Evan wouldn't go back to her. How could he possibly do that?

Shoving her insecurities away—the insecurities her sister had built up simply so she could toy with Paige—she rolled her suitcase back to her bedroom and started unpacking. A simple, routine act that would help ground her back into reality.

But Evan's imprint was on each piece of clothing. The hungry look in his eyes as he'd stripped her sweater away. The reverence as he'd traced the line of lace along the top edge of her panties. The deep emotion in his voice as he'd said, *I'm yours*.

The doorbell rang for the second time that evening. She closed her eyes and took a bracing breath. Whitney was back for more. Maybe she'd thought of some new threat. Clearly, she hadn't accepted that Paige was done taking her crap.

When she reached the front door, she threw it open, ready to do battle.

But this time, Evan filled her doorway.

And her heart.

"I was already on my way back to you when you called." His gaze was fierce and passionate and protective. "I shouldn't have left. But I swear to you, I won't make that mistake again. And I won't let her hurt you," he vowed.

Then he wrapped her in his arms and kissed her. The purest vow of all.

Chapter Twenty-Eight

Paige stole his breath right out of his chest. Just the way she'd stolen his heart. Both now *and* all those years ago, talking and laughing and connecting on a deeper level than he ever had with anyone else.

Evan made himself set her down, though he never wanted to let her go. "The thought of Whitney threatening you makes me crazy."

He'd already been on his way back, trying the whole way to convince himself that desire was what drove his urge to be with her again. But when Paige had called and told him about Whitney's surprise blitz attack? He'd finally realized, finally *accepted*, just how much he felt for Paige. How much he cared. How much he wanted her in his arms, in his bed, in his life.

And not just for one stolen weekend.

"You were the one she was threatening, Evan."

"She'll use you to get at me."

"She can try," Paige said, lifting her chin. "But it won't work."

He stroked her cheek. She was so brave. So strong. So honest. If only he'd realized nine years ago that *brave, strong,* and *honest* were traits worth fighting for. Even if you had to fight your own demons. Especially then.

"Tell me what she said."

She was silent for a moment that was heavy enough for him to what had happened between them. "She wanted my sympathy. She wanted to know where I was this weekend." Pausing, it was obvious she had to weigh whether to continue. Her chin lifted with her decision to tell him. "She wanted to know how I could possibly think you would have feelings for me when you could have her instead."

"I will crush her before I let her hurt you." He would give away all his money, all his worldly possessions if that was what it took to protect Paige. "I'm so sorry I wasn't here to protect you from her."

"Don't be sorry. It was good for me." When his eyebrow rose in disbelief, she clarified. "The things she said were horrible. But knowing I could stand up to her and defend myself? That was good. Great, in fact. Although," she added with a small laugh, "I'm not sure I'll be able to watch *Sleeping Beauty* again any time soon. I swear she actually looked like the wicked witch when she was yelling at me."

It was a good sign that Paige could laugh. "I've always known you were stronger than her. So has she, which is why she worked so hard to cut you down." He ran his hands over her hair, needing to touch her, to know that she was safe and unharmed.

"She didn't expect me to come back at her. Never thought I would tell her not to call me again unless she wanted to apologize to you and ask for forgiveness."

For Paige, that was huge. Family was everything to her. It was why she hadn't deserted Whitney when anyone else would have.

But then, as if some sort of dam suddenly broke inside her, she sobbed, the tears rising so quickly she couldn't stop them. *He* couldn't stop them.

"God, sweetheart, please." He didn't have the right words. He could only gather her against him.

"That story I told you about swinging into the creek." Her voice broke. "I wanted it to always be like that. I wanted to love her. For her to love me. I wanted us to be *real* sisters. I wanted that so badly that I was actually dying for her to come visit me that weekend at college when you met her. I thought we could actually be different together once we weren't living in the same house."

He closed his eyes, feeling her grief, his own, knowing what they'd both lost that weekend.

"And I wanted to do right by my mother, to keep my promise. But I never could. It was impossible. Whitney would never let me."

He held her, stroking her back. "It wasn't your fault." But she needed to let it out. He'd thought his own wounds were deep, but the scars Whitney had left on Paige might even be worse.

She breathed in, out, quickly, then sniffed. "I know

I'm not to blame. I think I've known it since the day I found out what she did to you."

And he'd been caught in a vicious loop of believing how wrong it was to be with Paige because she was his sister-in-law. But the only wrong thing was Whitney. *Wrong* had never been finding pleasure—and peace—in Paige's arms.

He was so freaking tired of feeling shitty, of feeling guilty, of feeling foolish. Most of all, he was tired of imagining that his future could only get worse, like he was still that little kid hiding in dark corners trying to avoid the beating that was going to come anyway.

With Whitney, he had no doubt that she would fight him in as many dirty, nasty, underhanded ways as she could think of. But though he'd fight back with every ounce of his will, he'd also take the light, the joy, and the sweetness of the present with Paige. Every last moment that he could have with her—and he swore he would appreciate every single one.

He wiped the tears from her cheeks and took Paige's lips again, slowly, lingeringly, tasting every inch of her mouth. "You're so fresh, so lovely, so real. You can't know the number of people I meet who are phonies. Who just want something from me. But you've never asked for anything except my friendship. And you gave me yours without question."

She shook her head. "I've always wanted more, Evan." Yet again, her bravery astounded him as she squarely met his gaze. "I still do."

He kissed the corner of her eye, the tip of her nose, then her lips. He wanted to give her the promises she needed to hear, but he couldn't lie to her. The only thing he knew for sure was that he couldn't walk away.

"You're the most important person in the world to me, Paige."

Her smile warmed him, a smile that came even though he hadn't given her the word *love*, as she'd given it to him.

"I know I am." Her hands moved to cover his. "But I love hearing you say it out loud."

"I don't know what I'd do without you. I can't stand to even think of that."

"Then don't."

She made it sound so simple.

Was it?

Could it be?

Simple or not, he hauled her up until she could wrap her legs around his waist, locking her bare ankles behind him.

"I love it when you do that," she said. "When you act like you can't get enough of me."

"I can't." Nothing had ever been more true. And there was so much more truth she needed to know. "I love that we were friends first before lovers. That I know you so well. That you're part of my family."

She kissed him as he carried her into the bedroom, then he let her feet down until she was standing before him.

"I want you so badly, need you so much." He couldn't believe what he was about to admit. But he could be honest with Paige. Always. No matter what. "I don't know where to start to show you how much I need you."

Whatever he expected her to do or say in response, it wasn't the way she scrambled back onto the mattress and grinned up at him. "Where do you *want* to start?"

Sex had never been fun. It had been a minefield like all the other minefields in his life. But even after a harrowing confrontation, after tears, Paige was full of life and playfulness. Damn if he didn't need that. Badly. They both did, needed to banish the darkness once and for all. Together.

He climbed over her, straddling her body on hands and knees. "Here." He slid his hand up under her sweater and cupped her breast through the lace of her bra.

"Or," she said in a naughty voice that revved his engine hotter and faster, "you could start here." She drew his hand out of her sweater...and over the hot, damp apex of her thighs.

"You always were the smarter of the two of us." He enjoyed teasing her with his words as much as his touch. "You have too many clothes on."

She gazed up at him, her eyes hot. "Let's see who can get undressed the fastest."

He'd never seen her look quite so free before. He was proud of her for standing up to her sister, for having the courage to cut her off. But he'd tell her later, after he ravished her.

"You're on," he said, whipping his shirt over his head while he kicked off his shoes.

She simply started tearing everything off right there on the bed, throwing clothing every which way.

"I beat you." She lay dazzlingly naked in the middle of the bed, completely unabashed.

"That's only because you were barely dressed from the last time I devoured you."

Had it really been only an hour ago that they'd fallen on each other in her entryway? It seemed like a lifetime.

He started to climb back onto the bed, but she held up her hand. "Wait."

He stopped, one knee on the mattress. "What?"

"I want to look at you." Her gaze stroked him like the touch of her hand. "You're like a Greek statue. You always have been."

He worked out every day to get this way. He and Matt had been the puniest of the Mavericks when they were younger. "Back in college, I didn't have nearly enough time to work out."

She reached out, running her fingertips over his pecs, his abs, his muscles leaping beneath her touch. Wanting more. Always *more* when it came to Paige.

"Even in college, you were magnificent. And now I know how you feel, how you taste." She licked her lips. "Even in my dreams, it wasn't this good."

"I dreamed about you too. When we were in college."

"You did?"

"How could I not? And then this week, I couldn't stop dreaming again, couldn't stop fantasizing." He came back over her, kissing her mouth before raining kisses down over her neck, her shoulders, the swells of her breasts until she gasped. Moaned her pleasure. "You made all those hot little sounds in my dreams." He slid a hand down between them. "I touched you here." He stroked up, gliding over her aroused flesh until she arched, her breasts caressing his chest. "Then I did this." He rolled her to her stomach beneath him, brought her up to her knees.

Sliding down between her legs, he parted them and breathed her in. Her hair fell over her back, and he brushed the silky locks aside to kiss her spine, loving the way she trembled with need.

He licked and kissed and nipped, then rose up over her. "You're so ready. So hungry. For me. Only me." He rubbed his hard length along the slick folds of her sex. "Just like you were in my dreams."

He poised at her entrance, held himself there, glorying in her heat. Then he slid home inside her.

"*Evan.*" His name fell from her lips as she took him deeper than he'd ever thought it possible to connect with another person.

"I kissed your neck just like this." His words were raw, overwhelmed with desire as he peppered her neck with kisses. He pushed deeper, and her hands fisted on the sheets. When he pulled out, he forced himself to go slow, to tease her, stroke her. "I told you how gorgeous you were." He buried his face in her hair. "I told you how you filled up every empty space inside me."

She cried out, her body shivering around him. And he almost lost it. Lost himself completely in her. But he needed her to know what she did to him. How much she meant.

"In my dreams, I told you how much I loved the sound of your voice." He groaned as she let go of the sheets and laced her fingers with his. "I told you how I loved talking with you, just sitting, just being. Loved the way you listened."

He tried to hold on, but he couldn't help spinning out of control, rocking them both across the bed, keeping her hands tightly laced in his, the spasms of her body turning him mindless.

"I told you— " Then he couldn't remember anything else.

Except that he'd made the wrong choice long ago. At long last, he'd finally made the right one.

Paige was everything he could ever want, everything he could ever need. He was the luckiest guy in the world that she could still want to be with him after all the ways he'd screwed up.

But would the heat, the joy, the power of their connection, be enough to erase the mistakes—and the darkness—of his past?

Chapter Twenty-Nine

Whitney's lawyer was a shark, complete with big white teeth and fleshy lips large enough to hold them all. Randall P. Craig smiled with evil glee as he pushed duplicate copies of Whitney's new demands to Evan and his lawyer across the wide expanse of the conference table.

She was dressed for performance in a couture suit, her lips painted a deep red that would leave marks on a man's skin. Just the way her nails would. And her lies.

She dabbed at the corner of her eye with a small silk handkerchief that Evan was sure Randall P. Craig had provided for just this purpose. He also noticed a lipstick stain on her teeth. She'd be horrified, so he didn't tell her. It was petty but liberating.

"Due to Mrs. Collins' emotional distress after learning of her husband's perfidy—" Evan could barely hold back an eye roll at Randall's description. "—my client is asking for damages in addition to her rightful fifty percent. We believe one hundred percent would be just recompense. After all, Mr. Collins has been sleeping with her *sister*." Randall infused as much shock and horror as he could into the word. "Probably for years."

Evan's lawyer, Henry Gerhardt, was the best of the best in divorce court. Miles better than Whitney's lawyer would ever be. Henry hadn't been thrilled to find out that Evan and Paige had begun a relationship, even if it hadn't started until New Year's Eve, long after the divorce papers had already been filed. Knowing his lawyer would need to be armed with all the information, Evan had explained everything, from the wedding weekend at Susan and Bob's, to Whitney spying on them at Paige's condo.

Evan knew what Henry would have said if he'd asked for advice. That Evan should leave Paige alone until the divorce was final. That it was the only way to keep her safe from the ugliness.

Evan hadn't asked, and Henry hadn't offered. Likely because even the lawyer could see it was way too late for that. Evan couldn't stay away.

Paige made him feel too good. And not just because of their incredible lovemaking, but simply being with her.

Yes, he'd had wickedly sexy dreams about Paige. But he never would have acted on those dreams, not in a million years. Not until Whitney blew up their marriage.

He'd be damned if he'd let her mess with his life or his happiness again. He'd already given her too many years. Now he wanted to be with Paige. And if their relationship fell apart, it for damn sure wouldn't be because of Whitney.

It would be because Evan screwed it up.

God help him, he didn't want to mess up. Not with Paige. Not this time.

At least where Whitney was concerned, Evan would—finally—make all the right moves. Last night, he'd gone through his inventory of artwork and valuables and determined everything she'd taken. If Whitney wanted a fight—and she obviously did—she was on.

"Do not bring your sister into this." His words and demeanor were calm, despite the fury burning in his gut over the way Whitney dared to hurt Paige.

"*You* brought her into this," Whitney snapped. "I saw you kissing her. You disappeared into her condo and came back out with that look you get after sex."

They both knew he'd never had that look with her when they were married. What he shared with Paige was miles beyond simple physical release. "Long before I ever kissed Paige, I found out you'd lied about three miscarriages and a tubal ligation you never even bothered to discuss with me."

Whitney would never get one hundred percent of his holdings. She wouldn't even get fifty. He'd meant it when he told Paige that he'd hand over every penny just to protect her—but he knew Whitney, and even if he gave her everything he had, she would still stop at nothing to destroy her sister.

Whitney sniffed, affecting the injured party again,

just as her lawyer said, "We could argue about this all day, but there is an alternative. Mrs. Collins will forgive everything you have done and you will agree to forget all your *alleged* claims against her—*if* you reconcile." He spread his hands. "Problem solved."

Evan shouldn't have felt like the floor had opened up and his chair had plunged eighteen floors to the marble lobby of Hart, Pool, and Gerhardt. He should have known this was coming. That Whitney would think of the most devious way to play this out.

Not to mention the most hurtful to Paige.

"We could start fresh, Evan." Whitney looked at him with watery eyes. "The past would all be erased. Wouldn't you like that? To go back to the way we were in the beginning? Before Paige came between us? We were so in love. We can have all that again. That's what I really want. And I know, in your heart, you do too."

At long last, the shock wore off and his brain started working again. He licked his own teeth, then pointed at hers. "You've got some lipstick on your teeth."

Looking horrified, she reached for her mouth to rub it off.

He could have gotten nastier. He could have told her to go screw herself. He could have said that she was the last woman on planet Earth that he would ever consider touching again. He could have made it clear that he'd rather be celibate for the rest of his life than get back together with her.

But he was a Maverick. And he knew better than anyone how to control a negotiation.

Even when he was sitting across from the devil.

"I'm going to pass."

She stared at him a moment, as if she couldn't even begin to fathom that he would turn her down. It was her turn to plunge eighteen floors.

Her eyes narrowed, and her lips pressed into a thin line as the real Whitney came out to play. "Then I will drag your lover, *my sister—*" She stabbed her chest with a pointed finger. "—who you've been screwing behind my back, through the mud. I will ruin her career. I will destroy her."

It was his worst nightmare. That Whitney would hurt Paige again. And that she would annihilate anything he and Paige could have together.

His hands were starting to tense when he stopped. Breathed. Thought of Paige.

Paige, who was as caring as Susan.

Paige, who'd only ever tried to help him.

Paige, who had remained his friend through everything.

Paige, who had risked opening her heart to him completely.

Paige, who was fearless. Magnificent.

And who loved *him*.

"Two can sling mud," he said in a deliberately soft voice. "Do you really want your friends and all of San

Francisco high society to know why I left you? The gossip magazines would have a field day with that."

She eyed him like he was a rattler she'd suddenly found coiled at her feet. "It's your word against mine," she said, but her tone wasn't quite so haughty anymore.

Keeping his gaze on her, he held his hand out. "Henry, the folder, please."

Henry was perfectly professional as he fished a folder out of the stack in front of him and laid it in Evan's hand. Still, his lawyer couldn't quite contain the gleam of victory in his eyes.

"You really shouldn't have left a paper trail." Evan set the closed folder on the table in front of him. "And you shouldn't piss off people who might later be willing to testify against you."

Her face turned a sickly shade of pale.

"While I was out of the country, Henry was hard at work on my behalf. It's amazing how much documentation he found regarding the *little* lies you told."

"Now just a minute," Randall P. Craig started to bluster. Not so much of a shark anymore, was he?

Evan put his finger to his lips. Then he turned back to Whitney. "The divorce settlement is already more than generous. I've even decided to throw in the Atherton house in exchange for the San Francisco flat. You can keep all the artwork you stole while I was away, except the Dali. I suggest you take this offer. Or you won't have anything left when you lose. Nothing at all." He gave her a long look. "Because, make no mistake, Whitney, if you want to fight, I will fight."

Her lawyer looked like he was about to have a coronary as he said, "Mrs. Collins—"

She held up a hand. "Let me think."

"Go ahead and think, Whitney." Evan's voice was deadly. "Think of your reputation in this town when all your lies come out. Think of all the parties you won't be invited to. Think of how everyone will laugh. About *you*."

She drew in a deep breath, glared at him, then let her breath hiss between her teeth. Teeth that still had a smear of red across the front. "All right."

"I also want a nondisclosure agreement. You say one word about Paige, and it's all over."

"I said all right," she snapped through clenched teeth, her voice louder, sharper. "The nondisclosure applies to you too."

He could live with that. "Agreed."

"When do I get the house?"

"After everything is final."

"What about the Mortimers?"

"They don't belong to the house."

She huffed out a breath, then waved her hand. "All right, fine."

He felt the urge to laugh. Paige hated that word. *Fine.* So did he. Although, right now, he'd happily take it from his ex.

"I'll make the agreed upon amendments to the settlement immediately," Henry said, "and have them sent over by courier this afternoon."

Whitney stood, shaking off her lawyer's touch as he put an assisting hand on her elbow. On her mile-high heels, she stalked out ahead of him.

Good-bye, Whitney. And good riddance.

Henry clapped him on the back. "I'll send you the new draft for approval in a couple of hours. Then we'll get her to sign immediately."

The sooner the better.

He wanted Whitney out of his life.

And he wanted Paige *in*.

Chapter Thirty

The red light on Paige's desk phone flashed, indicating her next patient had arrived. Except that she didn't have another patient. Edward Wood was her last of the day, and they still had fifteen minutes to go.

But she never interrupted a session unless it was an emergency. If need be, her receptionist would have called instead of simply flipping on the light.

Turning her focus back to the middle-aged man in her office, she said, "How did you feel when she said that, Edward?"

His wife had just left him for a younger man. A *much* younger man, to the tune of twenty years. Edward was still sorting through his emotions, which was one of his wife's—ex-wife's—complaints, that he had no emotions.

"I guess I deserve it. She always said this would happen if I didn't change myself. And she was right."

"Perhaps," Paige suggested, "you could try thinking of it in another light. How about this?" Over the next few minutes, she detailed an alternative to his self-destructive thinking.

Her specialty was family therapy, but she never turned away anyone in distress. Edward was definitely in distress, even if he couldn't figure out exactly why. Yet.

When their remaining fifteen minutes were up, she ushered him out.

And her unscheduled patient stepped in.

"Evan."

She threw herself into his arms. Didn't stop to think it over. Didn't hesitate even the slightest. She simply gave herself wholly over to what felt right. To what she *knew* was right.

He pressed a kiss to the top of her head, and when she pulled back, his expression was serious.

"Your assistant said you're done for the day," he said in a deep voice that rumbled through her deliciously. "But I was hoping you could squeeze me in."

"Of course I can." Her heart was racing as she took a step back. Then she closed the door. And locked it. Whatever he wanted to say to her, it was obviously something big. Important enough that he didn't want to say it over dinner or in bed. She gestured to the couch, then took her usual seat.

"Please," she said ever so professionally, "tell me what I can help you with." Was it something to do with Whitney? Or his birth mother?

He was gorgeous in a dark blue suit, white shirt, and striped tie. And more serious than she'd ever seen him as he said, "I have a terrible confession to make."

"This is a very safe environment. You can say absolutely anything to me without fear, Evan. Anything at all."

His deep gaze pierced her. "I made a huge mistake nine years ago."

Her face felt overly hot, and her pulse beat against her eardrums as he continued.

"Despite everything Susan and Bob did for me, there was still a part of that little boy who didn't feel loved, who didn't think he deserved to be loved, who thought it was his fault that he'd been left behind. And yet I *needed* love so desperately that it made me blind to what real love was." He paused. "Right from the beginning, Whitney said everything she thought I wanted to hear. Her tactics were brilliantly insidious. Other women would only use me, she claimed, but not her. She made me believe she was the only one who could fill my deep, dark void. Made me believe that she would never hurt me the way I'd been hurt before."

Yes, that was Whitney. Absolutely. She figured out a person's biggest weakness and their deepest need and exploited both. "I wanted to warn you what Whitney was like," Paige interjected, "but I was jealous. I knew that had to be coloring my emotions. I hoped she might have changed. That maybe finding someone as good as you had worked a miracle."

"Even if you had warned me, I'm not sure I would have believed you. If there's anything worse for a guy than admitting he's weak, I don't know what it would be. But it's a fact—I was weak with her. And she knew it."

"You're not weak."

"Not anymore," he agreed, emotion swimming across his face. "Because of you. Because of your love."

"Did you know?" Her words were soft. But she had to say them, had to know. "Did you know I loved you all this time?"

"I couldn't let myself even think about how you felt. I didn't believe I could ever be good enough to deserve you. Whereas with Whitney..." A muscle jumped in his cheek. "Her darkness matched mine."

"*No.*" Paige bristled with outrage at that statement. "Nothing about your insides, nothing about who you are, matches anything about Whitney."

"I know that now." Regret was steeped in every line on his face. "I'm sorry it took me so long to see the truth, Paige. To see *you.*"

She went to him then, tossing out the pretense of being therapist and client, because he was absolutely everything to her. "I love that you finally see your true worth, how good you are. I love that you finally see me and my love. That I don't have to keep my feelings a secret from you. And that Whitney can't hurt either of us, because we won't let her."

He was holding her on his lap, his arms around her waist, hers around his neck, their lips close enough to touch. "You're damned right we won't." A hit of renewed fury sparked in his eyes. "Today, I kicked her out of our lives."

Our lives. How she loved the sound of that.

"We went head to head with the lawyers. And she never stood a chance."

"Of course she didn't." Her heart ached for him, though, as she guessed, "Even in battle, you were kind, weren't you? Too kind."

"I'm giving her the house, but it was always *her* house, not mine. The only room I liked was the library. Because of the time you and I spent there together."

She'd never forget all the precious moments she'd shared with him in that library. When she was just his friend…and he was always so much more to her.

"I'm glad she can't hurt you anymore."

"I won't let her hurt you again either. Not," he added, "that you need me to protect you. You're so strong, Paige."

"I am." She knew that now, with a certainty that no one and nothing could ever take away from her. "When she came to my condo, she admitted that she knew I was in love with you all along. From the day she met you in my dorm room. She told me it only made it better to take you for herself. To make sure I could never have you."

"Jesus, Paige." Grief and guilt welled up in him. "I was so freaking blind."

"You just wanted to be loved." She held his face in her hands. "But you always have been. I love you. Susan and Bob love you. Your friends love you." She wanted to tell him that Theresa loved him too, despite the way she'd hurt him. But for all his epiphanies today, was he ready to hear that one?

"How?" He looked at her in wonder. "How can you be so different from her?"

She stroked her hands along his arms. "She was the baby, while I had to be the responsible one. She felt entitled and privileged because my parents indulged her." Paige shook her head. "Why on earth do you think I became a psychologist? To figure her out. And to get her to change. But I couldn't do either."

"I know how hard that is to accept about someone in your family," he said. "That they're a monster who can't be changed."

They weren't talking about Whitney anymore, but about his father. Before she could speak, he brushed the hair back from her face and said, "Talk to me, Paige. I wasn't ready to listen before, but I am now. I want to know what you think. What you feel. With nothing held back anymore."

Anyone else would have made their declarations, their apologies, then happily moved on. But Evan wasn't just anyone. He was a brilliant, brave man. A Maverick.

And her one true love.

She had to kiss him then. To let him know, without words, just how much he meant to her before she pushed him to go to even more uncomfortable, raw places.

"Your epiphany about how a low sense of self-worth held you back from finding real, honest love is wonderful. The way you've dealt with Whitney and banished a powerful emotional vampire from your life is amazing."

"But?"

"No buts." She threaded her fingers through his. "How good does it feel to be free of Whitney?"

"Best feeling ever."

As much as she ached to do it, as much as it would hurt him, she had to ask, "How good do you think it would feel to forgive your mother?"

Chapter Thirty-One

He'd known what Paige would say. Because he'd deliberately opened the door for her.

Knowing a tornado was coming, however, didn't make its power any less fierce. It still whipped you up, spun you around, threatened to destroy you completely.

Only Paige could have kept him grounded. Only Paige could have kept him whole when everything inside of him was threatening to break apart.

"Whitney was the easy one," he finally said. "Everything with her ended up being black and white. Cut and dried. But with my mother, there are so many shades, so many sides, to what happened."

"Each betrayal is different." Paige's voice was soft, reaching inside him. "Some people are worthy of a second chance. Some aren't worthy of any kind of forgiveness. Whitney was calculated, plotting. But your mother was a beaten woman. Her choices weren't necessarily rational."

"No, she wasn't rational. She couldn't be when she was scared out of her mind." He leaned into the silky feel of Paige's hair against his cheek, her warmth. She made everything seem good, even when the bad threatened to overwhelm. She was solid, even in the midst of chaos. Her hands on his arms, the caress of her fingers—even through his shirt, the sensation worked some sort of alchemy on him. She made all his jumbled thoughts and emotions seem so much clearer. "What my mother did by leaving me was wrong." That fact would never change. But there were more facts that he needed to give his mother credit for. "Before she left, she did her best to protect me from my father by hiding me or taking the beatings herself. And when she found out she was pregnant, she made the only choice she could for the twins, two defenseless babies, to protect them as best she could."

Paige soothed him with her touch. "I'm so sorry for what that man did to you both."

"I am too." He pulled back, stroked his fingers over her cheek. "He had too much power over her, over me, while he was alive. He's been gone a long time, and both of us need to stop letting him have that power. We both need to move on. Fully. Completely." He forced himself to acknowledge the painful memories one more brutal time. And then he finally let them go. "My mother did an amazing job raising the twins. They're good people. Because of her."

"Do you realize that you've been calling her your mother? Instead of Theresa?"

"Maybe," he said slowly, "my feelings are changing." *He* was changing, with Paige's help. "But I'm afraid she'll continue to make bad choices."

"If she does," Paige said, "do you think you can love her and forgive her anyway?"

The answer hit him like a lightning bolt aimed straight at his heart.

"Yes. I can." After all these years, he suddenly saw things clearly. "Because she isn't the only one who's made, and who will likely keep making, mistakes."

"No," Paige said, emotion brimming in the short word. "She isn't. Not even close. We're human, so we make mistakes. All of us."

"I'm sorry," he said again. "Sorry for all the mistakes I made with you. Sorry for all the mistakes I'll make in the future."

"I forgive you. For all of it." Her lips trembled. "Just as I hope you'll forgive me for not telling you how I felt nine years ago. And for pushing you again and again to face the darkness when I know how hard and painful it is to walk back into the shadows."

"I love you."

Her eyes widened, then her tears spilled over.

"I love you, Paige."

He wanted to say it again and again. A billion times. Now that he'd finally said the words, he couldn't stop. He never would. She would just have to get used to hearing those three little words a thousand times a day. Days, weeks, years, decades that he couldn't wait to spend with her. To explore with her by his side. In his heart.

"I love you so damned much. I love you for being so damned brave. I love you for being so damned steadfast. I love you for pushing me to see that my mother deserves my forgiveness. And that I do too, for being so blind that I picked the wrong woman. I love you, Paige, for being joy and light and wonder." He held her tight to his heart, his body, his soul. "I love you with everything I am."

* * *

Evan loved her.

He'd forgiven his mother. He'd changed his life. He was whole.

And he was hers.

Finally.

"I love you," she said as he dipped his head to kiss her throat. "You're everything I could ever want."

"Tell me what you want, Paige." He lifted his face to hers. "Tell me, and I'll give it to you. Anything you want. Everything you want."

Didn't he know? "All I want is you."

"I'm yours."

She wanted to revel in this moment forever. Wanted to block out the rest of the world, if only for a short precious time, and focus everything on love.

When she smiled, it was full of emotion. And a touch of naughtiness too. "I've never made love in my office before."

He kissed her hard. "I want to be your first. Your only."

"You are. You always have been." This moment between them was potent with meaning—and with joy. So much joy that it was perfectly natural, instinctive to tease. "I can't stop fantasizing about having you ravish me with my clothes on. Like we're doing something totally illicit." And so beautiful her heart swelled with it.

"Paige." He murmured her name into the vee of her neckline, licking her skin. "I love how you're not afraid to make love fun. To play, even as you make me hotter than anything or anyone ever has."

"Play with me," she urged him.

On a lust-filled curse, he rolled her beneath him on the couch. She felt so soft, so sexy beneath his hard, heated muscles.

He bunched the material of her skirt in his hands and tugged it up slowly. "You made me crazy when I first walked in here. This pencil skirt and silk blouse you're wearing. They're sexy as hell. I could barely restrain myself from ripping them off you."

"I wanted to rip your suit off too."

He stopped a moment, his features serious again as he braced himself above her. "Don't ever stop being exactly the way you are. Don't ever stop making me laugh, making me crazy. My sweet, sexy, wild, *perfect* Paige."

Her heart contracted, and tears pricked at the corners of her eyes. No one had ever wanted her just the way she was. She'd lived her whole life in her sister's shadow.

But Evan loved her just as she was.

"I am sweet," she said softly. "And sexy." That came out louder, firmer. She was already rolling them over so she could straddle his hips as she said, "And wild for you."

He pulled her down and gave her a sizzling, open-mouthed kiss, tasting her with his tongue, filling her. "You forgot one," he said when he finally let her come up for air. *"Perfect."* He threaded his hands into her hair. "My every dream, every hope, every prayer, come true."

"Then love me now," she whispered, looking down into his beautiful face, her gaze caressing his lips.

The next thing she knew, zippers were unzipped, buttons were unbuttoned, and fabric was pulled out of the way so that they could come together.

They made love to each other with lips, hands, hearts. Joy, pleasure, love—there were no boundaries anymore. No more shadows. Only the wild, *perfect* rhythm of their lovemaking, their sounds of pleasure, their whispered words of love.

And when they fell, they fell as one.

Chapter Thirty-Two

Paige sat in the passenger seat of Evan's Tesla the following night as they zipped along to Modesto. He'd asked her to come with him to see his family. He'd said they were as much hers as they were his, that they would love her as much as he did. Even now, it made her tear up.

"I'm so proud of you for taking this step. I know how hard it is."

Evan picked up her hand to kiss her knuckles. It was such a beautiful gesture, one she could never have imagined a month ago. But she'd dreamed of it a million times.

"With you by my side, it's not hard." He twined his fingers with hers on the console. "I want to know my brother and sister better. And it's time to reconnect with my mother. I'm ready to start a new life with a new family." He gave her the look that melted her heart every single time...and heated her straight through. "And with you. Especially with you."

She knew her heart was shining in her eyes. "I wonder what everyone will say about us being together."

"They'll ask why it took so long. Especially Susan. I'm pretty sure if we didn't get our act together soon, she was going to lock us in a bedroom and not let us out until we found our happily ever after."

"She didn't just adopt you and the other Mavericks," Paige said in a soft voice. "She adopted me too, a fully grown woman who was desperate for a family. For a home." Paige lifted her eyes back to Evan's. "Our family is going to be as happy as theirs."

"It is. Because we've learned from the best."

He pulled over to the curb a few moments later where all three members of the Collins family were outside waiting by the short hedge around the small lawn in front of Theresa's house. A flower box edged the porch, ready for spring flowers in a few months.

Paige and Evan were received with smiles all around and hugs from Tony and Kelsey, then they all trooped inside.

"Have you eaten dinner?" Theresa had obviously wanted to hug Evan too, but she'd held herself back.

"We have," Evan said. "But I brought dessert." He set a pink bakery box on the kitchen table. "Mrs. M's trifle is legendary."

"How lovely. I've put coffee on."

Kelsey flipped open the bakery box. "Oh my God. It looks like a billion calories." She laughed. "I'll just have to run an extra five miles tomorrow, because I'm not missing this."

"Need some help, Mom?" Tony asked, then automatically helped her get down the mugs, setting them on a plastic tray.

The house wasn't large, with an L-shape for dining, kitchen, and family room. There was no formal living room, but Paige thought rooms that didn't get used except on formal occasions were a waste of space anyway. Everything was neat and clean, the tile counter sparkling, though it had a couple of cracks in it. The appliances were older, but who cared as long as everything worked? The place was homey, and that was the most important thing.

Tony carried the tray of mugs, bowls, a cow-shaped creamer jug, and a sugar pot into the family room, setting it on the coffee table. Theresa brought the coffee carafe, and Kelsey followed up with the trifle.

"Would you like to do the honors, Evan, since you brought the dessert?" Theresa held out a big serving spoon.

"You go ahead, Mom."

She faltered, her hand trembling as she looked at him in shock. Then with joy. Her eyes shone with moisture as she smiled and said, "All right, dear. Big piece or little?"

"Huge," he said. "We're celebrating." He grinned at Kelsey. "All the calories are free tonight."

Sitting next to him on the sofa, Kelsey leaned over to kiss his cheek. "Thank you, big brother." Paige knew the show of affection had nothing to do with the cake and everything to do with their mother.

After Tony had poured coffee and passed around the cream and sugar, Evan held up his mug. "I'd like to make a toast." They all raised their mugs as he said, "First, to our mother. You did a fabulous job of raising your children."

"Oh Evan." A tear slid down Theresa's cheek. "I didn't raise you."

"You did for nine years. Then you let me stay with Susan and Bob, who finished the job. I will be forever grateful for that opportunity to become the man I am." Theresa swiped at the tears streaming down her face, and then he reached for her hand. "I know now that you did the absolute best you could in difficult circumstances and that you made the only choice you felt you could at the time. I don't want you to feel guilty about that anymore. I had a great life with Bob and Susan, and I'm looking forward to an even better life going forward, with you in it, along with my brother and sister."

Paige was so proud of Evan that her heart felt close to bursting with love.

He raised his mug again. "To Tony and Kelsey. I'm honored to have you as my brother and sister, and I want to get to know you both much better."

They clinked their mugs with his, and Paige thought Kelsey might start crying too. Even Tony's eyes had grown shiny.

"Thanks for not kicking us out the day we showed up at your house uninvited." Tony grinned and lifted his mug higher. "To family."

Evan's grin was a mirror to his brother's. "To family."

They all cheered.

"One more toast." He turned and faced her. "To Paige. The woman I love with all my heart. You have been my friend, my best friend, for years. I'm damned glad that by the time I finally woke up and realized I couldn't live without you, I hadn't lost you. Because you're everything to me. *Everything.*"

Paige didn't think twice—she simply leaned over and kissed him right there in front of his family.

"It's about time," Kelsey said, as if she'd known they belonged together that very first day she'd met them.

"I'm so happy for you both." Theresa squeezed Paige's hand.

"Me too." Tony's grin was even wider now as he held his cup aloft in another toast.

"You're all as lucky as I am to have her." Evan looked at Paige with all his emotions in his gaze.

Pretty soon, she'd be crying buckets too.

Then Evan reached into his pocket, and when his hand reappeared, Paige recognized the plastic T-Rex on his palm. And her tears fell for this big, beautiful, wonderful, forgiving man.

"You remember this little guy, Mom?" He handed

the trinket to her.

"Oh Evan," she whispered, grabbing a napkin to blot her eyes as she held the dinosaur close to her heart. "You kept it?"

"I've never been able to let it go," Evan said as he reached for Paige's hand.

"The Field Museum in Chicago," his mother told Kelsey and Tony. "We went to see the dinosaurs."

"It was the best day ever," he said, punctuating the words with a squeeze of Paige's hand. "We're going to have a lot more of them from now on."

"Yes. We will." His mother sniffed and used the napkin to dry her eyes, her gaze finally bright and alive.

Paige's heart bloomed with love. She was so proud of Evan. He'd banished his shadows, and in doing so, he'd banished his mother's too.

"I've been thinking," Evan said, looking at his mother, his arm anchoring Paige to him. "Modesto is too far out. Would you consider a job closer to the Bay Area?"

"You want me closer?" She looked like she'd just been given yet another of the greatest gifts in the world.

"I do. Very much. Although, I understand that you feel a great loyalty to your employer's company since he was such a help to you."

"You've said it's just not the same since Hugh died," Kelsey reminded her. "It would be great if you lived closer to Tony and me."

"My friends would love to meet you," Evan said gently. "You'd like them all. And I'd be there every step of the way with you, finding you a great job, helping you sell this house, or rent it out, if that's what you'd like to do."

Evan would take care of everything, Paige knew. And leaving Modesto would also help get Theresa away from any temptation to let Greg back in her life.

"Why don't you take some time to think about it?" Evan said, obviously working hard to let her come to it in her own time.

But Tony wasn't afraid to push. "It's time, Mom. You stayed there because you liked working with Hugh, but he's gone."

"I know," she said. "But adjusting to a new company..." Theresa didn't have to finish the thought. Change was frightening.

"We'll all help you find the right fit," Kelsey said. "I bet Evan has a million contacts. You could even live with me, if you'd like."

Theresa looked at them all, and her arms moved as if she wanted to throw them around her entire family. And when Evan moved into them, Paige felt his forgiveness envelope his mother, final and complete.

It was all she could ever have hoped for him.

And for herself, to be loved by this beautiful man.

★ ★ ★

They gobbled the trifle down to the bare bowl and

finished the carafe of coffee. Peace settled over Evan as he surveyed his new family.

Pure love for—and from—Paige had melted his icy heart.

"I've got a present for you, to say thank you for all you did for us." Kelsey reached down beside the sofa to produce a flat box. She leaned over to lay the gift on his lap. "I hope you like it."

The box was fairly heavy, and he tore off the paper. He hadn't needed anything in return for what he'd done to chase off Theresa's abuser, but the offering warmed him.

He lifted the lid to reveal a collage photo frame filled with pictures. He gaped at Kelsey. "Where did you get all these?"

"I told Susan what I wanted to do, and we went through her photo books when you left for the hotel after Yahtzee."

"What a beautiful idea." Paige leaned over to look, her scent weaving magic around him. "You guys sure were hotties even back then."

Front and center was a photo of the Mavericks taken shortly before they'd all left Chicago. Their hair was longer, and he and Matt weren't nearly as well built yet, but they'd just made their pact and were ready to take the world by storm.

The other pictures were in a satellite around the center, including one of the Spencers—Bob, Susan, Daniel, and Lyssa—and a photo of Susan and Bob on their twenty-fifth wedding anniversary just a couple of years ago. Kelsey had also included a shot of herself and Tony when they were about ten. His hair was longer than he wore it now, hers shorter. Right below was a photo of Susan and Theresa from the past weekend, the two women who had helped shape him.

"Thank you." He was beyond touched. "You couldn't have given me anything better."

"It was Tony's idea. But I collected the photos. It's a family portrait. All your family." Kelsey's words showed her understanding of how important the Maverick clan was to him, while also bringing to light his future. His brother, sister, and mother weren't eclipsing anything, they were extending.

Then he saw the photo in the upper right. Paige was seated next to him on Susan's sofa, the Yahtzee dice in her hand. She was laughing at something he'd said, her gaze on him, her love for him written in her smile, her laughter.

Just as his love for her —the love he'd thought he needed to keep secret, even from himself—was written on his face.

Kelsey had obviously seen it too, capturing the moment with her cell phone.

Paige traced the edge of the picture. "That's a nice one," she said softly. Her voice and her touch, the heat of her body beside him, the slight lift of her gaze to his, showed she also recognized the emotions shining through.

His feelings had been there all along, deep inside. He'd lost his way for a very long time. But now he was found.

In front of his family, he declared himself again. "I love you, Paige."

As she said the words back against his lips, he kissed her, and his family cheered beside them. He would say it, think it, feel it every day for the rest of his life. He would thank God or the universe or whatever power was in charge for allowing him to finally see how much he needed her.

And he would be forever thankful that he hadn't been able to resist the sweet, sexy, wild woman who tempted him so.

Because they were meant to be.

Epilogue

Daniel picked up a champagne glass from the tray Mrs. M was handing around for the Valentine's Day toasts.

"We're going to turn the formal living room into a library," Evan told the group filling the room under discussion.

The new library would be small compared to the one in Evan's old Atherton house. But this place fit Paige and Evan better than his previous residence would have.

"Here's to a great new home for you both," Will toasted, all fat and happy after six weeks of marriage. All right, he wasn't fat, but he was damn happy. And Harper was beaming like a thousand watts of joy.

Everyone raised their glasses in salute and drank.

"Here's to your new life together." Tony Collins held his glass high, and everyone cheered with him.

That Evan had a brother and sister, twins no less, had taken some getting used to. Hell, Evan could have been Tony's twin they were so much alike. While Kelsey resembled him, she was also a very beautiful young woman.

The photo montage of the family that she and Tony had made for Evan had been an inspiration. It showed an understanding that seemed far beyond their years. They were both good people, smart, funny, and terribly protective of their mother.

Still, Daniel wasn't sure what to make of Theresa Collins. Her life had been hard, and the years had taken their toll. She was his mom's age, but she looked five years older. Evan had forgiven her for leaving him, but Daniel wondered when he'd get there himself.

He'd seen the bruises Evan's dad had left on him. Sometimes it was harder to forgive the things done to your friends than it was the things people did to you. Especially when Daniel had grown up with the best parents possible. He simply couldn't understand beating your kid or ditching him to save yourself. But his mother counseled forgiveness, so Daniel was working on that.

"Here's to finding family and discovering the love of your life in the process," his mother toasted.

She wore a beautiful smile for the happy reunion, but there was also a special gleam in her eye, as if she'd known all along that Evan would come to his senses and finally recognize the woman of his dreams had been right beside him all along.

Hell, they'd all known Paige was the sister Evan should have married long before he figured it out. He was a wiz with numbers, investments, and cash flow— but the guy was definitely slow on the uptake where matters of the heart were concerned.

At least he got there eventually. Just like Will and Sebastian and Matt had. It was about time that Evan found happiness. He'd never looked more relaxed, less serious, even close to carefree. And Paige had never looked more beautiful. She wore a celebratory red dress, and Evan had matching hearts in his eyes.

Yeah, his friend had found a jewel, which was a rarity in this world when the majority of women Daniel met wanted his money first and him second. Or third, after his connections.

But not Paige.

Evan had paid cash for the house so they could make the move in time to host a Valentine's party. Daniel, though he had no Valentine sweetheart—and didn't need one, thank you very much—had come stag, as usual.

After the toasts, everyone explored the house and property. The house itself, located in the Los Altos Hills—was far more modest than the Atherton behemoth, not more than five thousand square feet. But it had home offices for both Paige and Evan, a couple of extra bedrooms for family to stay, and a granny suite over the garage for the Mortimers, who of course, had come to the new place. There was also a garden out back and a yard that would easily fit the playsets and soccer games for the children Daniel hoped his friends would soon have.

The home suited Paige perfectly. And Paige suited

Evan. He'd never laughed as hard, never smiled as big.

Daniel's parents had flown in from Chicago—though Lyssa hadn't been able to make it, due to the job she still needed to dump. Jeremy had come with Harper and Will, but Noah had commandeered him, along with Jorge, the son of Ari's friend Rosie, dragging them both into the dining room, where they were seated around the table building some mysterious creation out of Lego blocks.

Ari's brother, Gideon, had sent his regrets. He was a quiet one and difficult to know. But Daniel had found him to be a hard worker since he'd started at Top-Notch. Ari's friends Rosie and Chi were welcomed too. They were fast becoming extended family, right along with Rosie's dynamo kid, Jorge.

The Mavericks were expanding exponentially. Pretty soon, he thought with a grin, they'd have to find his parents a bigger house in Chicago just to handle the holiday parties.

Francine Ballard accompanied Sebastian and Charlie. Daniel loved Charlie's mom, and he plopped down on the sofa beside her while Charlie was off getting the elderly woman a plate of food.

"How's my favorite lady doing?" He took one of her arthritic hands in his.

"Oh, I'm in good shape for the shape I'm in." She laughed, giving his fingers a squeeze, at least as much as she could. Charlie's mom was a doll, pushing her walker a mile a day, never giving up, always offering a smile, no matter how much pain her arthritis caused.

She looked at Evan with his arm around Paige. "They're glowing, aren't they?"

"They are."

"And Evan's new brother and sister are darling."

"Darling is exactly the right word for it." Daniel smiled at her charming expression.

"They certainly take care of their mother. Such good children." Then she leaned close to whisper, "I wonder how the other wife would have handled it all." The *other* wife. What a diplomatic way of referring to Whitney. "I met her once, you know, at Charlie's opening. She ran for the hills." She laughed again. "Beautiful people who are as vain as she is are terribly afraid of old bags like me. They see their future in the lines on my face."

"Promise me you'll never again call yourself an old bag," he admonished, raising her hand to his lips. "You're a lovely lady. We're so glad you've become a Maverick right along with Charlie."

"Did I hear my name?" Charlie arrived carrying a plate laden with appetizers—meatballs, spring rolls, chicken skewers.

"Hey, you brought enough for me." He gave her his most devilish smile. "Thank you."

"Get your own," Charlie chided him, handing her mom the plate and a napkin.

"Thank you, dear. Daniel's a growing boy. He can share. I can't eat all this."

He was already reaching for a spring roll when Charlie said, "You are so bad."

"I am. Totally." Daniel's grin widened. "That's why no woman will have me."

A hand moved around Charlie's waist, and Sebastian was right behind her. "Are you stealing Francine's food, Daniel?"

"I offered," the little lady beamed, spearing a meatball for him, which he happily ate. "Charlie brought too much," she whispered as if they couldn't hear.

Charlie smiled down at her mother indulgently, and Sebastian kissed Charlie's cheek.

The Mavericks did know how to pick their women, even if it had taken Evan a couple of tries. The dark shadows Sebastian had once carried were gone now too. Charlie had banished them forever.

Matt suddenly broke up all the conversations with a clink of a fork against his champagne glass. "Ladies and gentlemen, we have an announcement." Taking Ari's hand in his, Matt raised it to his lips, kissing the backs of her fingers. Both of them were almost sparkling they were so happy together, like two shining stars.

"I'm beyond pleased to let you all know that Ari has agreed to be my wife."

A chorus of hurrahs went up. Rosie and Chi hugged each other, then group-hugged Matt and Ari.

"We're planning the wedding for the summertime because we'd like to have it in the puppet theater at

Noah's favorite petting zoo in San Jose."

Noah jumped off his seat at the dining room table and threw his arms in the air. "Yay! I love the zoo and the puppet theater. Daddy and Ari take me there all the time. They have talking parrots, and you can pet the animals, and the puppets are funny." He turned to Jorge, grabbing his hand and pulling him to his feet. "This is *awesome*."

Everyone laughed at his enthusiastic *awesome* as they surrounded the happy couple with good wishes. It was so like Ari, Daniel thought, to turn her wedding into an event just as much for Noah as for her and Matt. Matt was a lucky guy, no question about it.

"You, young man," Francine said with a poke at his ribs, "are the holdout. When are you going to find your special sweetheart?"

"You're sitting right here."

Though she blushed, she poked him again. "Answer the question."

"I'm not looking right now." And it was the truth. He enjoyed women, of course, but not all the entanglements that came when they inevitably wanted more than he did.

His parents were the blueprint. Unless he found what they had, he wasn't interested in anything more than a sexy fling.

"That's exactly when it happens. When you're not looking."

"Maybe," he said, only to appease her. "But I'll tell

you what I'm really looking for." He swiped a piece of chicken from one of her skewers. "Some time to get back up to Lake Tahoe to work on my cabin."

The exterior walls were up, the roof was on, and with a space heater, he could work on the interior until the snow melted and the weather warmed up. He couldn't wait to have a quiet space. A place where he could go to think. To get away from it all.

He loved his family, but he needed this too. Needed something that was all his own. Away from business meetings, away from women in clinging dresses. Just the sun and the sky and the lake and the mountains.

Francine meant well with all her talk of love. They all did.

But Daniel hadn't yet found anything that matched his parents' love for each other.

And he wasn't sure he ever would.

★ ★ ★ ★ ★

For news on Bella Andre's upcoming books, sign up for Bella Andre's New Release Newsletter:

BellaAndre.com/Newsletter

For news on Jennifer Skully's upcoming books, sign up for Jennifer Skully's New Release Newsletter:

bit.ly/SkullyNews

ABOUT THE AUTHORS

Having sold more than 6 million books, *New York Times* and *USA Today* bestselling author Bella Andre's novels have been #1 bestsellers around the world. Known for "sensual, empowered stories enveloped in heady romance" (*Publishers Weekly*), her books have been *Cosmopolitan* magazine "Red Hot Reads" twice and have been translated into ten languages. Winner of the Award of Excellence, *The Washington Post* has called her "One of the top digital writers in America" and she has been featured by *Entertainment Weekly*, NPR, *USA Today*, *Forbes*, *The Wall Street Journal* and, most recently, in *Time* magazine. She has given keynote speeches at publishing conferences from Copenhagen to Berlin to San Francisco, including a standing-room-only keynote at Book Expo America, on her publishing success.

Sign up for Bella's newsletter:
BellaAndre.com/Newsletter

Visit Bella's website at:
www.BellaAndre.com

Follow Bella on Twitter at:
twitter.com/bellaandre

Join Bella on Facebook at:
facebook.com/bellaandrefans

New York Times and *USA Today* bestselling author Jennifer Skully is a lover of contemporary romance, bringing you poignant tales peopled with hilarious characters that will make you laugh and make you cry. Writing as Jasmine Haynes, she's authored over 35 classy, sensual romance tales about real issues like growing older, facing divorce, starting over. Her books have passion and heart and humor and happy endings, even if they aren't always traditional. She also writes gritty, paranormal mysteries in the Max Starr series. Having penned stories since the moment she learned to write, she now lives in the Redwoods of Northern California with her husband and their adorable nuisance of a cat who totally runs the household.

Newsletter signup:
http://bit.ly/SkullyNews

Jennifer's Website:
www.jenniferskully.com

Blog:
www.jasminehaynes.blogspot.com

Facebook:
facebook.com/jasminehaynesauthor

Twitter:
twitter.com/jasminehaynes1